———————— ★ ————————

DEAD END

Caroline was at the desk. No longer sitting but slumped.

Rain ran into my eyes and suddenly the whole room was suffused with red. The red of the blood which surrounded her. Red on the white paper in front of her, red in her hair, red on her gloved hands, her fur coat still on and bloodied as any slaughtered animal. I was used to blood, but in the right place, at the right time.

Fear seemed to slow me down. The few steps to her body took forever. I saw the weapon that had killed her—the crowbar—bloodied and thrown on the floor.

———————— ★ ————————

"For those who like the lighter British fare, this new series will not disappoint you."

—*Mystery News*

Previously published Worldwide Mystery titles by
CHRISTINE GREEN

DEADLY ADMIRER
DEADLY PRACTICE

CHRISTINE GREEN
DEADLY PARTNERS

WORLDWIDE.

TORONTO • NEW YORK • LONDON
AMSTERDAM • PARIS • SYDNEY • HAMBURG
STOCKHOLM • ATHENS • TOKYO • MILAN
MADRID • WARSAW • BUDAPEST • AUCKLAND

DEADLY PARTNERS

A Worldwide Mystery/May 1998

This edition published by arrangement with
Walker and Company.

ISBN 0-373-26274-4

For David.
Thanks for the memories!

ONE

THE VOICE wavered away on the answer machine. Not that I minded: the elderly woman was offering me a job.

'Hubert!' I called out as I heard his footstep on one of the creaky floorboards. When his sombre face finally appeared around my office door I announced, 'Someone's making me an offer I can't refuse.'

'What sort of offer?' he asked suspiciously.

'A few weeks by the sea offer.'

He raised an eyebrow. 'Bermuda?'

I shook my head.

'Mauritius?'

Again I shook my head.

He smiled. 'Tenerife.'

'The Isle of Wight.'

Hubert smirked in a horribly satisfied way. 'The Isle of Wight,' he repeated, as if I were about to spend time in a Siberian salt mine. 'It won't be much fun on your own in December. I hope you'll be back by Christmas.'

'Hubert,' I began, as I stood to my full five-foot-four, 'in my frail financial, social and emotional condition, fun is not something that I'm looking for. And yes, of course I'll be back for Christmas.'

Hubert raised an eyebrow then stared down at my feet as I swung round on my swivelling office chair. 'You won't find much fun anywhere in a pair of moccasins,' he said in his dourest voice.

I sighed. Hubert Humberstone, funeral director, divorced, tall, thin, pasty-faced, fiftyish, foot fetishist, now in love with employee and transsexual Danielle, was my landlord, my best friend and often irritated me. But I knew I couldn't run my Medical and Nursing Investigation Agency without him.

'Not everyone finds shoes exciting, Hubert,' I said with conviction. 'In fact, some odd people just find shoes... well...utilitarian.'

Hubert's eyes narrowed slightly and he looked puzzled. 'What's church got to do with shoes?'

It took me several seconds to comprehend. 'That's *Unitarian*,' I said. Hubert was by now grinning. He loved me to fall into his little traps.

'Tell me about the case, then,' he said. 'What do you have to do to earn your few weeks out of season by the sea? Be a companion to some old biddy?'

'It's a PI job, not a nursing job.'

'Yes?' said Hubert impatiently.

By now I was beginning to feel just a tiny bit tetchy with Hubert. I did have to do occasional nursing jobs to pay his rent and be able to eat, but my enthusiasm was always fired by thoughts of a new investigation and I wanted him to be just a little impressed.

'It's a missing person case,' I announced. 'A Mrs Elizabeth Forrester wants me to find her nephew, Nigel Carter.'

'Did he miss his annual visit?' asked Hubert.

'No,' I said swiftly. 'Auntie hasn't heard from him in three months and he previously rang her once a week at least.'

'Perhaps she's a bit of a pain and he's just...well, opted out for a while.'

'Lizzie thinks he's been most definitely opted out—like in dead, deceased, passed away, respirationally embarrassed—killed, even, as in...murdered.'

Hubert did have the grace to look impressed then. 'What makes her think he's been murdered?'

I was a bit stumped on this point. After all, it had been a fairly brief message and I had been more interested in the chance of a breath of sea air and a generous daily rate plus expenses; so mere details seemed to have passed me by. 'Mrs Forrester's writing to me; I should get the letter soon. She's making my hotel reservation and sending me money.'

'Don't count your chickens before they hatch, Kate.' Hubert was a real master of the corny homily.

THREE DAYS LATER I felt my chicken eggs had definitely been sat on. There was no letter or money or even another phone call from Mrs Forrester. It was as if that message had been a figment of my deluded imagination. The message was still on the tape but by now all thoughts of a holiday on the Isle of Wight had receded from my mind. Much more urgent and pressing was how to pay the rent.

On Saturday morning, when grey clouds and driving rain gave Longborough High Street that 'End of the world' aura and a waitressing job in Spain seemed the pinnacle of ambition, the phone rang. I recognized the wavery voice immediately.

'I'm so sorry, Miss Kinsella,' she said. 'I've been too poorly to phone before, but I've organized everything. I've reserved you a room with a sea view. I'm sure you'll be very comfortable, and I've sent you two weeks' money in advance...' She paused, obviously breathless.

'Would you like me to call round and see you before I go?'

'No, no,' she said quickly. 'I'm not well enough for visitors.'

'What about your address and phone number?' I asked.

'I'll keep in contact with you, Miss Kinsella. But please do your utmost to find him. I think I'm dying and I would so like to see him before I die, or at least…know the truth.'

'I'll do my best,' I murmured. 'The police do know about your nephew Nigel being missing…don't they?'

There was a slight gasp from Mrs Forrester. 'Of course they know,' she said. 'I haven't been remiss in my efforts to find him.'

I mumbled an apology.

'I'm sorry too,' she said. 'I didn't mean to jump down your throat. It's just that the police aren't interested in adults who go missing unless there are real grounds for suspicion.'

'And they couldn't find any?'

'It seems not,' she said. 'But I know one thing, Miss Kinsella. Nigel would have phoned if he were able to. Deep down I suppose I know I'll never see him again but one has to try, and, if he has been murdered, as I suspect, then I want his killer brought to justice.'

'Fair enough,' I muttered, thinking with a sinking heart how bringing a killer to justice sounded an awesome responsibility, and was I up to it?

There was a throaty pause for a few seconds which gave me a chance to formulate vital questions such as where exactly on the Isle of Wight was I meant to be staying, where had Nigel worked and where was he last seen?

The answer to the first two questions was swift: 'Uplands Lodge Hotel, Ryde.' There was another pause. 'Of course I didn't *see* much of Nigel; he didn't leave the Isle of Wight very often.'

'How long was he there?' I asked.

'Ten years. He's thirty-six now. He was drifting before

but I gave him some money and together with a friend of his, Stewart Michaelson, they bought Uplands Lodge and I believe it's quite successful now.'

'When was he last seen, Mrs Forrester?'

'I'm really not sure. Stewart will be able to give you all the details...' Her voice tailed off. 'I get *so* tired now.'

When she spoke again the voice sounded even more feeble. 'I'll ring you at the hotel for progress reports. I don't mind how long it takes you, Miss Kinsella...within reason. I'll try to keep going until he's found.'

'I'll do my best, Mrs Forrester.'

'I should hope so,' came the sharp reply and for a moment I experienced the same emotions as I'd had when receiving one of those 'pull up your socks' pep talks at school. Did any pupil ever take a whit of notice? But this was really serious stuff: 'doing my best' this time meant finding Nigel, dead or alive.

I sat for a few minutes after the phone call and made a list of jobs to do and things to pack. I didn't go away very often and I couldn't afford to forget anything vital. Then I went downstairs to find Hubert. He was standing with grieving relatives in the hallway just outside the Chapel of Rest, so I decided to go home and begin packing.

'Home' is a small terraced cottage in a row of four in the village of Farley Wood. It overlooks the church and of course the graveyard. When I write to my mother, who is in Australia happily doing various forms of menial work, she is horrified by my proximity to death, but I try to explain that familiarity with death and its bits and pieces makes you appreciate life more, and, strangely, less worried about dying. She isn't convinced.

Once home I didn't find my list particularly useful since I'd left it in my office, but I tried to remember the main

points—'check knickers' was first on the list. Is it just me,
I wondered, or does everyone get paranoid about knickers
and underwear when they plan to stay in a hotel? Perhaps
it's the packing itself, I thought, as I laid out bras, slips
and pants and noticed how nothing matched except one
greying slip with one equally greying bra. I discarded
both: the slip had a disgusting habit of riding up with
every step and I thought then how the demise of what
Hubert called the 'frock' could be attributed to the ever-
creeping-upwards petticoat. As for the so-called 'half
slip'—half of *what?* I've always wondered, since most of
them hang at least an inch below a skirt and have to be
hitched up at frequent intervals.

The packing didn't take as long as I thought it would,
partly because I needed new everything, from flannels to
toothpaste, and partly because the phone rang. It was Hubert offering me Sunday lunch at the Swan and a lift to the
coast.

ON THE JOURNEY down Hubert gave me more dire warn-
ings than a TV weather man on the eve of an earthquake.

'Hubert, it's the Isle of Wight I'm going to, not Marrakesh.'

'Where's Marrakesh?'

I didn't tell him.

He stared ahead at the road but mumbled, 'A young
woman on her own... Some men think are... You know,
Kate.'

'You mean an easy lay, Hubert.'

Hubert coughed, obviously embarrassed. I couldn't re-
sist going on. 'I should be so lucky. I mean, this is no
eighteen-to-thirty holiday, is it? If some young stud ap-
pears at Uplands Lodge Hotel and makes a play for me,
why not combine work and pleasure?'

'I hope you don't mean that, Kate,' said Hubert glumly. 'I worry about you.'

I shrugged. Hubert was saying in effect that he was going to miss me. I looked forward to the change.

TWO

AS THE ferry left Portsmouth harbour I saw Hubert standing by the quayside waving rather dramatically, I thought, as if I was on the last voyage of the *Titanic* instead of a thirty-minute ferry across the Solent.

I reasoned that on such a short trip I could do without a drink. A brisk walk on deck would be far more beneficial. I was trying to ignore the gale force winds and enjoy the sea spray on my face when I heard the sort of anguished babble that either starts a riot or means someone is in trouble. At first I couldn't quite see what was happening but then a little crowd moved away and I saw a young man, tall and gangly, sagging at the knees, fighting for his breath and obviously distressed. I moved closer. Although his eyes were panic-stricken, his colour was good—too pink, even—his breathing was deep and ragged but not wheezy like an asthmatic. No one rushed forward saying they were a doctor, or even better someone with a recent first aid certificate, so I edged nearer. A youngish woman grabbed me. 'He can't breathe!' she screamed. 'He can't breathe!'

'I'm a nurse,' I mumbled. 'What's his name?'

'Adam—he's my son—he's only fourteen. Please help him... *Please.*'

Adam had by now actually given way at the knees and I was swaying to one side as the boat dipped and dived, taking my stomach with it.

'Adam—you'll be fine,' I said firmly. 'I want you to breathe very, very slowly.'

In a quick aside to his mother I asked her to get a brown paper bag. She looked at me for a second in disbelief. 'Do it!' I yelled.

While the boat rolled from side to side I encouraged Adam to stay calm and prayed the bag would actually work when it did arrive. The seemingly long wait ended when Adam's mother returned clutching a brown paper bag and after a brief protest Adam began taking a few breaths of his own carbon-dioxide. Within a minute or so his breathing grew less panicked, more normal. I'd never used the paper bag technique for hyperventilation before, but I was impressed with the results because after a few minutes Adam was able to walk below looking more chipper than either his mother or me.

By this time the Isle of Wight had come into view, windy and capped by grey-black clouds. It *is* December, I told myself, but I was still irrationally disappointed in the weather and began to view my stay as the private investigator's equivalent of being offered a case on a tropical island only to find your stay corresponded with monsoon month.

Just as I left the ferry Adam's mother rushed up to me. Adam hung back, tall and awkward, looking far older than fourteen and desperately uncomfortable about it.

'I don't even know your name,' she said, as though we'd just had a one-night stand. Now that I could observe her properly I guessed she was, like me, in her early thirties and there the similarity ended. She had blonde hair that wasn't natural but looked as near as dammit, bright turquoise eyes and a figure that appeared neat and 36/24/36-ish even under a padded blue jacket. I mumbled my name.

'You saved my son's life. I'm really grateful.'

'He wasn't in too much danger,' I said. 'It's the paper bag that should get the praise.'

'No, you saved him. Where are you staying on the island?'

'Uplands Lodge Hotel.'

She nodded. 'We're...on holiday, so I've rented a bungalow. You must come for a meal one evening.'

'I'd like that.'

'Good,' she answered. 'I'll give you a ring at your hotel. My name's Caroline, by the way... Must dash—a friend's waiting in the car. Bye.'

I stood clutching my suitcase for a few moments and then saw a lone taxi. The driver didn't say a word during the journey, which was mercifully short. When we did arrive he managed to grunt, 'You get good nosh here.' That was something to be grateful for and the hotel was more attractive than I'd imagined. Ivy crept up over the walls and the white-painted balconies on the second floor somehow gave the hotel an aura of a vast cricket pavilion, minus sun, of course.

At the entrance were two white plastic chairs above which, hanging precariously and swinging with every gust of wind, was a basket of winter pansies. Quite unnecessarily I ducked my head and walked into reception.

Inside, it was warm and welcoming; large ceramic lamps with tasselled cream lampshades seemed to shimmer in the soft glow from a deep-pile cerise carpet. There was no sign of a receptionist so I stood by the desk staring at the elephant-shaped hand bell that was just asking to be rung, when the door opened and I recognized a familiar sound—the click of walking sticks and Zimmer frames. In those few moments warm and welcoming Uplands Lodge became Costa Geriatrica and although I was ashamed of myself I couldn't help feeling a vague sense of disappointment as greyish faces hove into view.

Three elderly people walked towards me, two women and a man. The leader of the trio, on the Zimmer frame and easily the tallest, was female, thin with a bent neck, a rolling gait and a very tight bluish perm. I hardly managed a proper look at the other two because she stopped in front of me, slowly raised her head an inch or two so that she could look me in the eye and said, 'Bar's open, dear, and we've got our own vodka so you'd better stick with us.'

Maybe she's a bit dotty and thinks I'm a relative, I wondered, so I tried to demur, but she smiled at me disarmingly and said, 'You look as if you could do with a drink.' I couldn't argue with that so I followed their slow-slow, click-click-slow to the bar.

A young woman with a badge that said 'Amanda Giles—Receptionist' was already there not drinking but chatting to the young barman. She smiled at me and informed me that my room number was 23. I said I would like to unpack and reluctantly she left the bar. Once I'd signed the register, collected my key and found my room on the second floor I felt more at ease, more legitimate, somehow. The single room was spacious, a little too pastel for my taste but I had no complaints—I could see the sea, a little distance away but there it was, a wide vista all grey and whipping up fiercely under a glowering sky.

Unpacking took no time at all, which is odd, I thought, considering what a chore the actual packing had seemed. I stared at those empty virgin drawers and placed my underwear there as carefully as if performing a religious ritual. Perhaps I just wasn't used to hotels, but I did find something disconcerting about spreading belongings around a strange room. I felt exposed. As if all the staff would be regaled with stories of my underwear. Would anyone really have any interest in my underwear? How could I be that paranoid? Was I normal? Hubert would probably say not, but who was he to judge?

I checked that the TV worked, that I could get direct dial on the phone, and that I had a Gideon Bible, because I'm superstitious about that. I once stayed in a hole where there wasn't a Bible in my room and I was convinced it was an ill omen. The fire alarm went off two nights in a row and then water seeped through my bathroom ceiling. I patted the Bible in my bedside cabinet, felt comforted and went downstairs to the bar.

The elderly trio sat on two sofas separated by a low table. There was enough space for me but I wasn't sure whether I was glad or sorry. The tall woman moved her Zimmer frame slightly and patted the empty space beside her. I sat down uneasily. I'd joked with Hubert about it not being an eighteen-to-thirty holiday but I hadn't expected it to be this bad!

'I'm Harold James, at your service,' said the lone male, who had the carefully laundered and manicured appearance that some elderly men achieve but usually only when a woman is regularly clipping and snipping stray hairs. His hair was strikingly silver, but dapper though he was, I didn't think he'd ever been very attractive. His features had a caved-in look, his eyes verging on blue but with bloodshot overtones. He insisted on buying me a drink, so I asked for an orange juice. He slowly made his way the few feet to the bar and just as slowly returned to hand me my glass, with a little stiff bow, and then sit next to the tiny woman opposite me. 'Take a few sips first, dear. I'm Mrs Nancy Patterson,' she said. 'And sitting next to you is Miss Margaret Bright.' Margaret managed to lift her head to give me a weak smile. Her name might have been appropriate once but now she was definitely less than sparkling.

'Drink up,' urged Nancy, as if my orange juice was the elixir of life itself. I quickly took two large swigs. 'Lower your glass,' she said. I lowered my glass. From her capacious bag she retrieved her vodka bottle and treated me to a glass-filling measure.

By seven o'clock I too was walking with a strange gait. I managed to follow them slowly into the dining room where a few quiet, totally sober souls were already on their first course.

'We're late,' giggled Nancy as she lurched sideways, her thin legs making her look even less stable. Nancy's legs suited the rest of her birdlike body. Her face was thin but she had good cheekbones, highlighted quite subtly with blusher, and she wore bright pink lipstick. Unfortunately she also wore a blue eyeshadow under pencilled brows, which had the effect of making her look like an aged porcelain doll.

I'd already found out that she was nearly eighty, had been married twice, no children, and had owned and managed a fish and chip shop for years. The fumes from the frying must have been beneficial to both hair and skin because Nancy had a wonderfully clear complexion and thick white hair cut in a boyish short hairstyle that made her look younger but not quite as young as her toy boy, Harold. He was a mere seventy-one but needed a new hip or two and used a walking stick—'When I remind him,' Nancy told me.

Over thin tomato soup Harold told me about his exploits as a plumber ('King of the gold taps'), and about how successful his business had been. Margaret tried to butt in a few times but the soup proved to be a trial and she stayed silent with her head bowed in its painful-looking position.

During a long delay while we waited for our main course she spoke at last.

'I've been here six months now,' she said.

'Yes,' said Nancy, 'and weren't you in a mess when you first arrived? You had more booze with you than the Co-op.'

'I did not.'

'You did! Sherry, whisky, gin. You'd got the lot. You were planning to do yourself in.'

'Don't exaggerate, Nancy,' said Margaret, obviously embarrassed.

'Harold agrees with me, don't you, Harold?'

'As ever, Nancy, as ever.'

Nancy shrugged her thin shoulders but still looked slightly peeved.

'Oh, all right...' said Margaret after a short pause. 'I admit I was depressed. I was old, deformed and lonely and then when all seemed lost I met you two.' She smiled across at the couple. Nancy smiled back with satisfaction.

'There you are, Kate,' said Nancy. 'I told you.'

I nodded, wishing at that moment Scottie would beam me up.

It was a relief when the main courses started to arrive, delivered with a fixed smile by a young waitress wearing high-heeled purple boots with her short black skirt and white apron. Hubert would have been enthralled.

Now that Margaret had started to talk there was no stopping her. 'Once I realized I didn't *have* to die I realized I could live quite comfortably in this hotel. The chambermaid was really helpful, the room was cleaned beautifully every day, my bed was made, I could even have my shoes cleaned and my washing done. And it was cheaper than anything social services could offer me.'

I smiled at her in complete understanding as I thought of some nursing and residential homes I'd worked in. I knew if I was old and had a few thousand brain cells left and the capability to stand up, I would infinitely prefer to be in a hotel like this than with my knees covered with a crocheted blanket, eating sloppy mince with a spoon.

During the main course Harold talked about plumbing, Nancy talked about the merits of frying with lard as opposed to oil, and Margaret tried, without success, to steer the conversation towards a pre-Christmas shopping trip to France.

Silence only fell as the dessert trolley came into view. Virtuously I chose fresh fruit salad *sans* cream and decided that I had tendencies towards being a calorie miser—save a few here, save a few there. The trouble was at the sight of a jam doughnut or a cream slice I'd soon be blowing all my 'savings'. Still, I thought, even a few calories saved was less round the bum to worry about.

My companions, who had the compensation of age making them less calorie conscious, chose sumptuous trifles and gateaux. I was just about to tuck into my healthy option when a tall, youngish man walked into the dining room. He was easy limbed, dark haired, dark eyed as far as I could see—and I was doing my best to see him; in fact, my eyes were out on stalks.

'Who's that?' I asked Nancy.

'That,' she said, 'is the co-owner of the hotel, Stewart Michaelson.'

'And his other half?' I asked casually.

'Poor Nigel, you mean.'

I raised my eyebrows quizzically, thinking as I did so how difficult it was going to be to snoop and sleuth without falling under suspicion myself. But then if the staff at Uplands Lodge had nothing to hide they wouldn't get too paranoid. Perhaps I could pass myself off as a long-lost cousin or similar.

'Why "poor" Nigel?' I asked.

She shrugged. 'I always thought of him like that. And then he just disappeared—'

'Now then, Nancy,' interrupted Harold. 'He didn't disappear, he just decided to...get out of the hotel business. People get what they call "burn-out" these days.'

Margaret lifted her head slightly. 'Is that the same as "going for the burn"?'

Nancy smiled indulgently. 'Come off it, Margaret. You know what it means. We go for the burn every morning just getting out of bed.'

All three of them laughed at this, causing Stewart Michaelson to glance our way. He wore a pale grey suit and a black polo-neck sweater. He looked faintly dangerous and very interesting and I tried in advance to think of something to say to make him think I was pretty interesting too. But life isn't like that and when he did speak to me I stuttered like an idiot. He'd only asked my name and if I was on business or pleasure, and stupidly I burst out with 'K...Kate Kinsella—just business.'

Luckily he smiled and merely said, 'Perhaps we could have a chat about that later in the bar.'

Being intermittently celibate and quite fancying him didn't stop me breathing a sigh of relief and thinking how delicious an early night seemed, because then I wouldn't have to think up any more lies or worry about what to do if at any time he decided to make a pass.

It was Nancy who said, 'You're well in there, dear. He usually avoids our table like the plague. I think he thinks old age is catching. We frighten him.'

'Surely not,' I said. 'You're so lively.'

She shrugged. 'Our minds might be lively but our bodies are only fit for the knackers' yard. Some people just see the wrinkles and the saggy bits. Nigel was different, though. He used to have a chat with us most evenings.'

'So where is he now?'

Nancy was about to speak when Margaret lifted her head and said slowly, 'I don't know where he is, but don't be misled, Kate... He wasn't particularly liked.'

'But I thought... Nancy gave me the impression...'

Nancy smirked mischievously at me. 'I never said I liked him. I only said he talked to us.'

Harold chuckled. 'You'll get used to us, Kate...you will. Come and join us at the bar. There's some live music tonight.'

I soon found out 'live' was a slight exaggeration. There was one man and his piano and rather than him tickling the ivories, they seemed to be tickling him. It made observing him a serious threat to one's mental health. Not that Nancy, Margaret and Harold thought that; they seemed entranced.

The evening passed aided by liberal doses of vodka added to my innocuous orange juice. I was just musing on the effect of the vodka—I'd begun to quite *enjoy* the pianist—when Stewart appeared. From being quite attractive when I was relatively sober, he now appeared totally irresistible.

'I think our trio are leading you astray, Kate,' he said, smiling cheerfully in all directions. 'You'll need all your wits about you while you're on the island.'

What was he talking about? I wondered. I must have looked perplexed because he quickly said, 'You're here on business?'

The lie came as easily to my lips as saliva at the thought of the lemon. 'Yes, I'm thinking of buying a hotel.'

'Really,' he said. I wasn't sure at that moment if he meant a 'Really?' or a 'Really!' Once you've told a lie like that the awful part is the nervous agitation it generates: Do I look as if I've got a few spare thousands? Will my underwear pass inspection? Do I seem to have the business acumen? Then, inspired now to tell even more lies, I did have a feeling this one could save the day—'I've just come into some money.' I thought that was enigmatic enough until I realized he might have thought I'd won millions on the National Lottery.

Stewart smiled at me disarmingly. 'Well, good for you. I won't embarrass you by asking how much, but obviously enough to buy a hotel.'

I nodded.

'Just say the word and I'll give you a behind-the-scenes tour of this place. Give you the low-down.'

'Thanks, Stewart.'

'My pleasure.'

As he left the lounge bar I watched him go, wishing I could have told him the truth.

'So you're rich,' said Nancy.

I shrugged, trying to look modest and rich at the same time. 'It's enough to buy a small hotel. It's something I've always wanted to do.'

She smiled as if she understood and I felt more than obliged to buy the next round of drinks. This time there was no vodka added to mine and I sensed a less-than-subtle change in their attitude towards me. Having lots of dosh, I realized, could cause even mere acquaintances to grow a little cool. Memories of childhood exhortations to always tell the truth came flooding back and I felt an urge to go back to my room, ring Hubert and confess all.

Later that evening when I did ring Hubert he wasn't sympathetic. 'You sound drunk,' he said.

'I am. I've been led astray.'

'You're led astray very easily, Kate. What's happened? You haven't been gone twenty-four hours. Even you can't be in much of a mess yet.'

'Have some faith in me, Hubert,' I said, beginning to feel that I'd already failed on this mission.

'Stay off the drink, Kate. You have the capacity of a pregnant frog so stick to fruit juice and keep a clear head. Now...what cock-up have you made already?'

'Hubert, you can be a real know-all pig at times...' I waited for his response, but he didn't give me that satisfaction. So I said, 'I've told Stewart Michaelson, Nigel's partner, that I'm interested in buying a hotel. That would give me a chance to nose around behind the scenes without arousing suspicion.'

'Nothing wrong with that,' said Hubert. 'Sounds kosher to me.'

'And then I told him I'd come into money and now I think he might think I'm a lottery millionaire.'

There was a long pause before Hubert spoke again.

'And then again, Kate, why should he? Put him straight, that's all you have to do. Say a relative died and left you a tidy sum. Not too much, mind, the residents might want to start borrowing from you. You haven't given them a figure, have you? Like ten million or something?'

'No.'

'Good. Give them a figure, say...five hundred thousand. That should be enough to buy a small hotel and you won't have much left over.'

'That sounds sensible.'

'It is. Now you get to bed, Kate. I'll ring you tomorrow.'

As I lay on the bed waiting to feel slightly better before I slept, I thought of Nigel. Had he wanted to disappear? And why did it seem the only person clamouring for his return was an elderly aunt. Did the man have a serious problem? Like being ten feet underground or ten fathoms deep. Who would be chief suspect? I wondered. Had he had a violent disagreement with Stewart about the future of the hotel? Or was there more to their relationship than just being business partners? After all, they were two single men both in their thirties. At least I *assumed* they were single. So far I'd only wined, dined and told a lie. But tomorrow was another day and I planned to stay well clear of Harold, Nancy and Margaret and concentrate all my efforts on finding out more about Stewart's relationship with Nigel.

A warning voice somewhere in the part of the brain that should have been named the Vale of Sensibleness or something Latin and grand sounding told me that Stewart *was* dangerous. But in my state of male deprivation that only meant one sort of danger. That delicious feeling of finding a man your mother would never have chosen for you.

THREE

LIKE ALL resolutions made in that relaxed state just before sleep—such as going on a diet or promising yourself you'll write those letters or do your tax form—when the morning comes the resolutions are about as tangible as a dream. In a hotel, I reasoned, self-discipline was even harder to achieve, especially when the smell of bacon and toast seemed to creep under my door so tantalizingly.

Breakfast was certainly the highlight of the day, for after that followed a guided tour of bedrooms and kitchens which became very prolonged, primarily because Stewart kept getting called away, telling me to 'Stay put, I won't be a moment.' His 'moments' weren't my moments and I soon got bored waiting for him to return from his various missions. The more I saw of him, the more Mr Average he seemed, and I changed my mind about my mother disapproving of him.

I found it more than hard to bring Nigel into the conversation when discussing the merits of various laundry services or how many of the staff had taken the Basic Food Handling and Hygiene Certificate and therefore knew how to defrost a chicken. I did manage to find out that Nigel kept the accounts and was a keen cook, occasionally lending a hand in the kitchen. That didn't help me much, but I did manage to deduce from that information that he might, if short of money, be able to find work in a restaurant or hotel. Undoubtedly that would mean on the mainland and a choice of several thousand establishments. Chances of him using his real name were zilch, so that was a line of enquiry I wouldn't be able to use, especially as my client didn't have the odd decade to spare.

I'd decided to skulk back to my room well before lunch, when the phone rang. It was Mrs Forrester, my client, and judging by her brisk-sounding voice perhaps I was wrong about her prospects on the longevity stakes.

'What exactly have you found out, Miss Kinsella?'

'Do call me Kate.'

'Very well, Kate. Progress?'

'I have to admit, Mrs Forrester,' I began apologetically, 'as yet I've only spoken to one or two members of staff and the co-owner, Stewart, of course, and...I haven't found any reason to believe that Nigel has come to any harm.'

'In that case,' she said sharply, 'you need to work a little harder.'

'I have only been here a day,' I muttered.

There was a pause while Mrs Forrester coughed and then she said, 'True enough, Kate. Perhaps I am being a little unfair. The police couldn't find any cause for concern either, but I do know my sister's boy would have maintained contact.'

'I'm sure he would, Mrs Forrester, but apart from you who else would he have contacted?... Girl friends, male friends? At the moment I can't ask these personal questions in case they arouse suspicions. I've told Stewart I'm on the island to buy a hotel.'

'Yes, I do see...' she mumbled. 'He did have a girl-friend. I really don't know how serious it was.'

'Could you send me a photograph of Nigel? It would help if I knew exactly what he looked like and of course I need one to jog people's memory.'

'Yes, yes, of course. I should have thought of that.'

I was about to say goodbye when I found myself suggesting that maybe the media could become involved in the hunt for Nigel.

'Do you mean newspapers?' she asked in obvious disgust.

'They can be helpful.'

'I never read newspapers, Miss Kinsella, and I would be mortified to see my nephew mentioned in some scandal rag.'

As she put the phone down I was left wondering... Whatever did Nigel visit her for? She seemed quite sharp mentally but I found her somewhat disconcerting and couldn't quite work out why.

During lunch that day I sat with Harold, Margaret and Nancy. I had tried to avoid them but they called over to me, obviously afraid I'd be lonely. They were polite but I noticed not quite as friendly as they had been.

'How's the hotel hunt going, Kate?' asked Harold.

'I haven't seen anywhere yet, but this afternoon I'll be going to the estate agents.'

Nancy stared at me for a moment with a bland expression, pressed her napkin to her mouth, placed it in her lap, looked up at me and said, 'You're not aiming to buy *this* hotel, are you?'

'Why, Nancy? Is it for sale?' I asked innocently.

'We'd be the last to know, wouldn't we?' she said glaring at me.

'Come now, Nancy, don't upset yourself,' said Harold, patting her hand. 'We always knew that was a possibility.'

I smiled reassuringly at Nancy. 'I've certainly got no intention of buying this hotel and as far as I know neither has Stewart of selling it.'

Margaret looked up slowly. 'It was Nigel who wanted to sell up.'

'I thought he just wanted changes made.'

'That's what he told everyone but he told me he wanted to sell his half of the business.'

'Why would he tell you that anyway?' said Nancy. 'He hardly spoke to us about anything important.'

Margaret smirked knowingly. 'I exaggerated. He didn't actually tell me... I overheard him talking to someone.'

'Who?' Harold looked up sharply from his battered haddock.

'His girlfriend,' answered Margaret.

'That girl with the plaits and the long skirts,' said Harold, giving his haddock a teasing poke with a fork.

'I do wish you wouldn't do that, Harold,' said Nancy.

'Do what, dear?'

'Give your fish a poke before you eat it.'

'The batter's so thick the air gets underneath—I'm just deflating it a bit,' he explained.

Nancy still looked irritated, so I asked as casually as I could, 'Was his girlfriend called Claire? I'm sure Stewart mentioned a Claire.'

There was silence for a moment, then Margaret said, 'She wasn't a Claire—'

'She was Charlotte,' interrupted Nancy.

'That wasn't her name,' said Harold.

'How would you know?' said Nancy. 'The only names you remember are what's running in the two-thirty.'

'You said you weren't going to nag me about my little flutters, Nancy. I don't like the mood you're in today.'

Nancy's eyes flashed daggers but she merely said triumphantly, 'I *do* think her name was Charlotte.'

Harold began shaking his head and then stopped at Nancy's fierce expression. It was Margaret who settled the argument.

'You're right, Nancy. I remember now. He called her Charlotte—honeybunch.'

'He would,' said Nancy in disgust.

'What was her surname?' I asked.

Nancy shrugged. 'We don't know. Does it matter?'

'No, not at all. I thought maybe if I found his girlfriend I could find Nigel.'

'Why do you want to find Nigel?' asked Harold with a hint of suspicion in his voice. I paused, continuing to chew on my mouthful of chicken breast, and finally thought of a reason.

'Stewart recommended him as a bit of an expert on finance, especially hotel finance and I thought if I could find him he'd be really helpful.'

No one spoke for a while but eventually Margaret said, 'I don't know her last name, but I think she was a student. Older than average. She looked in her middle to late twenties and I do know she was in her final year.'

'What course?'

'I'm not sure. It was on the mainland... Art...no. I remember. Performing arts, that was it.'

'Where on the mainland?'

'I don't know that. But Portsmouth or Southampton, I suppose.'

I shrugged nonchalantly. 'Oh well, finding Nigel is no big deal. There must be others on the island who are in the financial know.'

'Yes, indeed,' murmured Margaret. 'And you are in a position to pay for advice, aren't you?'

I knew she was being catty, but I didn't let on. I smiled and said, 'When you've always been poor it's hard to get used to having money.'

She nodded her head in her own peculiar way and I

assumed that meant she felt some sympathy for my erstwhile poverty.

After lunch I slipped away, murmuring something
about estate agents but really I just planned a walk by the
sea and a review of my progress to date.

The walk took longer than the review. The sun shone
thinly with a watery bleakness, the sea looked more green
than grey, seagulls screeched and whirled and I wandered
lonelier than any cloud, more alone than at any time I
could remember. I really missed Hubert's long face and
our trips to the pub and our usually good-natured banter.
I'd ring him later, I decided, and have a long chat on
expenses.

After the sea and the beach I window-shopped, sticking
mainly to bakers' shops and idly wondering if having a
cream doughnut plus three huge meals a day was greed
on such a grand scale that I'd be ousted from the pearly
gates. I fought temptation as bravely as any tested saint
and merely gazed at the cakes and walked on.

It was still only three thirty. Back at the hotel the rest
of the day spread before me as long and tedious as a wet
Sunday. It was no wonder, I thought, that the trio needed
copious supplies of vodka. I'd just approached the stair-
case when Stewart appeared.

'I wanted to catch you,' he said smiling. 'I thought we
might have a meal together.'

'Here?' I queried, wondering quite what the point of
that might be.

'I thought a seriously good restaurant might make a
change.'

I smiled. The hotel food was good but not very original—swordfish and parsnip galette were unlikely to fea-
ture on the menu.

'Are you sure there is a seriously good restaurant on

the Isle of Wight?' I asked in all innocence as if I'd be able to recognize a seriously good restaurant anyway.

He gave me a mock stern look. 'Kate, this island may not have changed much since 1950 but the passage of time has let through balsamic vinegar, virgin olive oil and last week I heard someone had acquired a small jar of sun-dried tomatoes. So, no more insults. I'll meet you in reception at seven.'

Was this a date? I wondered. When it seemed to take me hours to get ready I thought perhaps it was. I couldn't make up my mind what to wear. Stewart's idea of a 'seriously good restaurant' might not mean swish and expensive, but of course I couldn't be sure. I only had two dresses; one is black, and was the only one I'd brought with me, so if I was to wear a dress my choice was limited. Even with that decision made I vacillated. Should I go out and buy something? I stared at my alarm clock. It was five twenty; there was no time before the shops shut. I'd wear the black.

I stared at myself in the dress. My dyed red hair was looking unruly as usual, my skin seemed pale and my eyes bright, as if I'd been crying. I looked funereal. With Hubert by my side we would have been dead ringers for the Munsters. I was forcing a smile at that image when the phone rang. Telepathy, I thought, as I threw myself across the bed to answer the phone. But it wasn't Hubert.

'Hello, Kate. It's Caroline…'

Caroline, I thought, who the hell is Caroline? I don't know any Caroline.

'Caroline—Uxton,' she repeated. 'On the ferry. Adam's mother.'

'*That* Caroline,' I said. 'Nice of you to phone. How is Adam?'

'He's fine. I rang to ask if you'd like to come to dinner tomorrow evening.'

I didn't pause to think as I don't usually turn down invitations to eat. 'I'd love to,' I said.

'We're staying in a bungalow not far from Uplands Lodge. Just walk down the slope for about quarter of a mile. Number five, Jonquil Gardens. I'll give you my phone number just in case.'

I wrote down the number. It was only when I'd put the phone down that I began to regret saying I'd go. I didn't know the woman at all. She seemed OK but did we have anything in common? If I was to be the only guest it could be a bit of a strain. On the other hand, I reasoned, I didn't know Stewart either but I was eager enough to have dinner with him, although I convinced myself that was because over wine and candlelight I could find out much more about young Nigel.

It was as I was going down in the lift that I remembered I was meant to be a woman who'd just come into money. Should I offer to pay the bill? Would he think I was flashing my money around if I did? And if I didn't offer to pay would he think I was as tight as a gnat's arse? It was a dilemma, but when I saw him standing in reception looking rather handsome and carrying a purple orchid I decided to stop worrying, enjoy myself by *acting* as if I was on a date but actually behaving like the professional investigator I tried to be but often failed abysmally.

Stewart put an arm round me as we sat in the taxi but the journey was so short that that was all the progress he did make. We stopped and there in front of us was the green and gold awning of the Royal Sahib. I smiled. I loved Indian food, had always thought French food overrated, but I'd obviously been brainwashed because I'd assumed a 'seriously good restaurant' *had* to be French.

Over poppadoms and that wonderful shredded onion plus mint and mango chutney I got to the point with Stewart.

'I'm a little worried about buying a hotel on the island,' I said.

'Why's that, Kate?'

'I've heard rumours about Nigel.'

'What sort of rumours?' asked Stewart sharply.

I took my time in answering. 'Well...that you...may have had something to do with his disappearance.'

Stewart nearly choked on his poppadom. 'Who the hell said that? It's rubbish, of course. For God's sake, he's a friend of mine and the only minor disagreements we ever had were about the future of the hotel.'

'I didn't mean to upset you. I just overheard a conversation. Someone saying it was strange Nigel hadn't contacted his friends and relatives.'

'What relatives? He hasn't got any relatives.'

I tried to answer casually. 'I'm sure I heard he had an aunt on the mainland.'

Stewart smiled. 'Aunt Lizzie. I forgot her. I can't imagine her noticing Nigel hadn't been in contact. She's a bit senile.'

I realized then, even before our main course had arrived, that Stewart had a serious problem with the elderly, and I had to say something. 'You really don't like old people, do you?'

'I wouldn't say that at all,' he said defensively. 'I don't particularly like the gruesome threesome at Uplands but I wouldn't like them if they were thirty somethings.'

'I think they're rather sweet.'

He raised a quizzical eyebrow but our food was being wheeled towards us and the pungent smell of frying onions and wonderful spices seemed to halt his response somewhere in his olfactory system.

'This is really really good,' he said as he tucked in.

We ate hungrily for a while with the odd 'delicious' and 'lovely' said almost as huskily as if we were nibbling each other's naked flesh.

Becoming more talkative the fuller we became, we were giving each other a run-down on our respective lives by the time the last few grains of rice and crumbs of nan bread were left on our plates. I wasn't being completely honest, of course. I told him about Hubert but gave him the impression I'd been a full-time nurse until I got lucky. I still didn't say where the money came from and he didn't ask, so I began to relax.

'You seem fond of old people,' he said. 'I'm surprised you don't want to buy a nursing home.'

'Too much legislation,' I answered blithely.

'Hotels are nearly as bad these days. The fire regulations are a nightmare—'

He broke off as a male voice shouted, 'If you think I'm eating this—I wouldn't give this to a dog.' I swung round to see a drunken man lurching to his feet. I stared at him. He was, I supposed, between forty-five and fifty-five—I mean his approximate age and waist size. He made Hubert look handsome. 'I want to see the owner!' he yelled. 'Get me the owner! I want the little bastard to see what I've been served.'

Everyone in the restaurant now took an interest in the proceedings. Some of the turbaned staff gathered by the entrance like Gurkha warriors and I heard vague mutterings about retribution. Our waiter came over to us and whispered, 'Please don't worry. He's a very nasty man. Very drunk.'

'Should someone call the police?' I asked as the dissatisfied customer hurled more abuse along with a couple of chairs and finally the table. 'No, no,' said the waiter. 'He'll go now.'

And indeed he did, but not without help. Two of the staff grabbed him by the arms and began dragging him to the door. The door closed, the staff began to right the table and chairs and within seconds all seemed normal again.

Stewart smiled. 'There you are, Kate—violent disorder. Do you still want to buy a hotel here?'

I nodded. 'I think I can stand the excitement. Was that Nigel's problem, do you think? The island being too quiet?'

Stewart shrugged. 'To be honest, I don't know what he thought. We were friendly but not that intimate. He was never very forthcoming and for the last few months before he...left, I couldn't interest him in the day-to-day running of the hotel. He obviously had other things on his mind.'

'What things?'

Stewart shook his head. 'I don't know, but just before he disappeared he'd seemed a bit worried and preoccupied. He spent more and more time in his cabin. I did ask him what was wrong but he wouldn't open up.'

'Cabin?' I queried.

'Yes, at the bottom of the garden behind that row of pine trees. He couldn't afford to buy a place away from the hotel and he liked his privacy. He kept all the books there.'

I noticed the past tense. 'So you've moved everything?'

Stewart shook his head. 'I must admit since Nigel went I've only been down there twice, just to leave some paperwork. I suppose I'm still hoping he'll come back before the annual audit.'

'Do you think he had woman trouble?'

'Maybe.'

'What about you? Do you have woman trouble?'

Stewart laughed. 'Who doesn't? I do have an ex-wife, if that's what you mean.'

It wasn't, but it was vaguely reassuring. Even so, I didn't want to pry. 'What about Nigel? Was he ever married?'

Stewart laughed briefly. 'Nigel didn't like to be tied down. In fact I think he preferred a succession of one-night stands.'

I smiled. 'You sound disapproving. I get the impression you didn't hold Nigel in much esteem.'

'I didn't mean to imply that, but to be honest Nigel could be an arsehole. He's good with figures, though. He got part way through his accountancy exams but quit when the going got tough.'

'So you think he's quit now and just gone walkabout.'

'It's his style.'

'What about Charlotte?' I asked.

Stewart's eyes glinted. 'What are you talking about?' he asked.

'Nigel's girlfriend.'

'Never heard of her,' he said sharply. A little too sharply. Of course he's heard of her. And in that instant I knew I had found a motive for murder.

FOUR

Now that I guessed Stewart did have a reason to murder Nigel my ardour was well and truly cooled. He didn't seem to notice, though, as he smiled and held my hand for one brief but rather suggestive moment.

'I thought,' he said, 'we could go back to the hotel and look at the books if you want. If I haven't made the hotel trade seem too dull and you're still interested, of course.' The 'still interested' sounded ominous and I wondered if he was the sort of man who thought that buying a girl a curry and a few poppadoms was a passport to other Eastern delights. There were to be no Eastern or Western delights with Stewart, I decided. He was, after all, el primo suspect and I couldn't afford to lose track of my main objective.

'I'm certainly still interested, Stewart…about the hotel but quite honestly it's a bit late for me to look at accounts which I wouldn't understand anyway. Perhaps during the day time?'

He nodded but looked a little disappointed. 'A club, then, or we could just go back to the hotel and have a drink in the bar?' This time he squeezed my hand with considerably more suggestion.

'This is really awkward, Stewart… I…well, I promised to visit someone after I'd had dinner with you. Someone I met on the boat coming over.'

'Male?' he queried nastily.

'Female.'

'I see.' His answer was so pointed I didn't need any signposts and I was annoyed.

'Stewart,' I said, 'for the price of a curry and a few poppadoms I'm not game for one night of passion. *And* I take exception to being thought a lesbian just because I prefer to spend time with a woman than with you.'

At that moment the bill arrived. I fumbled in my handbag, found my purse and managed to dredge out a twenty-pound note. 'That should cover it,' I said as I flourished the money on to the plate.

Stewart, I could see, was embarrassed and now I'd said my piece I was beginning to regret it.

As the waiter walked away I stood up and said politely, 'Thanks for a lovely evening. I'm sorry for my outburst. I do hope we can still be friends.'

He didn't answer for a while, then said, 'I'll get my taxi to drop you off.'

'There's no need,' I said with a suitably grateful smile. 'I can walk, it's not far.'

'There's every need. The pubs are closing and if anything happened to you I'd feel responsible.'

'OK,' I said, still feeling guilty about being so sharp with him. 'Thank you.'

In the taxi he didn't speak and I felt I'd been too hasty. He may have had a motive to murder Nigel but how was I going to find out more if I'd alienated my prime suspect and my prime source of information.

As the taxi stopped outside 5 Jonquil Gardens I said, 'Perhaps tomorrow we could have a talk about this, Stewart?'

'I suppose so,' he muttered grudgingly. 'Have a good night.'

I shivered in the cold night air outside number five and watched as the taxi drove slowly away.

The white bungalow, in a row of six, had a balcony with five wooden steps up to the front door. Having clomped noisily up them I expected Caroline to answer the door, so I stood gazing out at the black and treacle-like sea for a while until I realized she hadn't heard me arrive.

I knocked loudly but when she did open the door she didn't seem to remember me. She wore a brilliant-white towelling robe, which didn't make *her* look fat and shapeless. She'd drawn back her hair with a blue ribbon, she wore no make-up and she still looked fantastic. When she did remember me, she was overcome with embarrassment. 'Did I say tonight, Kate, I'm awfully sorry I thought it was tomorrow.'

I really warmed to her then. At least an embarrassment shared, I thought, is an embarrassment halved. 'No, please don't apologize, after all it's nearly eleven and I came here to…escape from someone.'

She smiled a wide friendly smile. 'There's no need to say any more Kate. I know all about that sort of thing. Come on in and tell me all about it. I'm really glad of some company. I'm all alone, Adam's staying with a friend.'

Caroline showed me through to the sparse living room that clearly said 'rented' in its cheap threadbare carpet and furniture. She'd tried to brighten the room with two vases of flowers but my eyes and spirit lifted only at the sight of a spindly coffee table on which stood a nearly full litre of white wine next to a long-stemmed wine glass and an opened box of chocolates. I felt comforted immediately—this woman could become a friend!

'You look as if you need a drink,' she said. 'You sit down, I'll fetch a glass.' She was back in a few moments with not only another glass but another bottle.

'I'll make a bargain with you, Kate,' she said, smiling and holding her head on one side so that I noticed her fair hair had dark roots. 'You tell me your troubles but I'll want you to listen to mine as well, and we have to finish off the wine and the chocolates.'

'How can I refuse an offer like that?' I said, feeling far more cheerful even before I'd started on the wine.

Caroline encouraged me to drink and eat and after a glass of wine and four chocolates I experienced a warm afterglow that was almost orgasmic and it loosened my tongue although I didn't tell her the real reason for my visit. I told her I'd come to the island to buy a hotel, that I lived in Longborough and lodged with an undertaker landlord called Hubert.

'Any hope of a romance there?'

I laughed. 'He's twenty years older than me.'

'But with money?'

'I suppose so. I've never really thought it. He's...a foot fetishist.'

She laughed as she looked down at my very medium-heeled shoes.

'Pathetic,' she said. 'That's really pathetic.'

I found myself springing to Hubert's defence. 'He's not pathetic, he's very kind and generous. He can't help his little aberration and anyway most people are pathetic in some areas.'

She smiled at me from behind her wine glass. 'You're obviously very fond of him even if you're not yet romantically inclined.'

I ignored the 'yet' and for some reason told her all about the death of my drunken boyfriend by falling masonry. I began to get quite maudlin and as I did she kept topping up my glass.

When I paused she asked, 'So what went wrong to-night?'

What *had* gone wrong? I wondered. I shrugged. 'I got scared, I suppose. Once bitten and all that. I meet a man, like him, even get a bit lusty, but then I think about the consequences. I fear involvement, I suppose.'

'Is this Stewart single?' she asked.

'Oh yes, he's divorced.'

She laughed loudly and I realized she was more tipsy than me. 'Most men are these days. You've done the right thing,' she said. 'I know, I'm in the process of getting divorced from a very violent, disturbed man. I'm always on the move, trying to escape from him. That's one of the reasons we've come here for Christmas. Mind you, he always seems to find me. I think he employs scumbag private detectives to follow me.'

I didn't blush, but I did begin to feel a little warm.

'Does he want a reconciliation?' I asked.

'He might want it, though God knows why, I've hated him for years,' she said angrily.

'Because of the violence?'

'That and the fact that he doesn't want me to work. He's got money, you see, not that he ever gave me much even when we were together. He wanted me either at home or working in an Oxfam shop.'

'What was your job?'

Curling her bare feet under her on the thin-seated sofa, Caroline settled herself back against the cushions before replying. 'Just secretarial,' she said. 'I'm working again now, thank goodness.'

'Why didn't he want you to work?'

She stared at me for a moment as if I was being stupid. 'He's insanely jealous. Even if the window cleaner said good morning he'd suspect we were having a rip-roaring affair.'

'Did he drive you into an affair?' I asked.

She laughed again. 'It was on the cards but he hardly let me out of his sight. Even when he was at work he rang me several times in the day.'

'What does he do?'

'He's a bank manager.'

I tried not to look surprised. 'Hubert has a theory,' I said, 'that this country's troubles are entirely due to the new breed of bank manager—"young, thrusting and greedy".'

'He could be right.'

'Hubert says twenty years ago bank managers were old fuddy-duddies but they were trustworthy. Now in Hubert's eyes that might as well be tally men or estate agents.'

Caroline laughed. 'Have some more wine,' she said, 'and tell me what you're going to do about Stewart.'

She filled my glass and I noticed I'd failed to see we were already on the second bottle. Strange, I thought, how I always had a sneaking admiration for anyone who had more than one bottle of wine in the house. One at a time seemed to be my maximum.

'Stewart,' I murmured thoughtfully. 'I'm going to try to get back in his good books because I do need his help on buying a suitable hotel.'

'Will you need a mortgage?' she asked.

'I'll probably have enough to pay cash.'

'Any left over?'

'I don't think there will be.'

'In that case you should get a mortgage, maybe a small one, but you'll need capital to start up. In hotels there's always something to replace, bills to pay, wages to find— you need a free flow of money.'

'I hadn't thought of that. You sound as if you know the hotel trade.'

'I wouldn't say that,' she said, smiling. 'But I did work as a chambermaid for a few months after I left school. I know about breakages—I was *always* breaking things. Seriously, though, much better to take out an affordable mortgage. I might be able to help you—I do have quite a few contacts in the housing market.'

'Thanks. At the moment I think I'll need all the help I can get. The hotel trade proved too much for Nigel. He disappeared three months ago.'

'Nigel?'

'Nigel Carter, the co-owner of Uplands Lodge.'

'Oh, I see,' she murmured. 'No one's seen him, then?'

'I've heard gossip-wise there was a woman involved. Perhaps they've run off into the sunset together.'

Caroline shrugged. 'Was he married?'

'No. In his thirties but not married.'

'Why has he disappeared, then?'

'No idea,' I said.

Caroline looked thoughtful. 'In my opinion, if it wasn't love it was money.'

'Why?'

'What other reason could there be? Either creditors or the like, or escaping from a lover's grip. I mean he hadn't already succumbed to marriage, had he? Perhaps he was weak, couldn't cope with any pressure.'

'He wasn't in debt, as far as I know,' I said thoughtfully and realized at the same time that really I knew very little about him.

'He was probably fiddling the accounts,' said Caroline confidently. 'People can be very dishonest, especially in business.'

'I suppose they can.'

I glanced at my watch. It was nearly one a.m. No wonder my eyelids felt waterlogged and my brain, temporarily I hoped, in a state of shutdown. I didn't want to go back to the hotel yet, because Caroline was proving to be quite useful, and I liked her.

'Stewart has offered to show me the books,' I said, 'and explain things in words of one syllable.'

'Is he good on the financial side?'

I shook my head. 'I think Nigel was really the money expert.'

'I bet he was.' She gazed at me thoughtfully for a few seconds. 'You're very naïve about business matters, aren't you?'

I smiled. 'I suppose I am. I've never had any experience. Nursing doesn't teach you business acumen.'

There was a long pause before she said, 'You do realize Stewart is setting you up?'

'What do you mean?'

'Taking you out to dinner, offering to show you the books. Next step, he'll offer to sell you Uplands Lodge at a knock-down price.'

'Surely not,' I said swiftly. 'It's not for sale.'

'Come off it, Kate. You arrive wanting to buy a hotel. His partner's done a runner. Stewart must know, or at least suspect, Nigel was skimming the profits in some way.'

I didn't answer at first. I was hurt. *Was* Stewart manipulating me? Offering to show me the books knowing a blind beggar would glean as much sense from them as I would?

'The bastard!' I said loudly as hurt pride quickly gave way to anger and the thought that maybe, if not me, then some other sucker. Perhaps he knew all the time where Nigel was. The thought occurred to me too that maybe

Nigel was devious enough to want to worry his aunt to death—hoping on her death to inherit her money and bail himself out, or that he and Stewart had hatched a plot *together*. Exactly why they should do that I didn't know but I'd find out.

'You can't let him get away with it, Kate,' said Caroline. 'I'll tell you what... How about if tomorrow night I come to the hotel and we have a look at the books together? I'm pretty good at bookkeeping.'

'How? As far as I know they're at Nigel's place.'

'Where's that?'

'He's got a cabin-type place at the bottom of the hotel garden. Sort of home plus office. We'd have to break in.'

'We'll get in somehow,' said Caroline.

I remembered my previous, very minor attempts at breaking and entering. I may have got *in* but it's *then* the trouble starts. Somewhere, though, in that wooden abode was a clue to Nigel's disappearance—either in the accounts or something more private, but just as important. A forced entry was at least worth considering.

'I'll think about it, Caroline. You could come to dinner at the hotel and perhaps we could discuss it.'

She smiled in a satisfied sort of way. 'We may as well finish the vino,' she said as she emptied the remaining wine into our glasses. Lifting the glass to eye level she said, 'To tomorrow night!'

'Tomorrow night,' I murmured.

'You'll stay the night,' she said. 'There's a spare room. The bed's made up.'

I didn't argue. As I'd stood up I'd felt quite giddy.

I remember lurching slightly as I found my way to the spare bedroom, and as I turned to close the door Caroline was right behind me, her turquoise eyes glittering slightly.

'Just wanted to make sure you made it to the bed,' she said, smiling.

FIVE

IN THE MORNING I woke up with a start wondering where the hell I was and why I had such an awful headache. I remembered the plain chocolates but conveniently forgot the wine.

In the kitchen Caroline, wearing her immaculate white bathrobe, was busy making coffee, boiled eggs and toast. We didn't speak much, she read her copy of the *Daily Mail* and commented on bits of lightweight gossip, I read holiday brochures, noticing her own 'holiday home' listed with the name and address of the landlord. As we washed up the breakfast dishes Caroline said, 'What have you got planned for today, Kate?'

I paused before answering. 'I might visit one or two estate agents and maybe look at a couple of hotels, if there are any for sale.'

Caroline laughed. 'You really are green, aren't you! There are more hoteliers going bankrupt than any other businessmen. Even those not up for sale would probably sell for a halfway reasonable offer.'

'I didn't realize it was as bad as that. The recession, I suppose?'

'That and the fact that so many families go abroad for holidays now. The eighteen to thirty crowd want Greece or Spain. No one wants the dear old Isle of Wight.'

I left the bungalow at just after eleven, promising to be in reception at seven p.m., so that we could be fed and watered before attempting our vaguely planned breaking-and-entering scheme. It seemed somewhat foolhardy now, *sans* wine, and I wondered why Caroline should want to help me. But perhaps it was the fact that I'd helped her out on the boat that made her so keen to help. If Stewart was trying to set me up with a failing hotel it would be as well to know, so that I could feel righteous indignation. Misplaced, maybe, because I was fooling him, but nevertheless I looked forward to it and, of course, to finding Nigel. If Stewart *did* know where Nigel was perhaps I could coerce him in some way. I couldn't quite imagine myself playing solo Russian roulette with him or smacking him in the mouth. In the end I'd probably have to make do with mere righteous indignation and find Nigel myself.

I had no intention of visiting estate agents that day, as it was bitingly cold with a wind strong enough to make eyes water and knees tremble, and anyway my first priority was going to be to find Nigel's girlfriend Charlotte. I lazily anticipated lying on the bed and finding her via a few calls.

In the hotel, the welcome warmth made me quickly remove my jacket and gloves. Amanda Giles, the receptionist, handed me an envelope with my key. I opened it there and then, saw that it contained a photo, turned my back to her and gazed at the blond hair and blue eyes of a youthful Nigel—so youthful he was still at school. Could I really tout Aunt Lizzie's favourite photo of Nigel aged fifteen around the Isle of Wight and suggest that people use their imagination? My only hope was to find a recent photo in our excursion to the cabin at the bottom of the garden.

My second disappointment of the day was due entirely to my misplaced optimism that a few phone calls to colleges and drama schools would find an aspiring actress called Charlotte. What they did find was rudeness and sarcasm, although I had to admit that 'You must be joking—we've got Charlottes behind every arras' was one I quite liked.

AT SEVEN I was waiting in reception. The wind had dropped; it was dark and clear outside, with frost already glimmering on far roof tops. Caroline arrived by taxi, wearing a fun fur which suited her. I'd tried one once myself but managed only to look furrily fat and like a less-than-expensive tart. Caroline managed to look elegant, sexy and rich all at the same time.

'This is exciting,' she said. 'I've got a torch and a crowbar, one in each pocket.'

'What if we get caught?'

She shrugged. 'We won't. If we do I'll bluff our way out of it. I'll say we went in to rescue a stray cat or something.'

I still felt wary. She was taking over and I was letting her.

Dinner passed pleasantly enough. Caroline did most of the talking, going through Adam's childhood from labour onwards. Labour tales, I thought, are akin to hearing about hysterectomies, haemorrhoids and triple bypasses, of absolutely no interest unless you've experienced them. But I nodded politely and privately thought her tales of her violent husband were more interesting—or perhaps the wine last night had affected my judgement.

We sat in the corner of the small bar afterwards, drinking coffee and watching the comings and goings. Harold, Nancy and Margaret sat together on a three-seater sofa, looking like the three wise monkeys and occasionally waving across to us as though we needed cheering. Harold fiddled with his glasses often and Nancy's voice seemed to get higher the later it got, probably because of their secret supermarket vodka. There were a few other residents I'd never actually spoken to. One or two non-residents seemed to have drifted in and I noticed the average age was mid-forties and rising. Frankie, the barman, was unusually busy but managed to keep smiling and, I noticed, gossiping. I could hear snippets in the restrained atmosphere. 'Well, there you are, John, it just goes to show I was right. She came in here all the time. I'm not saying she was a tart but they weren't playing Scrabble—were they?' A little later I heard him say, 'If you ask me I'd say Derek needs a new woman like a teetotaller needs a bottle of whisky.'

Why hadn't I noticed Frankie's gossipy tendencies before? I wondered. Then I remembered that previously I'd be in the bar with Harold, Nancy and Margaret and perhaps he knew about the illicit vodka or he just didn't like them, because he had seemed positively surly and unapproachable then. Now he was animated and talkative and someone I should cultivate.

Caroline murmured, 'Excuse me,' and walked off in the direction of the ladies. I looked at my watch. It was ten p.m.

A few minutes later she reappeared, closely followed by a short, stocky man with receding hair and rimless glasses. They were obviously rowing and an expectant hush fell on the customers. She turned around to confront him and he grabbed her arm.

'You bitch!' he screamed. 'You wrecked my life. You scheming, evil bitch!' He raised his hand and hit her hard in the face. A man standing at the bar began to pull the assailant away and others moved forward.

'I'm calling the police,' said Frankie in a high-pitched voice. By now I was at Caroline's side, the man let go and she slumped towards me. I sat her down and saw that she was crying. Her attacker was being bundled outside, and I rushed into reception, past the men who had removed him and through the main door. I wasn't going to let him get away!

It was dark and beginning to snow outside and I could see him staggering slightly along the wet pavements. He wore no overcoat, strands of sparse hair lifted in the wind and rain, his shoulders were slumped in abject defeat and suddenly he seemed more sad and pathetic than dangerous. I assumed that this was her husband. He'd obviously been drinking and my chasing after him, I reasoned, wasn't going to achieve anything.

Back in the bar Caroline sat looking pale and shaken with a brandy in front of her. 'I'm sorry about that, Kate. I told you what he was like. He must have followed me from the bungalow.'

'Don't apologize,' I said. 'It wasn't your fault. Are the police coming?'

'I asked the barman to cancel the call.'

'Why?'

Caroline shrugged. 'They'll just give him a warning. It wouldn't help.'

'But he might be waiting at the bungalow.'

'He's already drunk, he'll just get paralytic and fall asleep somewhere. Tomorrow he'll appear, all contrite and pleading. I'm used to it, Kate. One day, of course, he'll kill me.'

I sighed inwardly at her resignation. 'Caroline, you really should slap a restraining order on him. You can't live your whole live in fear.'

'I'm getting hardened to it,' she said and sipped her brandy.

Stewart suddenly appeared at the bar, spoke a few words to Frankie and then approached us. He sat on the arm of the sofa, gave me a rather forced smile, turned to Caroline and said, 'I'm the hotel owner, Stewart Michaelson. I'm so sorry about the...incident, and sorry I wasn't around to help out. I believe you told the barman to cancel the call to the police.'

She smiled, her eyes holding his. 'I'm Caroline Uxton. It's kind of you to be concerned, Mr Michaelson.' She paused. 'But unfortunately that man is still my husband and he's to be pitied really.'

Stewart looked impressed, 'I think that's very magnanimous of you, Mrs Uxton. Could I get you ladies a drink?'

'Call me Caroline. Yes, I'd love another brandy.'

'And you, Kate?'

'Coffee, please.'

As he walked away, Caroline turned to me and said, 'He's very attractive. I'm not surprised you were swayed by him.'

'I haven't been swayed,' I answered swiftly. 'And I'm not likely to be now.'

Stewart brought back the drinks moments later and then left informing us he had to check the menus for the next day.

'What time do you think the bar will be empty?' asked Caroline.

'You still want to risk it?' I said in surprise.

'Of course. I owe you a favour.'

I paused before answering. I *did* want to gain access to Nigel's place because then I could get a better idea about the sort of man he was, without arousing too much suspicion, but I was still wary.

'Come on, Kate,' said Caroline. 'It would be as well to know what sort of man you're dealing with before he begins his sales pitch. After all, it could be a very good deal. I've picked up quite a few tips over the years about buying and selling businesses—we could beat him down on price.'

I shrugged at her determination. 'Yes, I'm still game, but I've had no suggestion from Stewart that he *wants* to sell me this place.'

'Just you wait,' she said, smiling. 'Just you wait.'

At eleven thirty we left the bar, waving goodnight to Nancy, Harold and Margaret, who looked as if they were too tired to walk to their rooms without help.

Upstairs we sat propped up on my bed watching television for a while and I tried desperately to keep awake. I'd actually nodded off when Caroline shook my arm. 'Kate, it's one thirty. We should make a move.'

Rubbing my eyes and stretching, I staggered to my feet. At that moment I would have loved to have the strength of character to refuse, but I didn't. We slipped on our coats and I followed Caroline out of the room and down the Staff Only back stairs. They were narrow and dark and lit only by the light of Caroline's torch, but we were soon at the back door and out in the snow-covered garden.

I stood for a moment staring at the white lawn and from there to the pine trees beyond. On my right was a circle of apple and cherry trees, all dripping with snow and glimmering in the light of the quarter-moon. Caroline whispered, 'Stop staring at the view—come on.'

The sound of the crunch of our feet on the snow reminded me—footprints!

Caroline turned round and shone her torch at the ground. 'Don't worry, we can say we came down to investigate a noise and anyway it's thawing. By the morning the snow will have gone.'

In the right-hand corner beyond the fruit trees I caught a glimpse of the cabin tucked away behind more small pine trees like a large Wendy house. It was painted as white as the snow. As we got closer I could see the door, also white, had a black latch-type handle and above that was a black sign saying 'The Cabin' in gold letters. There were two small windows with drawn curtains and judging by the size of the cabin it contained only one room.

'Let's go round the back,' said Caroline as she shone her torch to light our way back into the dark place behind the cabin. Spiky bushes and a bumpy ground proved enough to make me stumble and as I put out my hands to save myself I felt a sharp pain in my wrist. By the time I'd sworn a few times the pain had become merely a dull ache. It didn't appear to be hideously deformed in the light of Caroline's torch so I presumed it wasn't broken.

'Are you OK?' asked Caroline as she brushed loose snow from my jacket.

'Fine,' I said. 'It's not broken—just throbs a little.'

'I'll do the hard work, then,' she said.

The back of the cabin itself proved to be bare white boards and one tiny high window. There was no way either of us could reach the window, let alone go through it.

'Let's abandon this, Caroline. Is it really worth the risk?' I asked, feeling unusually sensible.

'I'm the one doing the deed,' said Caroline taking the crowbar from her pocket.

The first crack of a split board sounded loud in the quietness of the night but somehow being at the back of the cabin gave me a certain feeling of security: like a child, I supposed, believing if you can't see someone they can't see you.

Caroline continued wrenching away and the next board she managed to crowbar off in one piece. Again the crack seemed ferociously loud. With three boards loosened, she edged her way in sideways. I quickly followed, although it was more of a squash for me and I could hear my jacket being ripped open by a jagged edge.

She scanned the room rapidly with her torch and then lifted a lamp from a bedside cabinet, placed it on the floor and switched on. A dull glow flooded the room. A room that encompassed a whole living area; bed, desk, table, a tiny kitchen area and in one corner a shower area with a white shower curtain that was pulled across.

The musty smell of damp reminded me of an old garden shed and rotting things and my eyes stared at the thin red carpet which covered the floor. Had anyone searched for Nigel under the floorboards? I wondered. I thought not, because only his aunt feared the worst, but as I stood in his previous home I experienced one of those slight body tremors, not quite a shudder but more than a single shiver.

'What's wrong?' asked Caroline.

'I'm fine,' I said, because by then the feeling had passed and although I no longer noticed the smell I did notice the curtains, plain, creased, and a putrid green colour. They told their own story. Nigel had been depressed because only a depressed man could have lived with those curtains.

Caroline's concern for me hadn't lasted long. She was already opening the filing cabinet next to the desk in the corner of the room with the aid of the crowbar. She removed several invoice books, a handful of files and a couple of A4-sized cash books. She placed them in a neat pile on the desk, then peeled off her black leather gloves, revealing underneath a pair of tight-fitting surgical ones. I wasn't wearing any gloves and the fact that I wasn't told me two things: I was a lousy burglar, and Caroline Uxton wasn't. She'd done this sort of thing before and for reasons of her own she'd chosen me to accompany her.

I dithered for a while, told myself here was a golden

opportunity to learn more about Nigel and then, resolving to make full use of the opportunity, began searching his domain in earnest.

In a small chest of drawers I carefully sifted through a few pairs of oldish cotton boxer shorts, two pairs of faded black silk boxers, assorted vests and a selection of socks, mostly old ones. I reasoned that like most people he had taken his best underwear with him. His single wardrobe revealed two suits, two pairs of shoes, only two pairs of casual trousers, plus three sad-looking sweaters.

Meanwhile Caroline sat reading the books and even though I tried to be quiet I thought my quest must be irritating her. She said nothing. She was far too engrossed.

I made mental checklists of what I had found and what I hadn't. The most striking missing object was any form of luggage. Unless Nigel hadn't owned a suitcase, which I thought unlikely for a man who wore silk boxer shorts, then he'd taken it with him.

In the bedside cabinet drawer I found two photographs of the hotel and a more recent one of Nigel. He wasn't alone. He stood between a small boat named *The Havana Belle* and a tall man with a beer gut that resembled a barrel of beer itself. I pocketed the photo and made my way to the shower area. I'd put off pulling back the shower curtain. Ever since I'd seen the film *Psycho* I'd felt that drawn shower curtains were a sure sign that some form of shock was in the offing.

I took a deep breath as I stood in front of the white curtain. Then I raised my hand and with a valiant flourish yanked it back.

There was of course nothing, except the shower itself. I opened the small bathroom cabinet. It contained a bottle of paracetamol, a packet of dental floss, E45 cream and a half-empty bottle of cheap aftershave. There was no razor—electric or otherwise.

Caroline continued to scan the books, oblivious to me and my search. 'How much longer do you think you'll be?' I asked.

'Hours,' she said, without looking up. 'You go back to bed, Kate. I'll come to your room in the morning.'

I bristled a little at that. I sat on the divan bed and watched her for a while. 'Surely there's something I could do?' I queried.

'Leave it to me, Kate. Unless you're an expert on double-entry bookkeeping.'

I wasn't, of course, and I sat for several minutes feeling totally useless and wondering what role I had let myself assume. Was I a burglar's mate? Or simply an accomplice?

Eventually I decided to leave. As I left via our back 'entrance' I glanced at Caroline, turning the pages of a ledger, still wearing her rubber gloves, and my only thought then was, What the hell is she up to?

SIX

THE SOUND OF heavy rain woke me at seven a.m. I'd only slept for about three hours but I felt strangely wide awake. Good, I thought, all trace of our footprints will be gone. I pulled back the curtains to see in the distance a black, choppy sea, matching sky and rain that had surely scoured every snowflake from sight.

There was no sign that Caroline had returned and although I admired her stamina, at this time of the morning she was in great danger of being spotted. And, of course, so was I.

The corridor was deserted and I felt like a criminal as I crept down the back stairs. I hadn't put on a coat just in case someone did see me, so that I could say I was lost and was merely looking for the dining room. As I opened the back door the rain beat at my face and I took a deep breath before running down the garden.

At the back of the cabin there was still some snow lying in wet clumps on the soggy ground. Rain ran down my face and I shook myself like a dog before attempting to get through the gap in the boards. This morning the space seemed narrower, so crouching down with my head only through the gap I called out, 'Caroline, come on out now. It's after seven—we'll be seen.' There was no reply. 'Caroline—wake up. It's time to go.'

By now the rain had made me cold and I quickly scrambled through. Caroline was at the desk. No longer sitting but slumped.

Rain ran into my eyes and suddenly the whole room

was suffused with red. The red of the blood which surrounded her. Red on the white paper in front of her, red
in her hair, red on her gloved hands, her fur coat still on
and bloodied as any slaughtered animal. I was used to
blood, but in the right place, at the right time—the oper-
ating theatre or a casualty department.

Fear seemed to slow me down. The few steps to her
body took for ever. I began to shiver and feel sick. The
blood was on her wrist but I went through the motions of
trying to find her pulse. Gently I lifted her head. One eye,
fixed and staring, caught mine. Her blonde hair was mat-
ted and still wet with blood. I gulped back the bile that
came into my throat and then I saw the weapon that had
killed her—the crowbar—bloodied and thrown on the
floor.

There was no telephone and I was in an agony of in-
decision. How could I explain my presence? Should I ring
the police anonymously? I stared at Caroline's body for
some minutes. Had she been attacked from behind? Had
she been sleeping? Had she been aware of what was happening? I hoped for her sake she knew nothing. As for
the killer, there was no doubt in my mind that her husband
Lyle was responsible and he couldn't be allowed to get
away.

I looked at my watch. It was seven twenty and I knew
from the fact that the blood on her hair was still slightly
wet that she hadn't died long before. At a rough guess I
would have said after six a.m.

I walked slowly back through the garden, no longer
caring if I got wet. Passing a room on the first floor I was
surprised to see Nancy and Harold emerge from the same
room. Nancy looked summery in a thin, short-sleeved
jumper of palest blue with a black and red floral skirt. She
wouldn't be cold, though; I knew that because the tem-

perature in the hotel was maintained at a constant 80°F. But I was cold; my wet clothes hung to me in a icy embrace.

'Are you all right, dear?' asked Nancy. 'You're so wet. Why didn't you put a coat on?'

Harold nodded as if in agreement. 'You should have a nice hot bath,' he suggested. 'Shall I get them to send you up your breakfast on a tray?' Strangely, I noticed he wore a powerful aftershave and his hair was slicked back as if gelled. I shook my head and walked on in a daze. I expected to find Amanda Giles in reception but Stewart was behind the desk.

'Where on earth—?' he began and then stopped as I interrupted him. 'Call the police, Stewart—There's been...a death.'

'Here? What's happened?' His face registered several emotions at once.

'Just call the police,' I said wearily.

He paused for a moment and then picked up the phone.

I sat down and tried to marshal my thoughts but Stewart had other ideas. He crouched down beside me and held my hand. 'Kate, what's happened? Where's the body?'

I realized I couldn't *not* tell him. 'It's Caroline Uxton, she's been murdered.'

'Christ,' breathed Stewart. 'Where? How?'

'In Nigel's cabin.'

'What the hell was she doing in there?'

'Stewart, I'm a bit shocked. I can't explain to you first and then to the police. You'll find out soon enough.'

He patted my hand. 'Would you like a brandy?'

I shook my head.

'Tea?'

I nodded.

I'd only drunk a few sips when the police arrived like

a swarm of excited bees. The queen bee hovered at the
desk wearing a grey pinstripe and an expression of grim
determination.

'Where's the body?' he asked Stewart. 'I'm DCI Formbridge.'

Stewart indicated the corridor to the back door. 'Cabin
in the garden.'

'You lot,' said Formbridge to his entourage. 'Cordon it
off. Don't touch anything. Let the video man in first and
then the scene of crimes. And watch where you put your
bloody great boots. And where the hell is the doctor?'

'He's on his way, sir,' murmured someone timidly.
Formbridge made a sound that was an expressive snort
and added a sneer for good measure.

By now I was feeling nervous. He didn't seem a very
nice man. He didn't look that pleasant either. He was thick
set with heavy-lidded eyes and a dark menacing look—
he'd have made a good extra in a Mafia film.

'Who found the body?' he asked of no one in particular.

By now a few residents were sauntering past towards
the dining room.

'Move along quickly, please,' he said. 'Police business.'

Turning to Stewart, who looked as awkward as a jilted
bridegroom, he said, 'Make sure they don't leave the dining room until we've got statements. And of course I shall
want to look at the register.'

Stewart nodded.

'Right, then. Who found the body?'

It reminded me of those situations at school when a
teacher demands someone owns up to a misdemeanour
and guilt surges through the innocent.

'I found the body,' I said and felt as if I were saying
'I killed her.'

His dark eyes fixed on me and I knew he was noting my wet hair and clothes. 'Did you know the victim?'

I nodded. At that moment a young woman carrying a medical bag arrived.

'Ah, there you are, Doctor,' said Formbridge charmlessly. 'The body's in the cabin at the bottom of the garden.' He pointed towards the back of the hotel. The doctor, without a word, turned and walked in the direction of the back door.

Formbridge turned his hooded eyes towards me and I quailed inwardly although I did my best not to show it.

'Your name?'

'Kate Kinsella.'

'Miss?'

He made the word sound like an insult. I nodded.

'Well, Miss Kinsella. Perhaps you'd better explain how you managed to find a body at the bottom of the garden on this wet, cold December morning, when most people only manage to find fairies.'

There wasn't a hint of humour in his voice or his eyes and I found myself saying, 'It wasn't my idea. Caroline was doing me a favour...' He fixed me with a cold stare and I was aware Stewart was listening to every word.

'Caroline is the victim?'

'Yes. Caroline Uxton.'

'In that case I'd better visit the victim.'

I'd just started a sigh of relief when he added, 'I get very nasty about murders on my patch. We are talking murder, Miss Kinsella?'

I nodded.

'Don't move an inch. I'll be back.'

Stewart and I stared at his retreating back and I could almost see the questions forming in Stewart's mind.

'What the hell's been going on, Kate? What did you mean it was her idea?'

I mumbled about being in shock but he ignored me.

'Out with it, Kate.'

I sighed. There was no way I could lie any more. 'I'm a private investigator, Stewart. I've been employed by Nigel's aunt to...find him.'

Stewart stared at me. 'So all that crap about wanting to buy a hotel was a pack of lies.'

'Precisely.'

'What about Caroline? Where does she fit into the equation?'

'She thought you might be planning to "offload" the hotel on to me.'

'Why would I do that?'

'Because Nigel had been fiddling the books in some way and you might have thought it would be in your best interests to sell up before the deficit came to light.'

Stewart frowned. 'Do you think I'm some sort of idiot? The finances of this hotel are just fine and dandy and I have, as I told you before, absolutely no intention of selling up. Nigel had his money given to him, I had to work extremely hard for mine and this hotel is my life.'

I was trying hard to think of a suitable reply when DCI Formbridge returned. 'I think, Miss Kinsella, you have some explaining to do. At the station.'

Stewart flashed me a 'serve you right' sort of look and I stood up, still feeling slightly removed from the situation, as though I were watching myself through a frosted pane.

A woman police constable called Alison Joiner, who looked very young but drove the car with grim determination and an equally grim expression, took me to the police station. I didn't think it appropriate to make smalltalk and she needed all her concentration to drive in the ferocious rain.

At the station I was led to an interview room and offered tea. Alison Joiner sat with me in total silence until it began to unnerve me. I almost asked for a cigarette, which for a non-smoker showed the sheer depth of my unease. Every time I opened my mouth to say something I realized it sounded fatuous in the circumstances, so I stayed silent. It was almost a relief when Formbridge showed up.

'You're in trouble,' he said. 'And I mean trouble.'

I waited for what I guessed was going to be an even more damning quote—and it came: 'It seems to me, Miss Kinsella...you are, as we say, our prime suspect.'

I stared at him. He didn't blink and I could see by the expression on his face he meant it. My mind raced and for a moment I felt genuine panic; cell doors clanged shut, a single light bulb shone in my eyes day and night, cold porridge or soggy cornflakes faced me every morning, not a man in sight, I'd have to wear prison-issue knickers, and would Hubert ever forgive me?

'Chief Inspector,' I began, trying to keep my voice firm, 'I'm a private investigator employed to find Nigel Carter, the co-owner of the hotel. I'm most certainly *not* a killer.'

In a voice heavy with sarcasm Formbridge said, 'I'm impressed. Perhaps you'd be willing to expound your theories on who the killer might be.'

'Her husband—Lyle—of course,' I said with confidence. 'He has a history of violence and Caroline told me he would kill her one day. He was at the hotel last night. He hit her and he wasn't in a pleasant mood.'

'So in your opinion as a private investigator this man is the murderer.'

'Who else?'

'Who else indeed.'

Formbridge's lips stretched somewhat, but to have called it a smile would have been a severe exaggeration. 'Perhaps you could explain, then, how this man Lyle Uxton could have been responsible, when he was safely in police custody after being locked up last night for being drunk and disorderly on the streets of Ryde and wasn't released until seven thirty this morning.'

SEVEN

I COULDN'T at that moment think of a suitable reply, so I just looked humble and murmured, 'Anyone can make a mistake.'

DCI Formbridge looked down his nose at me and frowned. 'Just start from the beginning,' he said. 'I want facts not half-truths. I want to find out exactly what happened last night. And I'm warning you,' he paused for fear-inducing emphasis, 'if I'm halfway suspicious that you're not telling the whole truth and nothing but the truth—you'll be sorry.'

I began at the beginning, my office and the phone call from Nigel's aunt.

'Hang on a minute,' interrupted Formbridge. 'Why *you,* if you run a medical and nursing detective agency?'

I shrugged. 'I'm the only one locally, I suppose. Either that or my fame has spread by word of mouth.'

He wasn't impressed. 'Carry on. You came to the Isle of Wight to find Nigel Carter. Have you made any progress?'

'Not really…I've been very low key, not wanting to arouse suspicions…'

'That's a joke.'

'No, it wasn't a joke,' I said coldly. 'If I'd said openly I was trying to find Nigel people would have clammed up. After all, he could have been murdered too.'

'We found no evidence to suggest that.'

'Neither have I…so far.'

'Where did you meet Caroline Uxton? Here or on the mainland?'

'On the ferry.'

'You'd never met her before?'

'No. I'd never met her before.'

'Is this your first visit to the island?'

'Yes.'

'And Caroline's?'

'I think so.' Had she actually told me? At that moment I couldn't remember, but I did recall her saying something about the 'dear old Isle of Wight.' No one says that sort of thing unless they are familiar with a place.

Formbridge fixed me with a stare as cold as a corpse. 'Last evening—what happened?'

I related the whole evening to him.

'I see,' he murmured. 'Two things spring to mind. Why didn't you simply *ask* Stewart Michaelson to see the books? If he was trying to "offload" the hotel wouldn't he have expected you to see the books? And, as far as Caroline Uxton is concerned, didn't you think it odd that on the same evening she was attacked by a man she is keen to do some breaking and entering solely in the name of friendship?'

I paused. He was right, of course. If I'd been attacked by a man I would have wanted to take to my bed.

'He wasn't a stranger,' I said. 'He was her husband.'

Formbridge's rubbery lips formed a thin stretched line. 'That makes it all right, does it?'

'I didn't say that. It was just that she always expected him to find her. It would have been more of a shock if she'd been attacked by a stranger.'

'But didn't you think it strange she had the nerve?'

I shrugged. 'She was a strong woman.'

'Did you provide the crowbar?'

'I did not!'

'It's no good getting indignant, Miss Kinsella...' He paused. 'Let's recap, shall we? Caroline provided the crowbar and did all the donkey work. You just observed for a while and then took yourself off to bed to reemerge a few hours later to find her dead.'

I could feel myself starting to blush with shame. Anything I said now would only compound my stupidity.

'Well, what have you got to say?'

I looked him straight in the eye. 'It seems that I made a mistake.'

'Made a bloody mistake! I'll say you made a mistake. A criminal mistake. I'm a man who sees things in black and white, Miss Kinsella. Right and wrong. You've admitted breaking and entering and you were the last person to see Caroline Uxton alive. I'm going to keep you here for further questioning and of course until we have some forensic results.'

'Am I under arrest?'

'Yes.'

He recited my rights, which seemed minimal.

'Am I entitled to make a phone call?'

He nodded.

In a narrow corridor outside was a pay phone. Formbridge stood behind me, unnerving me. The phone rang and rang. Please be there, I muttered to myself. Please! Eventually, when despair had reached astral proportions, Hubert answered.

The sound of his voice was reassuringly normal and, for Hubert, quite cheerful.

'Hubert...I...'

'Hello, Kate. Everything all right? Cracked the case of disappearing Nigel, have you?'

'No...I'm sort of...arrested.'

'Only sort of, Kate? What did you do? Hit a lamppost or do a bit of jay walking?'

'No, Hubert. This isn't trivial. I've been arrested for breaking and entering and far worse than that—'

'You are being serious, aren't you?'

'I wouldn't joke about anything so serious...would I?'

'Well, you do have a very odd sense of humour. Warped, even.'

'I'm ignoring that, Hubert. I really am in trouble. A woman I met on the boat and had dinner with last night...has been found murdered.' There was no response. 'Hubert, are you still there?'

'Of course I'm still here. I'm thinking.'

'Hubert...please. I need help.'

'You always do,' he muttered. 'I'll be there as soon as I can.'

'You will?'

'Yes. Just don't say anything until I get there.'

'I've already been interviewed.'

'Just keep your mouth shut from now on, then. I know it's difficult for you, but remember... Shut!'

I was about to thank him when Formbridge took the phone from me.

'Hubert coming to the rescue, is he? Your solicitor?'

'No. An undertaker. And, yes, Hubert is coming here.'

Formbridge gave a false cough. 'Coming from the mainland?'

I nodded.

He smiled with satisfaction. 'He could be delayed, of course. Gale force winds are forecast.'

'He'll be here,' I said firmly.

AFTER THREE HOURS in a cell I began to feel claustrophobic. The loud clicking noise as the spy hole was opened every twenty minutes made me jump. I couldn't just watch the minutes tick by, so each time the noise and the sight of two anonymous eyes checking to see I hadn't hung myself by my knicker elastic came as a fresh shock.

It was a relief when I was summoned out of the cell and led back to the interview room. I remembered what Hubert had said about keeping my mouth shut, but that was all very well in theory. If I refused to co-operate I guessed I'd be back in the cell before I had a chance to appreciate the delights of the relative normality of the interview room.

This time Alison Joiner sat in the corner and the tape recorder was on display. It seemed this was going to be a proper interview.

'Before we start, Chief Inspector, I'd love a cup of tea and something to eat.'

He nodded at Constable Joiner, who disappeared promptly, leaving Formbridge sitting across the desk from me looking smug.

Minutes later a tin tray with a pot of tea, china mug and cheese sandwiches was placed before me. It looked quite a banquet and even in my fairly dire circumstances I managed to enjoy the first few bites of my sandwich—until I became aware of them both watching me intently.

'Murder hasn't spoilt your appetite, then,' he said as I paused mid-sandwich. 'The death of a friend doesn't seem to have affected you much at all, does it, Miss Kinsella?'

'She wasn't exactly a friend. I'd only met her twice.'

'I see. So mere acquaintances getting themselves murdered don't matter.'

I took a deep breath. 'Chief Inspector, would you be kind enough to switch on the tape recorder. Then perhaps instead of being merely insulting you could ask me some penetratingly intelligent questions.'

Formbridge looked about ready to explode but he switched on the machine and in a carefully tight-lipped manner gave time, date, who was present, et cetera.

'What was your purpose in visiting the Isle of Wight, Miss Kinsella?'

'I was employed as a private investigator to find Mrs Elizabeth Forrester's nephew, Nigel Carter, co-owner of Uplands Lodge Hotel.'

'What progress have you made towards finding him?'

'None so far.'

'Did you tell anyone your real business in coming here?'

'No.'

'Why not?'

'I thought I could find out more...undercover.'

'But you found out precisely nothing.'

'The police and I had that in common.'

'Don't get smart with me. We made our usual investigations but—'

I interrupted swiftly. 'No one wanted to help you.'

Formbridge frowned angrily and crossed his arms defensively over his chest. 'I concede you may have a point,' he said, 'but since he'd packed a suitcase and was seen on a ferry leaving the island, and at that point he was still breathing, there seemed little for us to worry about.'

I murmured. 'I see,' and tried to keep my surprise from showing. Why hadn't Stewart told me Nigel had been seen?

The interview dragged on with questions ranging from how did Caroline and I get talking in the first place to who suggested the crowbar. During the questions I amused myself by giving Formbridge a background: his mother was Italian, his father English. He'd got three O levels, could produce a mean pasta sauce, drank red wine, beer or Scotch, was divorced (on the grounds of being a miserable old git) and had two teenage children he saw as little as possible.

'Do I have to repeat the question?'

'If you would, Chief Inspector,' I replied.

'What did you and Caroline row about?'

I stared at him. 'I didn't say we had a row.'

'I'm suggesting you did. I'm suggesting that you had a serious row. Maybe you went to the cabin much earlier than you admitted to and a row broke out. Or you stayed there all night and rowed when you were both tired and edgy. Perhaps one single blow killed her and then in a panic you had to make it look like a frenzied attack.'

'It *was* a frenzied attack,' I said tersely. 'But I wasn't involved. I hardly knew her. I liked her. I'd got no reason to row with her, nor did I have a motive for killing her. Even if I were lying about the times, which I'm not, I've worked as a night nurse and, believe me, I've got tired and edgy but I haven't battered anyone to death because of it.'

Formbridge managed a tight smile. 'No need to get agitated, Miss Kinsella. Just testing.'

Formbridge finally terminated the interview and left the room. This left Alison Joiner, gnome like, in the corner.

'Do you mind if I ask you a question, Officer?' I said as I turned in my chair so that she could see me face to face.

'Fire away.'

'Is DCI Formbridge divorced?'

She shook her head. 'He never married. He lives with his mother.'

'She's Italian.'

'Not that I know of. I think she came from Southend.'

I felt disappointed but not surprised. In my state of mind I felt that I'd got everything wrong. Was it my fault Caroline had died? If I'd stayed with her all night maybe I could have deterred her killer, perhaps I could have even saved her. It was a sobering thought.

'What happens now?' I asked.

Alison Joiner shrugged. 'Another cuppa maybe, or he might want you back in the cells.'

I thought of Hubert and made up a short prayer to guide a travelling undertaker safely to my side. Shortly after that when the door opened I thought my prayer had been successful—it hadn't. It was Formbridge.

'Take her back to the cells,' he said to Constable Joiner.

My heart sank. I dreaded going back to the cell. I dreaded spending a night there. If I closed my eyes I was sure Caroline's one staring eye would be upon me. That one dead eye was as potent as any conscience and I was beginning to feel as responsible for her death as if I had wielded that crowbar.

When the cell door clanged shut I broke down and cried.

EIGHT

I SPENT FIVE more hours in the cell. It felt like five days. I was too depressed to think and my nerves seemed as strung as a fiddler's bow. I sat on the edge of my so-called 'bed' feeling as if I were waiting for a train during a long and protracted train strike.

When the cell door did open I jumped in surprise. It was Formbridge looking tight lipped. He stood at the entrance to the cell with his hand holding open the door and his body blocking my view and my exit. I suspected he was going to give me dire news. Instead he said, 'Your Hubert Humberstone is in reception. And you're a very lucky lady. Due to Mr Humberstone's intervention my boss says you are to be allowed back to your hotel until we decide what action to take. There may be more questions to be answered.'

I struggled for a response. With such a mixture of emotions I thought for a second I'd lost my voice. I wanted to jump up and down and scream hysterically like a winning game show contestant, but I managed to keep my cool and say, 'Thank you, Chief Inspector,' while thinking joyously, 'Thank you, Hubert.'

Hubert stood in reception with what was left of his hair pressed firmly into place. He wore a navy suit, dark blue shirt and matching tie. Given a pair of dark glasses, he and Formbridge could have been two hoods you would walk over broken glass to avoid.

'Kate,' Hubert said as he placed an arm round me. 'Are you all right?'

I sagged against him for a moment so pleased to see him but not wanting to burst into tears or do anything dramatic. I took a deep breath. 'Thanks for coming, Hubert. Can we get out of here now?'

Outside, the air was clean and cold and I could smell the sea and the pungent smell of fish and chips overlaid with beer.

'Can you smell a pub?' I asked as I couldn't actually see one. He sighed and I had a strong feeling he was about to be disapproving.

'You haven't changed,' he said. 'I thought you might have taken this…débâcle seriously. You've no idea how many people I've had to speak to…'

'Were they famous?'

'Is it likely?'

I laughed. 'Just a thought.'

In the Pig and Whistle I thanked Hubert properly by ordering him steak and kidney pie and a pint of bitter. We managed to find a corner alcove, which although dim meant we could just about see our respective meals, and at least it was as private as a pub ever can be.

'I've no idea how you got me out, Hubert, but my gratefulness will definitely last until eternity.'

My fulsomeness didn't impress him. 'You worry me, Kate,' he said as he sipped his beer. 'You blunder in and then expect me to bail you out.'

I smiled. 'I'd do the same for you.'

He looked heavenwards but said nothing, and I knew that until I was put to the test he'd never know the answer to that one.

'You'd better tell me all about it,' he said.

I spared Hubert graphic descriptions of Caroline's body. He traded in death and I was sure there was nothing in her death that would shock or surprise him, but I did let him know how guilty I felt.

'Had you thought that maybe the murderer didn't mean to kill Caroline?'

I stared at him. 'Of course he didn't,' I said sarcastically. 'He just wanted to chastise her mildly with a crowbar.'

'I didn't mean that,' he said, obviously peeved. 'I meant that the killer could have been after you. Caroline was, in a way, doing your job.'

I paused. I really hadn't thought of that. 'No one knew what I was doing here,' I said sharply. 'Only Nigel's aunt.'

'Don't get upset,' said Hubert.

'I'm not upset. It's ridiculous. To everyone at the hotel, Caroline included, I was just someone with a bit of money who wanted to buy a hotel.'

I could see Hubert wasn't totally convinced. 'That thought never crossed your mind?'

'Can we drop this? Soon you'll be encouraging me to come home and forget about finding Nigel.'

Hubert didn't say a word. He didn't have to. I could see by the expression on his face he'd already decided where I'd be out of harm's way.

'I'm not leaving here until I've found Nigel and who murdered Caroline. I owe it to my client and to myself.'

Hubert shrugged. 'I can't stay here long to help you,' he said. 'I know I'm not indispensable to Humberstone's—' He broke off. 'Sod it! Of *course* I'm indispensable, I'm the boss.'

I almost told him I didn't need his help but resisted that urge and said, 'Yes, Hubert. I'm really grateful you could spare me the time.'

Hubert scanned my face, trying to judge, I guessed, if I was being sincere.

'How much headway have you made in finding Nigel?' Hubert asked, knowing full well I hadn't made any but I wasn't going to admit it.

'Some. I've been snooping a little and I've been generally alert.'

'Bullshit!'

'Hubert! You used to be such a gentleman.'

'You've changed me, Kate, and I think you've…I think you've been skiving. That's why you're in this mess. You haven't been professional.'

I seethed inwardly. Knowing he was right didn't help.

'I'm going to find Nigel if it kills me.'

'One death is quite enough,' said Hubert in a voice resonant with funereal tones.

I stood up.

'Where are you going?' he asked.

'To get you another pint,' I answered, knowing that with beer coursing through his veins Hubert would mellow.

Three pints later Hubert had indeed mellowed and the conversation dwindled to high-heeled shoes and the delights of Danielle's wonderful personality and 'her' unusually high arches. I wasn't sure which was topmost in Hubert's assessment of her attributes, but either way it was a lot less depressing than murder.

We walked back to the hotel and I was aware as I walked into a busy reception area that eyes were upon us, and I felt as if somehow they all held me responsible. Stewart wasn't there and Amanda glanced at me with thinly disguised suspicion. As Hubert signed the register she said, 'You're just next door to Miss Kinsella, Mr Humberstone.'

Straightfaced, he answered, 'Thank you. That'll be near enough to hear her snoring, then.'

Embarrassed, I elbowed him quickly towards the lift.

Once in his room he made it clear he didn't want me helping him unpack his Y-fronts or watching him doing it and I couldn't blame him for that, so I said, 'I'm going to wander down to the harbour. I'll see you later.'

The photo of Nigel plus 'friend' and boat was, I hoped, going to prove useful and I liked being near boats and hearing that tinkly sound they make even in the slightest breeze. No one had even remotely suggested Nigel was interested in boats, fishing or even paddling in the sea but it was a lead and the photo looked fairly recent. Could he even swim? If he was dead his death at sea was a definite possibility or at least the disposal of his body at sea seemed fairly likely. But why should he be dead? What had he done to merit death? A little voice told me to hang on and worry about Caroline instead. After all, Caroline was positively dead while Nigel could be laughing up his sleeve and sunning himself in the West Indies. What had *she* done to exact such a violent response? I hoped the police would swiftly chase up her husband because I had a feeling Lyle had hired someone to kill her. Unless, of course, it really was me who was supposed to die.

I stood staring at the boats, the *Saucy Sues* and the *Esmeraldas*, and I resolved that I'd do my damndest to find Caroline's killer and locate Nigel.

The boats continued to bob up and down on a choppy sea, their masts making that distinctive metallic sound seem as if the boats were communicating with each other. They needed to talk to each other because I couldn't see a soul fiddling with the riggings or whatever boat people do with boats. Surely, I thought, an old salt will be along soon. I wore my black padded jacket, scarf and gloves but

I still felt cold and I began to shiver. I walked backwards and forwards along the harbour edge but not a single old salt, or even a young salt, appeared and I'd just decided I was wasting my time when I spied a figure in the distance. I couldn't tell if the backside was male or female but it was human and I walked quickly towards the blue denim.

Even as I neared the rear which jutted out on to the quayside there was no movement from it. I could see now there was a can of paint in use. I could also see from his sockless hairy ankles that it was a man.

'Excuse me,' I said with that nuance of apology that almost needs practice. He didn't reply. I repeated my 'excuse me', this time more loudly and with more emphasis on the 'excuse'. He moved backwards on his knees, paintbrush in hand, and eventually stood up. He towered above me, but he had a splash of black paint on his thin nose so I concentrated on that and tried to avoid his eyes, which flashed like blue neon with a faulty circuit.

'What do you want?' he asked. 'Where's the bloody fire?' He seemed so angry I wondered if 'boat rage' wouldn't be next year's tabloid fetish. We'd had the year of mad dogs, the year of rape, the year of road rage—surely boats couldn't be far behind?

'I'm sorry to disturb you, but I couldn't find anyone else around. I'm trying to find a missing person and I—'

'Say no more, madam,' he interrupted. 'Was it a he or a she you were looking for?'

'A he, but I—'

He didn't let me finish but was smirking with a mouthful of yellow teeth and saying, 'You're in luck, dear. I've just seen him under my boat, stuck to the port side like a bleeding barnacle.'

I resisted a strong urge to kick him in the groin and,

finding him totally repulsive, moved backwards and side-wards. In doing so my foot caught the can of paint which scattered its contents over the side of his boat.

That definitely took the smirk from his face. I didn't hang around and as I began to run I called out, 'Thanks for your help.' His curses followed me and I'd only got to the end of the harbour before I'd doubled over with lungs in overdrive and a heart rate so fast it was more pearly gates than heart rate.

As I paused to hang over a low wall to recover I resolved two things: never to interrupt a man painting with his bum in the air, and to get fit. If he had decided to chase me I wouldn't have stood a chance. Next time it could be a knife-wielding maniac instead of a sockless boat painter.

As my bodily functions returned to normal sluggishness and I walked away from the harbour, I noticed tucked away behind a stone wall the Harbour Master's Office. A small, one-storey building with red check curtains, it seemed to be occupied by a man who took up most of the window space. He was obviously a hardened sea farer because the door was propped open, in the depths of winter, by a doorstop in the shape of an anchor. The round man who sat at the desk puffing on his pipe was the old salt I'd been looking for, although I doubted he'd been in a small boat since he'd upped his calorie intake. He wore one of those nautical navy jumpers with a 'boat' neck and the two pockets in the front, the sort advertised in the Sunday magazine supplements. His bushy white beard was neatly 'trained' below a complexion that had been well seasoned by wind, rain and sun.

'What can I do for you, my dear?' he said in a voice that sounded as if he had worn out his vocal cords shouting 'Land ahoy!' from a crow's nest. I wondered at this

point how hard he worked at his image. A wildlife pro-
gramme observing him would have named him 'Barnacle
paternalis'.

I came straight to the point. 'I'm a private investigator,
looking for a hotelier, Nigel Carter. He's been missing for
some weeks.'

He lovingly stroked the bowl of his pipe for a moment
and then glanced up at me via pale blue eyes that were a
touch reddened round the edges.

'Get Carter, is it?' I must have looked blank. 'You
know...the film.'

I nodded, remembering only vaguely.

He took a long puff, the smoke white and faintly aro-
matic drifting towards the open door.

'Sit down, dear. Do you fancy a cuppa?'

'I'd love one. I'd love one even more if I could close
the door.'

He smiled, showing crooked teeth. 'I like a bit of a
draught. I forget some people don't. You close the door,
dear, if you want.'

I closed the door and he swivelled in his chair to flick
the switch of an electric kettle on a shelf behind him. Two
mugs appeared from a drawer in his desk and in moments
we were drinking strong tea. Robbo Tyler began giving
me accounts of every sea swell, sea rescue, storm, sinking,
drowning, near drowning, type of rain, the sinister colour
of clouds, people mangled on rocks, bodies appearing all
bloated after, as he put it, 'The sea had had its way with
them.'

'That's really interesting, Mr Tyler,' I said, trying to
sound sincere. 'But as far as I know Nigel Carter had no
interest in the sea. But I did want to know about a certain
boat.' I handed him the photo and he stared at it for a few
seconds.

'I'll tell you something, my dear, there's not many on this island that aren't fond of the sea. It's got a strange pull on people. Fascinated, they are, by the sea.'

'I'm sure they are,' I replied, trying to hide the weariness I felt. 'But I'd be so happy if you could tell me who actually owns the boat.'

He puffed on his pipe again. 'Do you know,' he said, 'there's no legal requirement to register a boat.'

'I didn't know that.'

'Of course, those on the Continent want things changed, but here we like a free and easy approach. Boat owners do check names with Lloyds Shipping but otherwise anyone can have a boat.'

My spirits were already ten fathoms deep but I persevered, 'Mr Tyler, I really do need to know who owned *The Havana Belle*.'

'Of course you do, dear, and I can help. If that boat was ever in this harbour I should know about it. You come here and look at my ledger.'

I stood beside him to look at his listings. 'This is my ledger for the past five years, but I've got records going back years and years.'

'Great,' I murmured, 'but wouldn't it be easier to keep everything on computer?'

'Computer! Computer indeed. Wash your mouth out with soap, my girl. As long as I work here, and I hope that's till the day I drop, I'll have no computers. Computers break down and they get those nasty viruses—puts them out of action, you know—just like people.'

I kept a straight face. I had the feeling he thought computers could actually get the flu.

We scoured the ledger. Each boat had a name and a number, plus, alongside, the name and address of the owner. It took ages as Robbo regaled me with more sea tales than a land lubber should be forced to bear. In truth I saw the sea as being safer and more interesting from behind the comfort of a hotel window unless it was high summer, of course, when the sea did have its charms.

'Well, there you are, you look at this,' said Robbo. 'No wonder I didn't realize. I was on holiday at the time it was registered. My mate stood in for me.'

I stared down. The handwriting was different from that of the previous entries, but there it was, *The Havana Belle*—owner James Renton, Holly House, Ryde. I flashed the photo before Robbo's eyes. 'Do you know this man?' I asked.

He held the photo a minute distance from his face and I realized he was very shortsighted. 'It doesn't look much like him in the face,' he said uncertainly, 'but body wise it looks like him.'

'So you do know him?'

'I only know *of* him.'

I waited expectantly.

'He's rich, been on the island some years, does a bit of property developing and money lending, spends a lot of time in Spain…' He paused to puff on his now-dead pipe. 'I wouldn't recommend you have anything to do with him.'

'Why not?'

'I think he's a criminal, but he's too clever to get caught.'

I nodded and stared thoughtfully at the ledger. I peered closer. The entry was two years old, but there was a date and some tiny letters in one column. I managed to make them out—RIP.

'Does that mean he's dead?' I asked. 'It says RIP.'

Robbo smiled, the pipe still in his mouth. 'That's not for a person, that's for the boat. Let me have a closer look.' He raised the ledger and said, 'If you look closely you'll see a small F in the circle.'

I looked again and sure enough there it was.

'That means,' explained Robbo, 'there was a fire on board. I remember now. It didn't immediately come to mind because I wasn't on the island then, but my mate told me about it. Being a "Belle", which is a common boat name, I don't suppose I took much notice.'

'What exactly happened?'

Robbo frowned. 'Give me a minute, will you, dear? We've had quite a few fires in this harbour, I can tell you.'

He proceeded to tell me about fires on boats since the year dot. There was no stopping him. I did wonder whether he'd have been a bit more succinct if I'd been a big, ugly, six-foot man with a scar down my right cheek and bulging pectorals. Perhaps all my investigations would have been shorter and easier if I'd been a man. Since that wasn't a remote possibility I tried being firm.

'I am in a hurry, Mr Tyler. Just *The Havana Belle* fire, please.'

He looked disgruntled. 'I can't speak from firsthand knowledge, you know. I like to be a bit graphic in my descriptions...'

'I gathered that,' I said, with a smile that I hoped would coax a response. 'Just tell me what your mate said about it.'

'I'll just fill my pipe,' he said slowly. 'That'll help me remember.'

I watched in mild agitation as he began digging into the bowl of his pipe with some sort of thin metal, digger dagger or scraper. I wasn't sure if it had a name. Once he loosened the old tobacco he banged it loudly home into a metal waste bin. Then he took the stem of the pipe apart and began cleaning it out with one of those slightly furry pipe cleaners. Sighing inwardly I tried to remain patient.

'You have to do this properly,' he said, looking up from beneath less-than-well-trained eyebrows. 'There's no half measures with smoking a pipe.'

Eventually, after filling, packing and a ritual lighting, I realized that pipe smoking was not merely a habit, it was most definitely a hobby. He puffed away for a few moments as though trying to get the pipe into gear. Then, once satisfied with its pulling power, he murmured, 'Right, dear. That's better. I've got the old thinking cap back on. It was winter—November. You can see that from the date. My mate said this chap, the owner, came down to check the boat over. I think they had a chat, but I'm not sure. Anyway this chap—James Renton—went off to the boat. It was moored in number ten bay. About two hours later my mate saw him leave and shortly afterwards there was a small explosion. My mate didn't play the hero, of course, I mean when there's no one on board you don't, do you? He called the fire brigade but the fire took hold in a couple of minutes, there was lots of smoke and the flames were licking the sides before he'd put the phone down. *The Havana Belle* was a goner by the time the firemen arrived.'

'Did they find the cause of the fire?'

'A leaking gas canister, that's what they thought, dear. Gas canisters can be a problem on boats.'

'Was the boat insured?' I asked.

He laughed. 'Yes. I expect so. Can't insure against sinking, of course, or acts of God, but theft and fire…yes.'

'Did this James Renton buy another boat?'

'Not that I know of. It's not moored here, anyway.'

'And you never saw Nigel Carter here?'

Robbo looked puzzled. 'Oh, you mean the young chap

in the photo? No, I don't think so, but of course I meet so many people.'

'Could you make some enquiries for me?'

He smiled at me and then noticed his pipe had gone out. I could see the ritual starting all over again. Instead, he placed his pipe lovingly in the ashtray and stroked his beard thoughtfully. 'I can do that,' he said. 'I'll ask my regulars if they knew Carter.'

'You look worried,' I said as he frowned.

'I'm trying to remember something. You'll have to bear with me, dear. My memory isn't what it was, especially for fairly recent events. Ask me something about forty years ago and I'm your man.'

I waited while he stared ahead and rocked slightly from side to side as if he were at sea. Eventually he picked up his pipe, stroked the bowl with a loving caress and then said triumphantly, 'I've got it! A girl. My mate said there was a girl. She came after the fire to help the owner salvage something, only there wasn't anything to salvage. There was only the shell left.'

'What was she like, this girl?'

'He didn't say. He thought she was good looking, but then he thought all women were good looking unless they had buck teeth, cross eyes and a crew cut.'

'He didn't give you a name?'

'Sorry, my dear, can't help you there.'

As I stood up I said, 'Thank you, Mr Tyler. You've been a great help.' I wasn't yet sure that he had, but he'd had good intentions.

'Have I, dear?' he said. 'Jolly good. Do call again. I'm here to be of service.'

Just as I approached the door I knew I had one more question to ask. 'Mr Tyler, would you describe me as a girl?'

He smiled. 'What else? Of course you're a girl.'

I smiled to myself but the smile soon dispersed into a grimace as the cold air made me shiver. The boat masts clinked away in the ever-increasing wind and the sea looked as dark as the inside of a coal bucket. I consoled myself that while I may not have been much the wiser about Nigel, at least I felt younger.

NINE

I WAS WALKING BACK, my hands deep in my pockets, my thoughts just as deep, when I saw him. At least I thought it was him. After all, I had only seen the man once and then it had been a dramatic moment during which I'd been more concerned about Caroline. I took my hands out of my pockets and began walking faster. Formbridge had said he'd gone back to the mainland and that was where they would look for him, but what better place to hide than your exit point?

I continued to follow him as he walked uphill in the direction of the shops and Union Street. His strides were far longer than mine but I didn't want to break into a trot or cause him to notice me in any way.

Once in the main road it was easy to keep him in view simply because there was no one about. Ryde in winter could easily have been twinned with Longborough. The Christmas decorations swung miserably at every gust of wind and I sensed the general feeling that this was how it would be just prior to a nuclear attack.

He walked on rapidly and it was obvious he wasn't just window-shopping. It could have been the walk uphill or the cold weather but I realized, or at least my bladder realized, that I wouldn't be walking much further with a normal gait unless I found a loo. Perhaps, I thought, the female bladder was the real reason men reigned supreme in so many professions. The brain surgeon standing for hours is likely to be a man, and the long-distance lorry driver. Fictional detectives don't have bladders, of course, so gender wasn't a problem there, but I did, and the more I walked the more my thoughts became fixated below the waist. How far was he going? Could I nip in somewhere and still catch up with him? I thought it unlikely, so I carried on regardless, trying desperately to forget my discomfort.

It was then in the distance I saw the unmistakable tall figure of Hubert on the other side of the road. I waved to him and as I did so my quarry turned round. He was some yards in front of me and I still wasn't totally sure it was Lyle Uxton. He'd slowed down a little and as Hubert approached, wearing a dark navy trench coat with the collar turned up and one of those little furry hats on his head, I tried not to laugh.

'Hubert, I'm desperate for the loo,' I said in a rush. 'I'm following that man. Will you take over for me?'

With a mere suggestion of a raised eyebrow he nodded.

'Where is the nearest one?' I asked.

'You've been here longer than me,' he said. 'The hotel's as near as anywhere.'

As I rushed off I urged Hubert to 'Go...go...go!' which, judging by his expression, didn't please him one bit. I turned round just before going down one of the side streets that led to the hotel and saw him following but trying to look nonchalant. If I'd been the one being followed and I'd turned round and seen Comrade Humberstone behind me I'd have run like hell.

At the hotel I managed to visit the ladies' without a soul seeing me and I dashed in and out again and was back on the main street within five minutes. There was no sign of either of them, which I suppose wasn't surprising. I stood dithering for a few moments and then saw Hubert appear from a doorway looking more sheepish than sleuth like. I rushed towards him. 'Where is he?' I demanded.

Hubert continued to look sheepish. 'I lost him.'

'How could you lose him? Did he get swallowed up in the crowds of happy shoppers? Did an alien spaceship land and he just happened to be kidnapped?'

'There's no need to be sarcastic, Kate.'

'Hubert... What happened?'

'I got distracted,' he mumbled.

'What by, for goodness' sake? Something in sea shells? That's all the shops here seem to sell.'

Hubert looked away, embarrassed. 'It was these shoes, if you must know. I wasn't looking at them long. When I looked up he was nowhere to be seen.'

I didn't say anything. What could I say? After a few moments Hubert said, 'I'll show you where I lost him, shall I? Perhaps we could split up, one to the left, the other to the right.'

'He could be in the same "God knows where" place that Nigel's in by now.'

Hubert shrugged. 'I'll show you,' he said.

The shoe shop wasn't far, but all Hubert wanted was another glimpse. 'Look,' he said. 'Aren't they splendid?'

'Great.' He didn't notice the exasperation in my voice; he was too enamoured. There they were in the front of the window—Cindy and Kelly. Cindy was in black patent, open toed with a strap around the heel and just across the front of the foot. The stiletto heel was thin and sharp enough to have been a lethal weapon. Kelly had the same type of heel but was in red patent and was altogether more strappy. Any foot in such a shoe would have been on a vertical plane and any proud owner would have had to practise an unusual mincing walk.

'I think they're about four and a half inches,' murmured Hubert.

'Probably,' I said. 'Except that I couldn't care less. Cindy and Kelly have a lot to answer for.'

'I'll make it up to you, Kate,' said Hubert, his eyes still riveted to the shoes. I took him by the arm and had to firmly prise him away.

'We may as well go back to the hotel,' I said. Hubert didn't answer. He was obviously still in high-heel heaven.

Once back at the hotel he'd adjusted his mind because as we stood outside our rooms he said, 'I'm going to do some real snooping today and I think you should concentrate on just one person.'

'Who?'

'Stewart.'

'I think I'm persona non grata with him now.'

'You will be if you don't tart yourself up a bit.'

'What's that supposed to mean?'

'It means you'll never be Mata Hari in flat shoes and an anorak. Doll yourself up a bit and he'll tell you all about Nigel.'

'You mean seduce him?'

'You don't have to go that far,' said Hubert, sounding shocked.

'Hubert, you are such an old hypocrite,' I said, smiling. 'You fall in love with a pair of shoes but a tad of normality shocks you.'

'Rubbish.'

'Think about it,' I said as I opened the door of my room.

I sat on my bed and then looked at myself in the mirror. I had a red nose from the cold air, my hair had a flattened look and my eyes had need of mascara. Hubert was right.

Looking like I did I wouldn't tell myself any secrets. And secrets, I was convinced, was what this case was all about.

As I lay in the bath with closed eyes I tried to think about Nigel, but it was Caroline who haunted my relaxed state as if she were saying, 'What about me?' In my mind's eye Adam stood beside her. I'd only met him once but surely he would know if Caroline had any enemies, other than his own father, of course. Before seeing Adam, though, I planned to learn more about Nigel via Stewart. Perhaps one death connected with his hotel would make him more circumspect about helping me.

I was roughly drying myself (does anyone pat themselves dry?) when the word 'connected' resounded in my mind. Could Caroline's death have been connected in some way with Nigel's disappearance? Why the hell should it? came the retort. But then again why not? She'd seemed very keen to see the books as if somehow she had an interest herself.

Still wrapped in a towel I rang Stewart on the internal phone. 'Hi, Stewart,' I said, trying to make my voice sound as soft and enticing as Häagen-Dazs ice cream. 'This is Kate.' I paused for my identity to sink in. I didn't want him to think I was so conceited he'd know who I was straight away. 'I was wondering...I was wondering...'—oh God, I thought, spit it out—'if we could talk about things over a drink. I want to explain and apologize.'

There was total silence while I felt a sinking feeling in the pit of my stomach. Eventually, though, he said slowly, 'I don't see why not. I'm not saying I won't try to make a pass at you again, so don't try acting like an affronted virgin.'

I managed to laugh lightly. I was pretty sure Mata Hari

would have done that. 'You can always try,' I said flirtatiously, as though he was really in with a chance.

'I can't make it till after nine,' he said.

'Fine.'

'I'll meet you in reception. About nine.'

'See you then.'

As I put down the phone I felt just a tremor of excitement. Was it the hint of a sexual adventure or was it that I enjoyed the idea of sleuthing with lusty overtones? Or did I have a warped romantic view of being a femme fatale and sacrificing myself for my 'art'? Whatever the cause of my emotions, I decided, I wasn't going to be swept off my feet by a man who didn't wish to confide in me in an upright position.

When I told Hubert I was meeting Stewart for a drink he said, 'Don't worry Kate, I'll keep an eye on you.'

'I don't think that will be necessary.'

Hubert shrugged. 'I can see you need help, but I can't stay here for too long. Danielle's holding the fort. If she gets a rush on I'll have to go back immediately.'

I was peeved at the idea he thought I needed help but deep down I knew he was right. I wasn't exactly a high-tec detective. I'd got no bugging devices or anyone who could access bank or financial details for me. I only had Hubert.

'You could be right about my needing help,' I said after a long pause. 'I do need you to ask a few questions for me, find out the gossip about Nigel and Caroline—if there is any.'

'I'm not that good at smalltalk, Kate. You know that.'

'Talk bigtalk, then. I'm sure Harold, Nancy and Margaret would be interested in cut-price funerals.'

Hubert looked miffed. 'I try to be subtle. You can't just blunder in because someone's over seventy and suggest they need to make plans for their instant departure into the next world.'

'Do you believe in a "next world", Hubert?'

He shook his head.

'Do your best, then, especially with the staff. Frankie, the barman, seems to be very gossipy and I'm sure Amanda, the receptionist, knows more about Nigel than she's letting on.'

'Haven't you talked to them yet?'

'I've been too busy.' Hubert sighed. He wasn't impressed. 'Hubert, I've only just "come out". I can be more open with my questions now, but even I have to be a bit circumspect.'

'You just remember that when you're being wined and dined by the owner.'

'We're only having a drink.'

'You're dressed up for a drink,' said Hubert, but I noticed he only glanced at my court shoes with their two-and-a-half-inch heels. If I'd been wearing a bin bag he'd have probably only noticed the shoes.

Hubert and I sat at a table for two during dinner and I noticed that we were being talked about. I wasn't sure if it was because we looked like an odd couple or because I was notorious for having found a body under mysterious circumstances. Whichever way I looked, eyes were upon us. Was it the same the night I ate at the hotel with Caroline? The answer came back with worrying clarity—yes. And with a start I realized that someone in the hotel might have killed Caroline. We'd been seen that night going to Nigel's cabin and the murderer intended to kill one or both of us...

'What's the matter? You've gone all vacant looking.' Hubert's voice intruded on my thoughts.

'I was just thinking.'

He smiled. 'About time. Have you come to any conclusions?'

'Not exactly—just that it's got to have been someone
in the hotel. Someone who either saw us or overheard
what we planned to do.'

Hubert smirked. 'That took a lot of deducing.'

'There's no need to be sarcastic, Hubert. Doing this sort
of thing is like making a diagnosis. You can't just rush
in and suggest that a slight cough is indicative of pneu-
monia. You have to weigh up all the signs and symptoms
before even making a tentative diagnosis.'

'Yes, Dr Kinsella.'

'I'm being serious. Someone looking out from the back
of the building must have seen us.'

'Or followed you.'

'Yes, but it couldn't have been with prior knowledge,
because I didn't tell anyone and I'm sure Caroline didn't.
Someone overhearing us is a possibility, though.'

'She may have told her son,' suggested Hubert.

I shook my head slowly. 'I'd thought of that, but it's
unlikely she'd tell a fourteen-year-old she was planning a
bit of breaking and entering.'

'What about the friend Adam was staying with?'

'Now that is a possibility. I'm planning to see Adam
and meet the owner of the bungalow soon. Even so, I still
think this was an inside job. Someone wanted to prevent
Caroline finding out Nigel's darkest secrets. I've had a
vague impression all along that no one wants Nigel to be
found but why, I don't know. Stewart in particular hasn't
given me information...as if he's trying to protect him.'

Hubert ran a hand through the hairs on his head. 'In
that case, Nigel couldn't have been on the fiddle unless
Stewart was in on it and doesn't want to be implicated.
It's safer for him *not* to help to find his partner.'

I couldn't disagree with that and by eight thirty we were sitting in the bar and I was trying to work out who had been in the bar the evening in question. If I'd known what was going to happen I would of course have paid more attention. We had been fairly engrossed in our plans, though I remembered Frankie's gossiping and Harold, Margaret and Nancy sitting across from us. They couldn't have overheard us and no one sat directly behind us.

By nine thirty Stewart hadn't turned up and Harold and Hubert had got into conversation about bread and dripping, syrup of figs and bananas after the war. I fidgeted in my seat and kept looking round for Stewart until, at a quarter to ten, I'd almost given him up. 'I'll wait till ten,' I whispered to Hubert. I was a little upset at being stood up, even though it was purely business. But I couldn't help remembering other times I'd been stood up or had waited for phone calls that never came. The way I felt at the moment I was prepared to do battle on the strength of those other occasions when disappointment gives way to anger but there's no one to yell at.

At ten o'clock, just as I was about to go, Stewart walked in.

'I'm sorry to keep you waiting,' he said, like a GP with a long-suffering patient.

'No problem,' I said sweetly, keeping my pride intact. For God's sake why should I care anyway? PIs were meant to hang about.

'It's a bit public here. Come up to my flat.' He took my arm and I was like putty in his hands. I winked at Hubert, whose answering look was pure anxiety.

Stewart's flat was on the third floor. It was rather sparse, with a traditional mahogany table and only two chairs, one lamp with a blue fringed shade, no plants or flowers and two 'bucket' chairs, obviously hotel issue.

Once I was sitting down he asked, 'Glass of wine? White or red?'

'I'd rather have coffee,' I said.

'Please yourself.'

He disappeared into the kitchen and I moved over to the window, pulled back the blue velvet curtains a fraction and peered out into the night. I could see a side portion of the cabin and the lights from the hotel splayed on to the garden. *He* could easily have seen us that night.

'Enjoying the view?' he asked. I hadn't heard his footsteps and he startled me.

'I was wondering if you could see the cabin from here.'

'Come on, Kate, admit it. You were snooping.'

'I do it professionally.'

'You should have told me that from the start,' he said as he handed me a mug of coffee.

I merely smiled. Why should I defend myself?

He sat with a glass of whisky and stared across at me. 'Well, Kate Kinsella, private investigator, what exactly do you want to know?'

TEN

'I WANT TO KNOW as much as you can tell me about Nigel,' I said boldly.

He smiled. 'And I suppose you think I know everything about him.'

'You've worked with him for ten years. You ought to know him quite well.'

Stewart sipped at his whisky. 'What you're saying is that if you worked with someone for ten years you'd know everything about them. Well, we worked together. We went through some rough patches together, but that's all.'

'I think you're being evasive.'

'I don't give a damn what you think, but I will tell you a bit more about Nigel. I met him ten years ago when we thought Britain was dawning into a golden age. It was in a hotel in Southampton; Nigel was a chef. I was looking for a partner and he was interested in buying a hotel. We had a long chat and he said he had a rich aunt who would lend him the money. We decided to buy on the Isle of Wight because hotel prices were slightly lower and the potential was there.'

'Did you make a profit in the first year?'

Stewart shook his head. 'That first year was very hard. We worked sometimes sixteen hours a day. We had to redecorate the whole place, get the garden and kitchens organized. It was bloody hard work. My wife of two years walked out and financially we were really struggling.'

'Nigel wasn't married?'

'No. He didn't confide much but he did tell me he would never marry.'

'Did he say why?'

'No. Just "once bitten"—that sort of thing.'

'What about girlfriends?'

'I don't think there was anyone special. He saw a few girls over the years but I think he thought having his heart broken once was once too often.'

'What about Charlotte?'

Stewart shrugged and sat back with his hands intertwined behind his head. 'She wasn't his usual type and although I said I didn't know her I did catch a glimpse of her once or twice years ago—not that I recognized her in the hotel. She'd lost a considerable amount of weight and her hair was a different colour.'

'How long had they known each other?'

'I'm not sure,' he murmured, with a slightly puzzled expression. 'Strange, isn't it, just how little you can know about someone?'

I nodded in agreement. 'What about his interests generally? Did he like sports or sailing or—'

Stewart's deep laughter interrupted me. 'It's just as well you're not planning to buy a hotel. Running a hotel isn't just a job, it's a way of life. I manage most weeks to play an afternoon's golf. Admittedly it's quieter in the winter and in January I have been known to take a week off but now Nigel's gone that's gone too.'

'So you're telling me Nigel had no interests?'

'He went round the corner most evenings to the Pig and Whistle to escape from the residents, drank real ale, once or twice he went sailing but apart from that...he worked.'

I sat quietly for a moment. From Nigel's photo I hadn't

expected him to be a real ale man—with beard, sandals, a predilection for Morris dancing.

Stewart got himself another whisky and seemed to forget I was there for a few moments. He sat staring into the glass, looking slightly anxious.

'What's the matter?' I asked.

'Just thinking. Perhaps I should have seen it coming. He'd been getting depressed for some months before he went, not weeping and miserable but very quiet, sort of worried. Looking back I can see he was depressed.'

'Was there any reason for that?'

'Does there have to be a reason?'

'No, but sometimes there is.'

Stewart frowned. 'I know he'd have preferred not to have permanent elderly residents and he wanted to attract more conference holders, but that had been his stance for some time. I don't think he was depressed by it.'

'Could it have been a woman or family problems...? What about his parents?'

'He didn't talk about them, but I got the impression they were dead.'

'You didn't ask?'

'No. If he'd wanted to tell me he would have done.' He paused. 'Thinking back perhaps there was some major rift. Perhaps that was why he'd got depressed.'

'Being dead is a major rift,' I said.

'I didn't say they were dead, Kate. I just got that impression. For all I know they could be very much alive.'

'His aunt would have known, of course, but I'm sure she said Nigel was her only relative.' I thought about that for a moment. 'What about Nigel's male friends?'

Stewart smiled. 'Apart from me, you mean. Mainly, I think, the blokes he met in the Pig and Whistle.'

'Do you think he would have confided in any of them?'

'No way. We may not have been that close but he did trust me and I think if he'd wanted to I would have been the one to tell.'

'What about Charlotte? Wouldn't he have confided in her?'

'Kate, Nigel didn't trust women. He wanted a woman but he couldn't trust them.'

I sat for a moment giving Stewart the full questioning eye contact. After a very short time it unnerved him. 'What?' he snapped.

'I was just wondering why you let me believe Nigel just disappeared when in actual fact he packed his bags, his affairs were pretty much in order, and he was seen on the ferry.'

'I didn't see him on the ferry. The police told me he was seen on the ferry. That's merely second-hand stuff.'

'Did he go to the doctor's about his depression?'

'I wouldn't know that, would I? As I said, he wasn't going round like a sick man, he was just quieter than usual.'

'Quiet, as in worried or even scared?'

There was a long pause. 'You're right. He could have been scared.'

'Did he ever mention James Renton?'

'That shark! I told him to stay well clear of him. He's definitely bad news.'

'I found a photograph of them together standing by Renton's boat.'

'Would you like another coffee?'

I smiled. 'Don't try to change the subject, Stewart. Why did Nigel get involved with Renton?'

'He wasn't involved with him. A few years back Nigel wanted to build an extension, more rooms, more dosh, more suitable for conventions. He approached the banks but they'd got much more cautious and liked to say no, so eventually he sought out Renton.'

'What happened?'

'Renton offered to lend him the money but he wanted me to sign the loan agreement and I refused.'

'Did Nigel resent that?'

'He did at first, then he seemed to realize it was for the best.'

'He didn't hold a grudge against you?'

Stewart smiled. 'That wasn't Nigel's style. He seemed to accept the situation and settled back into a routine.'

'What about Nigel's personal finances?'

'You mean was he solvent?'

'Yes.'

Stewart's eyes lingered for a moment at my ankles, then he said, 'Nigel was very good at handling the hotel's finances, but on a personal level he always seemed short.'

'What was he spending his money on?'

'Keeping the Pig and Whistle in business, I should think.'

'Did you both take the same salaries from the business?' Stewart nodded.

'You manage on yours?'

He nodded again and smiled. 'Our salaries aren't that generous, but I can manage to save some.'

'Is it possible that Nigel had creditors he was trying to escape from?'

'Anything's possible, Kate, but how about changing the subject now? Tell me about yourself. How did you get into the detection business?'

I told him briefly.

'How do you manage the technical side?' he asked, as if he suspected I was a techno-moron.

I bristled. 'If you mean how do I manage bugging

phones and using long-range cameras, et cetera, I don't. That sort of equipment costs a fortune. As I build up the business I might buy myself a few gismos but at the moment I just have to manage with a little help from Hubert.'

'Is Hubert in love with you?'

'Don't be so silly,' I said, quite shocked. 'He's in love with someone called Danielle.'

As I placed my coffee cup on the small table in front of me Stewart leaned over and placed his hand over mine. I looked up to see his eyes bright and shining with a lusty luminousness. It took me by surprise and I held his gaze. After a few moments of eye contact it was obvious he wasn't content to just imagine; he wanted more than the window of my soul. We stood up as if in slow motion and just as slowly he took me in his arms. As he kissed me it came as a shock—it had been so long since I'd been in a man's arms. The contrast of the taut, hard body and his warm soft lips had me moving fast from 'No, no, I couldn't possibly' to 'Oh God, I can't stop now'. I also knew I was completely in his power when the fleeting thought passed through my brain that doughnuts and cream cakes couldn't compare with the warm lusciousness of his mouth.

It was then that his mobile phone rang from his back pocket. Startled, I pulled away from him and was immediately back in the land of the sensible.

As he answered the phone, I left. I waved from the door and blew him a kiss and wondered if, for me, it would always be like this.

THE NEXT MORNING at eight thirty DCI Formbridge called me. At first I thought he was at the station but he wasn't, he was in reception wanting to see me. I knocked loudly on Hubert's door but there was no reply.

It wasn't an exclusive: staff and residents were there en masse. Stewart was at the front of the small crowd and he smiled cheerfully at me.

'We do have a search warrant,' Formbridge was saying. 'Are there any objections?'

As if anyone would dare, I thought.

Formbridge's eyes scanned the faces as though one piercing glance from him could seek out guilt like radar finding a submarine. 'I suggest,' he said slowly, 'that everyone returns to the dining room and stays there until my men have finished.'

A slow shuffle began then, headed by Margaret who perhaps thought she might be trampled on in the rush. As I followed the others Hubert came up behind me. 'What's going on?' he whispered.

'Where have you been?' I whispered back.

'Paper shop. What's happening? And why are we whispering?'

'You started it,' I said. 'The police are searching our rooms. What they hope to find I don't know.'

I heard Hubert breathe in sharply. 'What's the matter?'

'You know,' he said.

'Are you ashamed of your Y-fronts, Hubert?'

'Oh, very funny,' he snapped.

I didn't say any more because I'd realized he didn't want people rooting through his personal things and neither did I. It definitely seemed like a violation if one's underwear could be violated.

Breakfasts carried on in the dining room, fresh tea and coffee were made, and then we sat and waited. It seemed a little like a siege or a disaster and even the staff moved round the tables chatting with the guests. Amanda Giles came to sit with us.

'This is a nuisance, isn't it?' she said. 'But at least it gives us a chance to talk to the guests.'

'Could be a mixed blessing,' said Hubert glumly.

'Have you worked here long?' I asked Amanda.

She smiled. 'Too long—more than five years now.'

'So you knew Nigel quite well?'

'You're looking for him, aren't you?'

I nodded and waited for her to answer my question. She didn't. 'Have you made any progress?'

Hubert cleared his throat noisily as though trying to warn me to be cautious. 'Progress has been slow,' I said, 'but steady. Nigel hasn't covered his tracks that well.'

'Hasn't he—?' She broke off, aware that in those two little words she had exposed a wealth of meaning.

'He was the careful type, was he?' I asked. 'You think he planned his disappearance and it wasn't just a spur of the moment decision.'

'He didn't confide in me,' she said sharply.

'Not even during pillow talk?' I muttered.

'What did you say?'

'I must have misunderstood, Amanda...'

'Misunderstood what?'

'I got the impression you and he were an item.'

Her face flushed angrily. 'Who told you that? It's not true.'

'I'm sorry. I did say it was just an impression.'

'Someone must have said something. Nigel and I were always friendly but not friends, if you know what I mean.'

I nodded. She was still agitated and she was still lying. I stared at her for a few moments and I could see her grow uncomfortable.

'I think I'd better circulate a bit,' she said then. 'Some of the oldies may be distressed by the police being here.'

I looked across to Harold, Nancy and Margaret. They

were laughing and chatting and were about as distressed as tropical fish in a luxury tank.

When Amanda had left our table Hubert said, 'What do you think?'

'I think, Hubert, no one wants Nigel to be found. That must be because...'

'Because they are trying to protect him from someone. Maybe this chap Renton. I'm not sure. Nigel could have been on a scam which hasn't been discovered yet but even so the people who knew him don't want him to get caught.'

'Does that include Stewart?'

'I think so.'

Hubert sipped at his coffee and then gave me one of his anxious looks. 'In that case, who would care enough about him to murder Caroline because she was getting nosy?'

'What are you trying to say, Hubert?'

'Caroline was an outsider. She's now dead. You could be next. Get too close to Nigel and it must be curtains.'

'You're being too dramatic. I still think her husband hired a hit man.'

Hubert raised his eyebrows. 'So you're saying that someone staying in this hotel is a hit man. Have a good look round. Who do you think it could be?'

ELEVEN

AFTER NEARLY an hour of the lingering smell of bacon and toast and the constant chinking of cups against saucers both Hubert and I began to feel restless. Frankie, with a hip-swinging walk and jaunty pony tail approaching our table, came as something of a high spot.

'Hi, you two,' he said in a boyish voice that I was convinced was an affectation. 'Mind if I join you? This is a bit of a pain, isn't it? I've got other things to do, you know. I mean, a barman's work isn't all beer and skittles.'

'You seem to enjoy it,' I said as I pulled out a chair for him. 'Have you always been a barman?'

'I was born a barman, sweeties. I see a glass and I have to fill it.'

'You're like Hubert, then,' I said, turning to smile at him. 'He's a born undertaker. He sees a corpse and he has to bury it.'

Frankie laughed loudly. Hubert scowled at both of us.

'Word has it you're a private detective trying to find our Nigel.'

I nodded. 'Word has it that if anyone knows Nigel's whereabouts...you do.'

His expression showed he was faintly flattered. 'I do like to pride myself on knowing what's going on, but our Nige kept his cards close to his chest.'

'Yes, but I'm sure he told *you* something. After all, the barman is everyone's friend.'

Frankie shook his head so that his pony tail swung

slightly. 'I try to be but Nigel wasn't talking much those last few weeks.'

'You mean he was depressed?'

'Yeah, I suppose so—quiet, anyway. I asked him what was wrong the night he disappeared.'

'You actually saw him that night?'

'He was here late. He'd come in from the Pig and Whistle and he stood at the bar for some time. I remember because he wasn't drinking, he just had a tomato juice. There were only two punters, both talking hanging and flogging, and Nigel didn't join in but every so often he looked at me as if he wanted to talk.'

'What about when the customers left?'

Frankie frowned. 'It's strange. He stood there for a while and I told him a few bits of gossip—you know, who's going with who, and he listened and smiled in all the right places, then he said he was going to bed, but as he turned to go he said, "You're a lucky sonofabitch, Frankie."'

'What do you think he meant by that?'

Frankie hesitated. 'I think the poor sod was having women trouble. I think he envied me.'

'In what way?'

'My lover.'

'Why should he be envious of your lover?'

Frankie smiled and looked at me in a faintly puzzled way as if I should know why. 'Darren's so beautiful and uncomplicated. We've been together now for four years. Nigel got on well with him. Occasionally on my night off we might pop into the Pig and Whistle. Usually we go to gay bars or clubs on the mainland but sometimes we went to the local.'

'What made you think, apart from that remark, that Nigel was jealous of your happiness?'

Frankie put his head on one side and looked at me quizzically. 'Now come on, sweetie, you know as well as I do that a heterosexual man without a woman is on a journey without a map, no means of transport and he's scared to ask the way. Whereas a woman without a man will make her own map and will ask the way if she's lost.'

'Does being a barman give you all these insights?' I asked.

He smiled. 'Lonely men drink in hotel bars and these days there are more lonely men around. The sad fact is they can't cope with women and they certainly can't cope without them.'

'Are you saying Nigel couldn't cope with women?'

'Oohh, Katie, I didn't say that, now did I? He wasn't gay, if that's what you're hinting at, but he did tell me once he didn't trust women. He was the ''love 'em and leave 'em type'', I guess.'

'So there was no one special?'

'He saw a girl called Charlotte occasionally but she doesn't live on the island. I got the impression she was a career girl and not the type to want to live in his wooden cabin.'

'I'm surprised he hadn't bought a house. That cabin isn't very homely.'

'He liked it,' said Frankie sharply. 'And anyway he didn't have the brass to buy a house.'

'Was he short of money, then?'

Frankie reached over and tapped me on the back of the hand. 'You're jumping to conclusions again, you naughty girl. I didn't say he was short of money, but...'

'But what?'

'I think he had some debts or outgoings he never mentioned.'

'Why do you think that?'

He shrugged. 'Sometimes he'd made comments about going on holiday if he could afford it. Once he said, "You make one mistake in your life, Frankie, and you pay for ever."'

'Perhaps he didn't mean money,' I suggested.

'I think he meant money and emotion, sweetie. My guess is someone screwed him up once and then it got to him, like a delayed reaction.'

'You're very perceptive, Frankie. So perceptive that I think you could make a very good guess as to where he is now.'

Frankie smiled, looking pleased. 'Well, I do have a theory. I reckon he's in a hotel somewhere working as a chef and waiting for his aunt to die so that he can start a completely new life.'

'So you know about his aunt?'

'Yeah, poor old thing. Not quite the ticket in the brain department but he's her only next of kin and he cops for the lot.'

'He could have waited here. Why do a disappearing act?'

'Search me, but you did ask and that's what I think.'

He looked about to leave the table and as my eyes caught Harold waving to me, I asked, 'Before you go, would you do me a favour?'

'I'm your man,' said Frankie cheerfully.

'Would you look round the diners here and tell me if you think any one of them could be a hit man.'

'You're kidding?'

'No, I'm perfectly serious.'

He flashed me a half-amused, half-puzzled expression but began table-watching immediately. 'The table for two on the right—that's Mr and Mrs Denks, staying here while

they have their dream bungalow built. Both retired teach-
ers, teetotal but fond of juice. Chatty at times but I can't
imagine he's got a Luger strapped to his waist. The table
in front of them, the two middle-aged men in smart suits.
They've got friendly with each other since they moved in
about three months ago. Their wives have given them the
elbow. They both drink till they get legless and Norman,
he's the bald, fat one, gets the shakes. The only way he
could kill anyone would be to fall on them. His friend,
Graham, is a timid bloke. I call him "duckie" and it
scares him. He thinks I fancy him but he's not quite the
suave older man I'm attracted to.'

I could see Graham certainly wasn't Frankie's type; he
was so ordinary, everything about him in the medium
range except for looking slightly crumpled and shrunken.
As if years of marriage had taken the stuffing out of him,
quite literally.

'Then, of course, to the right there's the amazing drinking trio—Harold, Margaret and Nancy. They quaff their
cheap vodka nightly and worry about money all the time
but it's romantic, isn't it?'

'What do you mean?' I asked nonplussed.

'Harold and Nancy. Didn't you know? They came here
separately, all miserable and within two weeks they were
sharing a double room. I've heard rumours they're planning to get married—just before Christmas.'

'That *is* romantic,' I said. 'And you don't think Harold's hit-man material?' I said it as a joke but Frankie
didn't laugh.

'He's an ex-soldier,' he said. 'He's the only one with
any potential at all.'

'His hips are too arthritic,' I said.

'He can manage some things. You should see Nancy's
smile some mornings.'

I laughed. 'What about the young couple at the table by the window?' The girl had a sullen down-turned mouth, frizzy hair and the habit of continually fidgeting. She also wore a collar that seemed to choke her. I was prejudiced against women like that—tight and buttoned up. Her male companion had small close-set eyes that travelled extensively over any female that breathed. He had lank, longish hair and an aged expression on his pallid face as if he'd already seen and done enough in his twenty-four or so years.

'Ah, the happy honeymooners,' said Frankie. 'They've been here nearly two weeks. They're house-hunting. Cheryl and Ian. Miserable little toads. Just look at them, they hardly speak to each other. I give that marriage a year at most.'

I didn't need to ask if either of them could be hit men. They just didn't seem primed to exercise any vigilance or manoeuvrings; they seemed more tired and jaded than the average refugee escaping from a war zone.

Not many suspects, I thought, on the paid killer level but the staff increased the numbers for amateur murder.

Frankie smiled. 'I hope that helped, sweetie.'

'Very much. You really have been a great help,' I said. 'Could I speak to you again? You might just remember something else.'

'I think I've told you all I know,' he answered, but as he spoke he looked slightly worried, as if he had told me all he knew and thought he'd said too much.

When he'd walked away the silent Hubert asked, 'What did you make of that?'

'I thought you'd died in the upright position, Hubert. You could have asked some brilliantly pertinent questions.'

'I was expecting you to do that.'

'I thought that chat went quite well.'

'You didn't ask him about Renton.'

I swore inwardly but refused to let Hubert see I was angry with myself. 'Why didn't *you* ask, Hubert? Honestly, sometimes I think you want me to fail.'

'That's rubbish,' he said crossly. 'I need your rent money.'

That was completely untrue and he had the grace to look slightly embarrassed as I raised my eyebrows in disbelief.

'If you must know, Kate, I didn't like him.'

'Why? Because he's gay?'

'No. I think he's a liar.'

'What do you think he lied about?'

Hubert thought for a moment. 'Perhaps he wasn't lying, but he wasn't telling you everything.'

'Why should anyone tell me anything? To them I'm just a paid snoop. Sometimes I'm surprised that people talk to me at all.'

'What are you planning to do when the search is over?'

'At this rate it'll be lunchtime. I thought a trip to the Pig and Whistle might yield a smidgen of info.'

'We'll see,' said Hubert glumly.

Somehow Hubert's glum response was merely a reflection of my own doubts. Would I ever find Nigel...? My thoughts were interrupted by the sight of the sour face of Formbridge at the dining room door.

'Ladies and gentlemen, the search of the hotel is over. I must ask you to bear with me now as we wish to briefly re-interview you all.'

A collective sigh seemed to echo round the room and soon a mixture of CID and uniformed police were descending on our tables as fast as wasps on a jam sandwich.

Formbridge settled on our table. 'Miss Kinsella,' he said, grim faced. 'Have you found Nigel Carter yet?'

He knew damn well I hadn't, but I didn't want to give him the satisfaction of actually saying so. For some reason I said, 'I'm pretty sure I know where he is.'

'Well, bully for you. I'm only interested in the murder of Caroline Uxton at the moment.'

'Is her husband totally in the clear?'

'So far.'

'I thought I saw him on the island.'

Formbridge stared at me unsmiling. 'He came back voluntarily to see us. Now...do you mind if I ask the questions?'

I waited while he took out a note book and found the right page. 'I'd like you to go back to the evening in question when you and Caroline were sitting in the bar. I want you to tell me exactly what happened.'

I paused. If I'd known what was going to happen I'd have been more observant.

'Come on, Miss Kinsella. You're paid to notice things.'

'So are you, Chief Inspector.'

'Just get on with it.'

I related the events of that evening as best I could. I tried to remember exactly who was in the bar and where they were standing or sitting, but it wasn't easy.

'Was anyone sitting behind you?'

'I've thought of that one, Chief Inspector. No one could have overheard us—we had our backs to the wall and anyway we didn't really discuss our...plan.'

'What happened when Caroline left the bar?'

'She went to the ladies' and when she came back her husband was beside her shouting and being threatening.'

'So he must have been waiting for her in reception.'

'Yes. The ladies' is just off the reception area. But of

course he could just have been coming in and seen her leaving the loo.'

'What did you do while the row was going on?'

I thought back. What did I do? Eventually I said, 'I sat there for a few moments. I was shocked. Then I stood up, but by that time he'd already hit her. I chased him out.'

'How far did you chase him?'

'Not far enough,' I muttered.

'What was that?'

'He was too fast for me. I lost him.'

Formbridge squinted at me. 'Don't lie to me. Lyle Uxton has already told us that although he dashed out of the building he stopped running once he was outside. He said he wanted to be caught.'

'Caught for what? Wife battering or to give him a good alibi for when his wife was murdered by a paid killer?'

Formbridge's answering smirk was so pronounced that I knew I was wrong. 'When you got back to the bar what did you do?'

'I went straight to Caroline to comfort her.'

'Was anyone with her at that point?'

'No...but someone had bought her a brandy.'

'So she was drinking brandy when you got back to the bar?'

'Yes.'

'What sort of state was she in?'

'Quite calm, really.'

'In fact, it was as if nothing had really happened?'

'Well, yes, I suppose so.'

'There's no suppose about it, Miss Kinsella. After all, it didn't stop her wanting to do some breaking and entering, did it?'

'No. I was a little surprised that she still wanted to go ahead with it.'

'It didn't occur to you that she was a hard case.'

'Well, I…'

'Come on now, Miss Kinsella. Were her reactions normal?'

'Chief Inspector, I'm not in court. You sound like a prosecutor. Caroline was a battered wife who was brutally murdered. You make it sound as if she were the perpetrator of her own murder and not a victim.'

Formbridge stared at me. 'Did she seem like a cowed victim to you?'

'Well…no.' I was beginning to feel defeated by this line of questioning.

'Precisely, Miss Kinsella. Caroline Uxton was no pathetic victim, except in death. And to add insult to injury I'm going to give you a little snippet of information.'

As I waited for him to impart his little snippet a uniformed sergeant approached the table. They whispered together and then the uniformed man left.

'What was I saying?' said Formbridge. He knew perfectly well; he just wanted me to react.

'You mentioned some information.'

'Ah yes. Caroline…' He paused. 'She never was Mrs Uxton. There is a Mrs Diane Uxton, Lyle Uxton's legal wife. Caroline Gordon changed her name by deed poll to Uxton. She was only his mistress.'

TWELVE

FORMBRIDGE, having imparted his little snippet, stood up, nodded at me in open triumph and walked away.

'Bastard,' I muttered.

Hubert, my erstwhile silent witness, now seemed to have had his switch thrown. He'd opened his mouth to say something which I guessed would either be a put-down or a startlingly obvious observation. For some reason I was annoyed with him.

'Don't say anything, Hubert. I've got to do a Garbo, "I vont to be alone."'

'We haven't been dismissed yet, Kate. And there's no need to get sarky with me. It's not my fault about Caroline.'

'What am I going to do?' I was aware my voice was high pitched and on the moany side.

Hubert shrugged. 'Perhaps the Pig and Whistle will provide a clue.'

'Pigs might fly.'

'If we drink enough they probably will,' said Hubert, and I smiled.

Eventually we were dismissed and filed out of the dining room as quietly as a well-behaved school assembly. On the way to the pub Hubert began giving me advice. 'It seems to me,' he said thoughtfully, 'you shouldn't even try to find Caroline's killer. You can't compete with the police and anyway you should finish one job at a time.'

He *was* right, I knew that, and I murmured in agreement, consoling myself with the thought that the sooner I found Nigel the sooner I could concentrate on finding Caroline's killer.

The Pig and Whistle had just opened and had a desolate air although the landlord had tried to brighten the place by stringing up some coloured lights, lighting a real log fire and adding an artificial Christmas tree in the corner with brightly coloured wrapped packages underneath—a few jolly customers would have helped. The landlord forced a smile for us and recommended we sat by the fire. He was thin and pale and wore round, thin-rimmed glasses. He had the appearance of an ageing intellectual and his *Times* newspaper with a nearly completed crossword confirmed he was quite bright. Hubert ordered the drinks, a pint of bitter for him and a warming rum and blackcurrant for me.

'I wondered if you could help me,' I said to the landlord. 'My name's Kate Kinsella and I want to find Nigel Carter. I've been told he was a regular of yours and possibly a friend.'

He peered at me from above his glasses, which had slipped down his aquiline nose. 'Yes, he was a regular and, yes, he was a friend. I say was not because he's gone walkabout, but because he borrowed five hundred quid and promised to pay me back within the week. That was more than three months ago and I haven't seen him since.'

'Had he ever borrowed money before?'

'Yes, and he's always paid it back.'

'So do you feel that something dire might have happened to him?'

'It's a possibility,' he said slowly as he handed me my drink.

I sighed. Now what? 'Could he have been harassed by anyone for money?'

'You mean robbing Peter to pay Paul? Maybe. But he didn't say.'

I had the strong feeling mine host wasn't planning to be helpful. 'I really do want to find Nigel. He could be in danger. Even if he's not, your five hundred pounds could become a little nearer to your pocket.'

The landlord picked up his *Times*. 'Are you good at crosswords?' I shook my head. 'I'm stuck on one. You solve my clue and I'll give you a clue.'

'It's a deal. How long have I got?'

'By the end of your first drink. Here, take it. It's eight down.'

I grabbed the paper and Hubert and I sat down at the table nearest the fire. 'Drink slowly, Hubert, this could take some time.'

He stared at the clue. I stared at the clue. Realization did not dawn. I glanced towards the landlord, who winked and waved to me.

'This is a complete waste of time,' said Hubert. 'I could go blind staring at these stupid little squares.'

'He knows something,' I said, 'and he wants to play this little game with us. It's got to be worth a chance.'

Hubert looked up at me glumly. 'I shouldn't be here at all. Just tell me what you've achieved so far. You haven't found Nigel, a woman we now find out was a liar has been murdered, you've been arrested, I've left my business at a lucrative time of year and my girlfriend is coping alone. Now we're sitting here doing a sodding crossword.'

'Don't exaggerate, Hubert. It's only one clue.'

'I want another drink,' he said, sounding petulant.

'Not until we've solved this clue. I think the landlord may know something and he's going to tell me but only if we show we're worthy of getting a clue he can't manage.'

'It's all very childish,' said Hubert, draining his glass quickly to show me he didn't want to play.

We toyed with words and fretted at our lack of intelligence. Eventually I'd finished my drink too and we were still no nearer an answer.

'I agree, Hubert, this is childish. We just ain't clever enough. I'll go and tell the landlord.'

An elderly man with a red nose was ordering a drink at the bar. The landlord glanced at me warily, I thought. When the customer wandered away clutching his drink the landlord raised his eyebrow. 'Well?' he said.

'We've failed. We just couldn't crack it.'

'Thank God for that. I would have been peeved if you had. I've spent some time on that one.'

Strangely, I wasn't that surprised, because I knew some people who consider themselves clever don't like to be outsmarted by those they judge their inferiors. And at that moment I felt intellectually inferior to a woodlouse, but I managed to force a wan smile and order two more drinks. While Hubert's second pint was being pulled the landlord said, 'I consider myself a generous type...' He paused and I thought maybe so but definitely pompous. 'I like Nigel, he was a good customer and I'd like to see him in here again, so I'll give you that clue, which isn't perfect but is half there.'

I waited. He handed me both drinks. 'On the house,' he said.

'Is that a clue?'

'No. That's me being generous. The clue is "The proletariat would be lost without it."'

I repeated it to myself, thanked him profusely and walked quickly back to Hubert.

Hubert raised his eyebrows to heaven and we sat for a while brainstorming and examining every single word.

'I think,' said Hubert, 'he's winding us up. I can't hang around in Ryde in the bleak midwinter while people need burying in Longborough.'

'You're right,' I agreed. 'It's not fair on you. I can manage now. I've got a couple of leads—James Renton, Adam's connections and the landlord's clue.'

'That's a joke,' said Hubert. 'You just take care with this Renton bloke and remember Nigel isn't an open, up-front type. If you ask me he's an arsehole.'

'Hubert, your language is deteriorating.'

He grinned. 'I blame you for that.'

HUBERT LEFT late afternoon and I had to admit I felt depressed. After he'd gone I forced myself into action. Christmas was coming and I didn't want to be in Uplands Lodge on Christmas Day.

I went first to the address I'd seen at Caroline's holiday home. I knew it would be impressive when the mini cab driver murmured, 'Nice,' as I gave him the address. And 'nice' it was. The sort of house that had room for six cars and a cottage, just in the front drive. Its mock-Grecian pillars signalled an owner who was slightly ostentatious, but who cared?

The man who answered the ornate brass knocker was silver haired at the temples, medium height and I didn't really notice the neatness or otherwise of his features because he had the bluest eyes I'd ever seen.

I didn't bother with any subterfuge. 'I'm Kate Kinsella, Medical and Nursing Investigations. I…knew Caroline. I found her body.'

'That's very succinct… May I call you Kate?' I smiled and nodded. 'I'm Alex Freeman. Come on in.'

Once inside the front door the marble floors, Persian carpets and pot plants tall as trees gave the vast hall a feel of summer and foreign lands. I muttered my admiration and Alex led the way to a kitchen: large, pine clad and so tidy it was obvious that a woman kept him organized.

I sat at the kitchen table, which was empty save for a basket of dried flowers, and he filled a cafetière with boiling water. While we waited for the coffee to brew he said, 'You're investigating Caroline's death?'

'No, not exactly. I'm investigating the disappearance of Nigel Carter.'

'Why you? It doesn't seem a medical problem.'

'I'm not sure,' I answered truthfully. 'His aunt employed me to find him. She's dying and I was the most local investigator, I suppose.'

'Are you any good?'

I laughed. 'I'm dogged.'

'How can I help you?'

'I've just found out that Caroline lied to me about being married to Lyle Uxton...'

He smiled. 'Caroline lied about most things, Kate.'

'I see.'

'You don't see. Most people find out about Caroline...when it's too late.'

'What exactly was your relationship with her?'

His blue eyes stared at me for several seconds. 'Nigel and I were once friends, a long time ago. We went to school together in Southampton.'

'And Caroline?'

He poured the coffee into bone china mugs. 'We both fell in love with Caroline—' He broke off as the sound of footsteps stopped at the kitchen door and in walked Adam and another tall boy. They wore 'grunge', baggy trousers and old sweaters with rampant holes.

'This is my son Tom, and Adam you've met, I believe.'

The boys eyed me sullenly. I felt I had to say something

to Adam. 'I'm sorry about your mother, Adam,' I said, knowing that the words were almost meaningless, but to not comment on her death would have seemed like ignoring her life.

He shrugged in response, a sullen look on his face. 'Yeah. So am I,' he said.

'We're going out, Dad,' said Tom.

'Don't be late back,' said his father.

When they'd left, Alex smiled and shook his head. 'Christ knows where they go but as long as they get in at a reasonable time I don't ask too many questions.'

'How has Adam been?'

Alex frowned. 'To be brutally honest you wouldn't think anything had happened. He seems his normal sullen self to me. They're not much trouble and I'm quite happy to have them in the holidays.'

'What about Adam's future?'

'He's Tom's best friend; they get on well. Adam can stay here for the duration if he wants.'

'Are you divorced?' I asked bluntly.

'No. My wife died when Tom was three years old. She was killed by a hit-and-run driver. No one ever found out who.'

I sipped at my coffee, wondering why he'd never married again. He must have read my thoughts because he said thoughtfully, 'I couldn't go through that sort of loss again. I've had girlfriends, but the moment they get serious I end it.'

'What about Caroline?'

'What about her?' he said sharply.

'I get the strangest feeling,' I said, 'that no one really cares that she's been murdered. And now it seems not even her son is grieving for her.'

He shrugged in the same way Adam had shrugged. 'She was a difficult woman.'

'Was she?' He didn't answer. 'She was very attractive,' I said. 'Lively and good company. I don't understand.'

'I knew her when she was young. She changed.'

'You were in love with her once.'

'Yes, once upon a time I was in love with her.'

'What happened?'

'She met Nigel and I was yesterday's man.'

'I see.'

'I don't think you do.'

'What about her so-called husband? Was he your first thought when you heard she'd been murdered?'

'Let's just say I wouldn't have been that surprised. I think she led him a dog's life.'

I was perplexed. 'She told me he was violent. She seemed very scared of him.'

Alex smiled at me as if he were soothing somebody extremely stupid. 'That was the impression she wanted to give. It suited her.'

'Why?'

'Perhaps she needed sympathy. She liked to be the centre of attention.'

'But I saw him being violent towards her. He hit her, he was screaming at her.'

'What you saw was a man at the end of his tether.'

I remembered then why I hadn't chased him. It was a gut reaction to a man whose body language spoke of defeat and misery.

A phone ringing in another room called Alex away and I sat there feeling not only puzzled but worried about my intuitive powers. I'd believed everything Caroline had told me, but now nothing seemed true or certain. Why should I believe Alex? Could he be a suspect? Why not? He could quite easily have known what Caroline was planning to do.

'Sorry about that,' said Alex on his return to the kitchen. 'It was one of my tenants. Being a landlord isn't always a picnic. I've some holiday lets and a few permanent tenants, so there're always problems.'

'Was it really Caroline's first stay on the Isle of Wight?'

He smiled. 'No, but I hadn't seen her in some time.'

'What about the night she was murdered?'

'What about it?'

'I just wondered if she'd told you what she was planning to do?'

This time he laughed. 'Oh, Kate. You really don't have a clue about Caroline at all, do you?'

'I didn't say I did. But I wondered if you could be a suspect?'

He didn't smile at that. He stared at me for a moment. Then he grinned. 'Do you think the police haven't grilled me on that one? I do have one of my tenants to thank for my alibi. That morning I had an early phone call about a leaking roof and I went to sort it out. The police have, of course, verified my alibi. And, of course, I had no motive to kill Caroline. I hadn't seen her for a year. I usually see her at the school sports day. The boys are boarders at the same school and although Adam has spent time here before, Caroline didn't fancy staying in one of my properties. This year for some reason she changed her mind.'

'You were telling me both you and Nigel had been in love with Caroline. Could you have been harbouring a grudge all these years because Nigel stole your girl?'

'Come off it. That was fifteen years ago.'

'People can hold grudges for longer than that.'

'Possibly, but not me. I'm a well-adjusted individual…'
He paused. 'You surely don't think…'

'Don't think what?'

'That I had anything to do with Nigel going missing?'

'It's occurring to me now that you may have.'

He shook his head. 'You're on the wrong track, Kate.
I saw Nigel occasionally. We even talked about old times,
but if anyone should be suspected of killing Caroline it
would be Nigel himself.'

Why hadn't I thought of that? Nigel disappears, Caroline is murdered, but who would suspect a man who
wasn't there?

'Why should Nigel want to murder his ex-girlfriend?
She was off his hands. I can't see why.'

Once more the phone rang and I waited impatiently for
his return. When he did come back he looked annoyed.
'I've got to go. This mad tenant will give me no peace
until I pay her a visit.'

'I'm sorry to have kept you, Alex. Please do me a small
favour, though. I've been given a cryptic clue to Nigel's
whereabouts and I haven't solved it yet.'

'OK, try me.'

'Here is it, then… "The proletariat would be lost without it."'

He rested his arms on the kitchen table looking thoughtful, then shook his head slowly. 'No idea, I'm sorry.'

'Oh well, thanks for trying.'

As I left the house I too was thoughtful. Although I
hadn't guessed what the clue meant I had a feeling Alex
had. Which meant that for some reason he was also
among the number who didn't seem to want Nigel found.

THIRTEEN

I'D ALREADY walked part of the long drive when Alex called out, 'I'll give you a lift if you like.'

'Thanks.' I was more grateful than he knew because I'd realized I'd forgotten the most important question of all. What was Caroline's permanent address?

We'd stopped at traffic lights and it was drizzling with rain. Ryde's Christmas decorations hung in bright profusion but the grey skies and nearly empty main street gave them a pathetic jauntiness like a flag waving above a sinking ship.

'Why do you want her address?' he asked suspiciously.

'I'm looking for Nigel and maybe the neighbours have seen him there. I mean, he did have a relationship with her once.'

'Why should he see her now? Their relationship was over years ago.'

'He might have sought her out if there was no one else. If he was in real trouble.'

'What sort of trouble could he have been in?'

'Money troubles. Someone after him threatening to break his legs.'

'I don't think he was a wild spender.'

'He was a regular in the Pig and Whistle and drinking flushes away money.'

Staring straight ahead, Alex said, 'This is a small place. I never heard any rumours he was drinking heavily.'

'Did he gamble?'

'I didn't hear any rumours about that either.'

He gave me the address just as we stopped outside Uplands Lodge. I wrote it down in my note book. 'The police will have been there,' he said.

'A neighbour might be helpful.'

Alex smiled and squeezed my hand. 'You are a little optimist, aren't you? Let me know how you get on.'

THE HOTEL reception area seemed as hot as a sauna after the cold of outside, partly because it had been invaded by a small crowd of high-spirited pensioners. Eventually Amanda handed me my key and whispered, 'They'll be staying over Christmas. Let me know if they make too much noise.'

I wasn't sure if she was being serious, but judging from the level of noise I thought she probably was. 'Are there any messages for me?' I asked.

She shook her head then said, 'I'm sorry, Kate, I forgot, there is one. Mr Humberstone left you this.'

She passed me a bulky envelope. There was a note amongst a bundle of twenty-pound notes:

Call yourself a private investigator? Buy a camera. Behave yourself!
PS. That clue—isn't there a French connection? Proletariat—isn't that French? What about Paris? Don't go there without telling me.

I smiled. Dear Hubert. As long as I lived I knew there would always be a soft mushy place in my heart for him.

I dithered for a few minutes, feeling an urge to rush out and buy a camera immediately, but I told myself my knowledge of cameras was limited to knowing that a Polaroid produced a photo within seconds and that itself I thought was a miracle. Zoom lenses were as foreign to me as the Internet and I knew that some eager young shop assistant would sell me some complicated camera that would need a degree just to understand the instructions. I persuaded myself to wait a while, decided to have dinner and plan meeting James Renton.

Later that evening I appeared at the dining room to the noisy chatter of the Christmas holidaymakers. I felt incredibly young. Apart from the staff I was the only one without greying hair or a blue rinse. I could see Harold at his usual corner table for four and after a few moments he waved at me and pointed to the empty chair beside him. I gazed round, looking for a lone alternative but there was none. I walked slowly towards his table, past the noisy new guests, and slid myself into the chair beside Harold.

'We were just talking about you,' said Harold.

I smiled. 'Nothing too bad, I hope.'

'Nancy was wondering if you lead an exciting life.'

'I wish it were, Nancy. I spend days sometimes just waiting for work. I get quite a few enquiries from people who want their partners or spouses put under surveillance to catch them…at it. And I'm not really that sort of detective…'

'What sort are you, then?'

'I prefer my assignments to have a medical or nursing background.'

'Why are you looking for Nigel?'

Why indeed? I wanted to say but instead I smiled at Nancy's eager face and said, 'Because his aunt is dying and that's as medical as it gets.'

'What's his aunt like?'

'I haven't actually met her. I've just spoken to her on the phone. She desperately wants me to find Nigel.'

Margaret, who until this point had been toying with a bread roll, lifted her head slightly and said, 'Why?'

I was taken aback for a moment. 'Why what, Margaret?'

'Why does she want you to find him?'

I stared at her sharp blue eyes. 'Because she's fond of him and is puzzled that he hasn't been in contact. She fears something nasty may have happened to him.'

'Better not to know, then. Finding out he was dead would probably kill her anyway. Why don't you lie and say he's gone to live abroad? You could get someone to send a postcard in capital letters and convince her it was from him.'

'Margaret, I'm shocked. That would be taking money by false pretences.'

She shrugged. 'What do you think, Harold?'

Our first course had just arrived and it appeared Harold was more interested in examining his fish mousse from all angles than answering. After a short pause he said slowly, 'Let's face it. Nigel was no real loss to anyone.'

'Why do you say that?' I asked.

'Who have you found who cares where he's gone?'

I was about to protest when I realized he was right. No one did care that much. 'No one really cared about Caroline Uxton either—'

'Not even her son?' interrupted Nancy.

'How did you know she had a son?' I asked.

She laughed briefly. 'I do read the papers. It was all in there.'

'Of course,' I muttered.

During the main course I thought I should say something about the forthcoming wedding. It seemed a low-key event and I couldn't help wondering if it was really true, although I now noticed Nancy was wearing an engagement ring. I hadn't heard them making plans so I thought I'd better be tactful.

'That's a lovely ring you're wearing, Nancy. Is it new?'

She smiled at me and then raised her hand to smile at the ring. 'We're getting married next week. Very quietly. Stewart's putting on some food and drink for us here. We're not having a honeymoon, though. We're having that now, aren't we, Harold?'

'Yes, my darling. We certainly are.'

Harold's hand touched hers and for several seconds they smiled delightedly at each other. Then Harold said, 'It was fate that brought us together.'

Nancy laughed. 'More like financial disaster.'

'In what way?'

'We both had businesses that were failing and we both tried the wrong way of saving them.'

'Was this on the island?' I asked.

Harold shook his head. 'No, dear. We both lived in Southampton, although we'd never met until we came here.'

'What happened to your businesses?' I asked.

'A loan shark took us for nearly everything we had.'

'The same one?'

Harold nodded. 'Yes. The same one.'

'Couldn't you have taken a civil action against him?'

'I talked to the police about it,' he said, frowning, 'but they more or less told me I had been stupid and although they knew he was crooked there wasn't much they could do.'

'So this loan shark is still working in Southampton?'

He nodded again and said quietly, 'He's still got offices there but I heard someone say he lives on the island now.'

'Don't let's talk about it any more, Harold,' said Nancy. 'You know how it still upsets you.'

Harold's brows lowered and his hands bunched into fists. 'If I ever see him again…I'll kill him.'

'Please, Harold, don't say that,' said Nancy, her voice sounding a little tremulous. 'If it hadn't been for him we might never have met, so it did have a silver lining for us.'

'And a gold lining for that bastard,' said Harold coldly.

Nancy patted his hand. 'It's all in the past now, dear. We have to look forward, not back.'

Harold managed a slight smile at both me and Nancy. 'Sorry, Kate. You don't want to hear our woes.'

'What was this loan shark's name? I'll make sure I avoid him.'

It was Nancy who answered me. 'James Renton.'

I RANG HUBERT later that night.

'So what do you think it means?' asked Hubert.

'I think Nigel borrowed money from Renton, couldn't pay it back and Renton threatened to break his legs or worse and Nigel had to do a runner.'

There was a pause during which I swore I could almost hear Hubert's thought processes.

'What did he want the money for in the first place?'

'Good question. That thought had occurred to me.'

'And?'

'Nothing's really come to mind unless he was fiddling the accounts as Caroline suspected.'

'Have the police got the books?'

'Yes. But they aren't going to give me any information, are they?'

'Is that surprising?' asked Hubert, sounding as if he was definitely talking from the high moral ground.

'How's business?'

'Busy. Full to overflowing.'

'Hubert, you could have just said "busy". I don't like the overflowing image.'

'You're only trying to change the subject, Kate. What are you going to do now?'

'See James Renton, of course.'

'And say what?'

'I'll think of something.'

'Just you be careful. That sort of man hires thugs to do his dirty work. He won't be breaking legs personally.'

'I'm glad to hear it. How's Danielle, by the way?'

'She's fine. I don't know what I'd do without her now. She's more like a partner than a receptionist.'

Again I felt a little pang of quite unreasonable jealousy.

'Bye, Hubert. Take care.'

'Let me know how you get on with Renton. And if I were you I wouldn't tell him you were looking for Nigel.'

'I wasn't planning to.' I was about to put the phone down when I remembered the camera money.

'Thanks for—' I broke off; the line was dead.

I scanned the local paper for a while and reading about a fire reminded me of the fire on *The Havana Belle*. Somewhere in this tangled mess that fire probably played a part. If it was an accident it wasn't worth following up; even if it was deliberate would it help me find Nigel or a murderer? I doubted that. I stared at the ceiling for a while trying to remember when exactly Elizabeth Forrester had last phoned me. Of course, she could have died in the interim. On that depressing thought I turned back to the local paper and ran through the Lonely Hearts columns.

I smiled at the tone of political correctness of some of them. 'Caring and sensitive. Great sense of humour' were a favourite tag. One woman wanted a 'clean', honest, sincere, caring man. What happened, I wondered, to dynamic, passionate men? Had they all gone the way of caring sensitivity? Those that weren't 'caring and sensitive' seemed sports-mad: 'Male, 28, tall and handsome. GSOH. Keen on fishing, cricket and rugby. Seeks like-minded female.' What an optimist! Any respondent would certainly need a sense of humour, even if he was handsome.

It was the opposite page then that caught my eye. There, amongst the bankruptcies, was a boxed message from a firm of solicitors asking a Brian Goody to get in touch with them. I could do the same for Nigel. Surely he would surface if he thought his aunt was dead. I know Mrs Forrester hadn't wanted me to get in touch with the media but this was discreet and all I had to do was find out which paper Nigel read and place an advert giving my Medical and Nursing Investigations address. If he'd left the Isle of Wight because of money troubles surely he'd be even more desperate now to get his hands on his aunt's money.

When I finally fell asleep that night, full of optimistic thoughts, I was disturbed twice by the noisy new guests staggering to their beds. After that I slept fitfully and had nightmares in which Caroline's head lifted from the table and her bloody mouth uttered three chilling words:

'What about me?' she asked, over and over again.

FOURTEEN

THE NIGHTMARE affected me badly. In the light of a grey December morning I stood staring blankly out of the window. It was all very well trying to find Nigel, who irresponsibly had disappeared, but what about Caroline? Had the police made any progress? Were the Isle of Wight CID capable of dealing with a murder case? After all, the IOW was hardly renowned as the murder capital of the world. This could well be Formbridge's only experience of murder. For goodness' sake, I probably had more experience than he! A little warning voice told me to be careful. Just because fictional detectives seemed to have all the suspects lined up like extras in a film didn't mean I could do the same. Had I even found one solid suspect? Stewart had to be in the running and James Renton, or at least one of his hench men, and Alex, of course, who professed to have loved Caroline once and lost her. He could quite easily have carried his bitterness with him through the years. And who was Adam's father anyway?

After an early breakfast I found James Renton's address in the phone book and booked a taxi. The driver, when he finally arrived, was as sullen and silent as the grey skies above Ryde. The journey into the island hinterland was thankfully short, taking only half an hour.

The house, in a hamlet of six or so houses, gave me the impression of 1920s middle-class gentility. There were wide bay windows and timbered gables. Inside I knew there would be high ceilings and deep skirtings, and an attic room where once a maid of all work spent her few measly hours of freedom. Now it would be a study or would house a billiard table. The illusion was shattered by two things: the satellite dish on the side of the house and the sight of two huge Rottweilers who loped excitedly towards me as I approached the front gate. There was a fence and trees and shrubs between the dogs and me, but their legs looked long and powerful and I had the feeling they could be over the fence in seconds. Just as I began backing away a man appeared. Renton. He was tall and wide, wearing gold-rimmed glasses and a dark grey pin-striped suit. He looked quite respectable until he opened his mouth and called the dogs. 'Here, Flash! Here, Thunder! Get inside.' I heard in his voice the sound of north London; although his accent was pronounced its pitch was the most striking thing; high, squeaky and it certainly didn't belong with his large head and body.

Once the dogs were inside he came up to the gate. 'Yes, love, what can I do for you?'

That was the crunch question? I looked past him at the house beyond. 'I was just admiring your home, it's wonderful. I'm staying on the island for a while—sort of house-hunting—and I came out here because someone told me there was a house for sale in Little Barstead. This *is* Little Barstead, isn't it?'

'Yes, love, it is. But my castle isn't for sale. Great, though, isn't it? But I don't know of any for sale round here.'

'Oh, I see.' I tried to look crestfallen. 'That's a real shame. I'm a nurse. My name's Kate Kinsella, and I was thinking of opening up a small nursing home. This sort of house would be ideal, but...' I sighed at this dramatic point.

'But what?'

'I've been turned down by two building societies already.'

He smiled knowingly. 'Ah well, my lovely girl, if you're trying regular building societies I'm not surprised you're being turned down. Have you got any collateral?'

'A small cottage, that's all.'

He opened the gate then, placed a beefy arm round my shoulder and said, 'You come with Uncle James to my office and we'll talk business. I'm sure I can find you a mortgage. You just have to know the people who, for a small fee—sometimes a larger fee—will be helpful. And of course it might be worthwhile for you to consider places already up and running.'

'I hadn't thought of that.'

'I think of everything. I'll move heaven and earth for my clients.'

'Clients?' I queried.

'I run a specialist company—helping people just like you.'

'Where's your office?' I asked.

'Cowes. We can go now if you like. I've got all the paperwork at the office and it's more businesslike.'

I dithered. In a car he might want to chat, which had a down side in that if I wasn't careful he might get suspicious. Conversely, if we chatted he might give away more than mortgage details.

'How long will it take?' I asked.

'As long as it needs,' he said, giving my shoulder another squeeze. 'I don't like to shortchange people.'

On the drive to Cowes in a white Porsche (not his only car, he informed me) he told me about his small empire which somehow he made sound like a cross between Dr Barnados and Help the Homeless.

'People contact me from all over the country,' he said.

'They know I can help them. I've got an office in South-ampton and Portsmouth as well as the Cowes branch.'

'Do you only deal with business mortgages?'

He negotiated a bend at an uncomfortable speed before answering me. 'My clients only have to ask and I'll do my best. Loans, second mortgages, bridging loans, you name it, love, I'll organize it.'

'I haven't got much capital, Mr Renton.'

'You call me James and let me worry about your capital.'

By the time we arrived in Cowes I'd almost convinced myself that buying a nursing home was my life-long ambition, and James Renton had certainly given me the impression that finding the money was a mere inconvenience that could easily be overcome.

Cowes was shrouded by a cold, misty pall, as if the sea had cast up a greyish gauze and the bulk of the population had scuttled indoors to await its disappearance, or spring, whichever came the soonest. A few rather weather-trodden people braved the outside, but the sky seemed to bow them down or perhaps it was pre-Christmas financial panic. Whatever it was, the town and the sea seemed far from welcoming.

James Renton obviously felt no shame about using his own name, because stamped in gold letterings on the opaque glass frontage were the words Renton Finance.

Inside, a young girl stood at the filing cabinet and turned towards us as we entered. She wore a very short black skirt, a white sweater with a sequinned butterfly over her left breast, and sported long red nails which I thought proved she did more filing than typing.

'Any calls, Angel?' Renton asked cheerfully.

'Only the police, Mr Renton,' she said. Her voice gave me the impression she had a mouth full of chewing gum.

For a second he seemed slightly flustered. 'It's since that murder in Ryde,' he explained. 'Unfortunately the victim worked in my Southampton office, so they keep tracking me down to ask me bloody silly questions.'

'I heard about that almost at first hand,' I said. 'A real tragedy.' I smiled and said lightly, 'They don't suspect you of killing her, do they?'

He affected a shocked expression. 'Come on now, Kate. Do I look the type?'

For a moment I gazed at him before realization dawned. He expected an answer! 'Of course not,' I said, trying my utmost to sound convincing. Then I added, 'But if you knew the victim quite well you're bound to be on their list.'

Now he looked faintly annoyed. 'She worked for me on a part-time basis about fourteen years ago and we did have a bit of a flirtation but I was married then and I soon saw sense. Now let's get down to business. Angel, two cups of coffee, please.'

Angel left the room on heels high enough to impress Hubert and I had to ask, 'Is that her real name?'

He smiled. 'One of the reasons I employed her. She's a lousy typist but she can take messages, make coffee, file and she doesn't argue with me.'

'So you don't have a partner?'

'I did once. It didn't work. I've got managers in my other two offices but I don't allow them too much freedom.'

'Why not?'

He smiled knowingly. 'You can't trust anyone these days. Someone always tries to rip you off.'

By the time Angel returned with the coffee Renton had handed me estate agents' details of three nursing homes. The prices were staggering and I nearly laughed.

'Take no notice of those prices,' he said. 'They're re-possessions. We can negotiate a good price for you.'

'You'd need to,' I said with a wry smile. 'Perhaps a small residential home is more in my price vision.'

'Vision is what you need, Kate. Just imagine yourself as queen of your own little kingdom. Self-employed, a good profit margin, no bosses to worry about, a holiday abroad twice a year, a decent car. I did it; you can do it too.'

I could feel myself being swayed. It sounded a lot better than struggling to find a week's rent and finding that a new crank shaft is a cause for complete financial collapse. Perhaps running a nursing home was more 'me' anyway. After all, in the finding of lost hoteliers I'd made as much progress as a Conservative government trying to resurrect the housing market. Now I sat here drinking coffee and feeling quite unable to bring either Caroline or Nigel into the conversation without arousing his suspicions.

Renton sat like some Eastern potentate while I flicked unseeing through the brochures. 'I'm a bit worried,' I said eventually. 'I know being self-employed sounds wonderful, but I've heard so many…stories about people getting into terrible financial situations.'

'What sort of stories?' he asked.

'Well…I was in the Pig and Whistle pub the other night in Ryde and I overheard someone saying a hotelier called Nigel Carter had disappeared taking with him a tidy sum belonging to the hotel. I can't help feeling slightly panicky when I hear that sort of thing.'

'Don't you fret, Kate. I'll be looking after you,' said Renton with a wide smile. 'I knew Nigel. He was a prat. I employed him once because he was good at figures, but I found out what he was up to and sacked him.'

'What was he up to?'

'He was doing little private deals on my time and with my stationery. He thought I wouldn't catch him but I did. No one, I repeat *no one*, gets the better of me.' His smile had long gone now, to be replaced by an ice-cold glare.

'Is that why you're wary of having a partner now?'

He smiled again, reverting once more to the jovial salesman. 'Could be, love, but I don't like talking about losers. Let's talk about you winning.'

At that point the phone rang. 'Renton Finance. May I help you?' intoned Angel in a sing-song fashion. She listened for a moment, then covered the mouthpiece. 'It's the Bottomleys,' she whispered.

'Tell them I'm in Southampton,' said Renton.

'He's in his office in Southampton, Mr Bottomley.'

Even from my position in the office I could hear the voice sounded irate. Again she covered the mouthpiece. 'He says you're a liar. He's in a call box round the corner and he's seen your car. He's on his way.'

'Shit!' said Renton. 'Sorry, Kate, love. The man's a nutter. I got him a bridging loan and now he can't pay it and he thinks it's my fault. I'll have to see you another day. How about tomorrow? In the meantime, you could see those ones you've got the details of.'

I nodded and picked up the brochures, aware of almost being bundled out of the door. Not quickly enough, though, to miss the Bottomleys. Mrs Bottomley was short, fragile looking and clung on to her tall, thin husband, whose face seemed to register both rage and despair. I noticed she'd been crying and although I walked away briskly I only went round the corner to a café where I could sit by the window and wait for them to come past.

I drank tea from a thick white cup and waited. Half an hour passed and I thought maybe there was another way out of the cul de sac. The café was an 'If it's not fried we don't serve it' sort of place and the smell of frying onions seemed to permeate even the tea.

It was five minutes later that the Bottomleys came into view, and they didn't look any happier. I left my window seat and walked out to them, trying hard not to appear as if I were pouncing on them.

'Excuse me,' I said as I barred their way. 'I'm so sorry to bother you but I noticed you going into Renton Finance and I wondered if you'd be willing to let me buy you a cup of tea and ask you a few questions.'

Mrs Bottomley, still tearful, gazed warily at her husband as if for confirmation.

'What's your connection with that piece of scum?' he demanded.

'Come into the café and I'll explain.'

They seemed to shrug in unison, then with only slight reluctance followed me in and I ordered tea and dough-nuts all round. I had a vague feeling of unease when Mrs Bottomley refused hers. Depression is, after all, a reason for eating jam doughnuts; to refuse indicates a very severe depression.

'Our lives are in ruins,' muttered the male Bottomley. His large lower lip trembled slightly, his eyes watered.

'I think you'd better drink your tea and eat that dough-nut,' I said, as though sustenance would solve all his prob-lems. He gave me a doleful look and Bottomley female sipped her tea and sniffed loudly.

'I'm Kate, by the way,' I said, hoping they would re-ciprocate with their Christian names, but they didn't.

I ate my doughnut and tried to guess their ages. I sup-posed they were in their early forties and as I tried to imagine them in more cheerful circumstances I still thought they would have that frayed-at-the-edge look. Mrs Bottomley wore a short beige coat and underneath a beige and brown jumper with a brown pleated skirt. Her spouse wore brown cords and a dull green jumper under a green padded anorak. As a child he could have been a train spotter.

His wife's doughnut plus his own seemed to lift his spirits slightly. 'We should have listened to our solicitor, dear, shouldn't we?'

His wife nodded miserably.

'What happened?' I asked.

He stared at me and sighed. 'We'd set our heart on this house on the island. We live in London and we love the peace and quiet here. We've no children and I'm about to be made redundant, so, with house prices being so much lower here, we decided to make the move. We had a buyer for our house at a reasonable price and we made several trips over here to find our dream house. And we found it, didn't we, dear?'

'Dear' nodded and smiled weakly at the memory and husband 'dear' continued. 'The owners of the house near Ryde were selling up and going abroad and of course they wanted a quick sale. So we were desperate for the house and made enquiries about a bridging loan. Our solicitor advised us not to, various banks and building societies turned us down and then just by chance we heard someone mention Renton Finance. Renton assured us he could get us a loan. We did have a buyer, so I thought that for just a few weeks we could manage.'

He paused and stared into his teacup. 'We did manage for a few weeks. The charges were far higher than we thought at first and with Renton's fees on top it was getting very difficult, and then the bombshell dropped—our buyers had changed their minds.'

'Oh dear,' I murmured. 'I can see that all this is disastrous, but surely in his way Renton did what you wanted.'

Mrs Bottomley sighed loudly. 'He says we should have read the small print but we did and it wasn't there.'

'What wasn't?' I asked.

'The ongoing fee to Renton, plus the security for the loan was…' She paused and glanced sadly at her husband. '…the house. We're going to lose the house. We can't afford to go on…we can't.' She broke down and sobbed quietly while her husband patted her shoulder with patient resignation that seemed born of practice.

'Have you see a solicitor?' I asked.

Mr Bottomley answered. 'Yes. We've even been to the police. Morally it seems Renton is in the wrong but not legally. We signed up, we have to pay the price.'

I tried to find something reassuring to say but could only remember vaguely from George Orwell's *Down and Out in London and Paris* a line which said that the fear of losing everything was far worse than the actual event. Once everything is lost the only way is up, I supposed was the message, but I didn't think it would particularly help the Bottomleys at this hiatus in their lives.

'We're not the only ones fleeced by Renton, you know,' said Mr Bottomley. 'He's wrecked other people's lives. We're collecting names and addresses. We placed an advert for people who'd become involved with loan companies—we didn't name Renton in particular, but in the replies he was the one most frequently mentioned. You see, men like him prey on the desperate. Those with County Court judgements, those already in arrears, those who don't earn enough to pay a mortgage, people in debt generally. People have committed suicide because of him.'

'I'm so sorry,' I said. 'I'm lost for something comforting to say. But if there's anything I can do?'

They both shook their heads in unison. 'We have to go back to London now,' he said. 'Losing our house is one thing, but that shark is obviously on a fiddle with estate agents and he'll pocket a large part of the proceeds. It's like he's stolen our life blood…all we ever worked for.' Mr Bottomley half stood up, glanced anxiously at his wife, then sat down again. 'Will you do me a favour?' he asked.

I nodded and smiled.

'Read these.' From inside his jacket pocket he produced a small bundle of letters. 'These are just a few of the answers I've received.'

I began reading and I soon realized that each letter contained tales of heartbreak, disappointment, broken relationships and broken lives. The bitterness of the letter writers was also reflected in the retribution they wished to exact, ranging from boiling in oil to castration and even decapitation.

When I'd finished reading them I said, 'At least you two do still have each other.'

He smiled wryly. 'Yes,' he said slowly. 'We do still have each other.'

I watched them leave, hand in hand. Their shoulders were hunched and their footsteps sounded loud on the cobbles. Somewhere in the distance I heard the faint sounds of a Christmas carol—'God rest you merry gentlemen, Let nothing you dismay.' It seemed hardly appropriate and for a moment their retreating backs reminded me of another occasion—when I failed to chase after Lyle Uxton because he, too, looked so defeated.

FIFTEEN

HUBERT RANG FOR an update that evening. I updated him, which didn't really take long, because although I'd found out that Renton was a loan shark whose financial gnawing was extremely frightening, I certainly had no evidence that he was violent or that he had anything to do with either Nigel's disappearance or Caroline's death.

'Hubert, he doesn't have to go in for the kill in reality. He goes in for the kill financially.'

'Don't get metaphysical with me, Kate.'

'I think the word is metaphorical.'

'Just don't try and be too clever.'

'Clever! That's a joke. I seem to have more leads to follow than a kennel full of dogs.'

'You should just stick to finding Nigel. There's no reason to dabble in murder.'

'Thank you, Hubert, for being so supportive. Given the connections between Nigel and Caroline, plus Renton, plus the rather strange Alex, I'm dealing here with a very complex case.'

'Perhaps you're making it more difficult. Have you solved that clue yet?'

'No, Hubert, my IQ isn't up to it.'

'Danielle's solved it.'

'She's obviously clever,' I said bitchily, 'as well as having higher insteps and a bigger cleavage than most women.' I'd nearly said most 'normal' women but at least I hadn't been that bitchy.

There was silence from Hubert until I mumbled, 'I'm probably just jealous.'

'Do you want to know the answer?'

'Of course I do.'

'She did it simply by word association—proletariat—French word—France—Paris—Metro—leave out the "r"—you get Metropole. Danielle says there is a Metropole Hotel just outside Southampton.'

She would know that, I thought, but I thanked Hubert and told him to thank Danielle.

'Are you going to visit the Metropole?'

'I don't know why he should be there but I'll go. After all, it was a clue given to us by a man to whom Nigel owed money.'

'You could be disappointed, Kate. After all, if someone really wants to disappear then it's easy enough to stay missing.'

'Yes, but why should anyone be after him? I don't think he'd imagine that his aunt would find a private investigator to track him down, so he must relax his guard after a while.'

Hubert murmured something about taking care of myself and suddenly I wanted to go back to Longborough and my cottage in Farley Wood more than anything else in the world. Except that Christmas was coming and there was only Hubert and now he would probably spend Christmas with Danielle. Perhaps I would be better off staying on at the hotel, I thought. At least I wouldn't be alone. By then I'd probably have found Nigel and discovered who murdered Caroline. And undertakers might suffer poverty!

THE CROSSING TO Southampton was rough, rough, rough. My stomach seemed to become part of my gullet and my bowels danced the twist. Thankfully my feet were soon back on unyielding concrete, but even there the winds were strong enough to cause me to sway. I waited with a few other disembarked passengers at a taxi rank, wondering if they felt more disembowelled than disembarked, for they had strange expressions on their faces as if they had just relived a disaster movie and they weren't quite sure if they played survivors or victims.

The Metropole Hotel had a grey frontage that was, I think, meant to be white. It did have a red awning and a lit Christmas tree outside. Inside, the red carpets and red lamps gave it the aura of a bordello, a hot bordello, as the heat seemed overwhelming after the cold outside. In one corner of the reception area was another Christmas tree at least six feet tall and decorated with silver and gold baubles, and on the reception desk itself stood a tiny artificial tree covered in silver and gold stars. I did wonder idly as I stood there if the trees were to compensate for the lack of staff—there was no one about.

It was five minutes before anyone did appear. I smiled at her when she did. She was in her late twenties, I supposed, with a slightly shaggy blonde haircut, pale face with red full lips, and she wore a black and white waistcoat, white blouse and black skirt. Pinned to her waistcoat was a small sprig of holly.

'Welcome to the Metropole Hotel. Would you like a single or a double room?'

'Single. Just one night...provisionally.'

She seemed vaguely disappointed, but smiled at me very professionally, hoped I would enjoy my stay and would I please sign the register.

My room when I found it in the maze of silent corridors was poky, hot and stared out on to a brick wall. The cream furnishings were restful but in the two minutes it took to unpack my overnight bag I felt claustrophobic. I wandered back downstairs determined to continue on into the kitchens.

The kitchen door was slightly ajar and I could hear voices. I peered through. A couple of pans as large as cauldrons were bubbling away, there were frying pans in action, vegetables being chopped and two fat men and a boy working as hard as if Fanny Craddock's ghost haunted them.

'Excuse me,' I called out casually from the doorway. 'What time will Nigel be in?'

'No idea, sunshine,' said the least fat man who had a sweaty bald head and wore a less-than-white jacket. 'I've never heard of a Nigel working here. Have you, Mick?'

Mick wiped grubby fingers down his trouser leg and merely shook his head

'Thank you,' I said as I determined to give dinner at the Metropole a miss.

So much for publicans' clues, I thought, as I braved Southampton in the wind and the cold. Or maybe, of course, Danielle had been wrong. Metro, Metropole, Metropolitan... I'd check the phone books. Maybe there were other hotels of that name or maybe it was somewhere else entirely—a restaurant or a company.

I spent the rest of the day visiting anywhere with a hint of France—the French Quarter Café, Paris Bakery, and a restaurant called Metropolitan Gateway. No one had heard of Nigel Carter. And I had to admit I was getting sick of the sound of his name.

Back at the Metropole I sat miserably in my room and wondered if I could face dinner there. Eventually I decided to visit the bar and make up my mind after a couple of drinks.

The bar was hot, dimly lit and crowded. Various offices

were obviously having their pre-Christmas tipple and there seemed to be giggling girls and loud back-slapping men everywhere. The queue at the bar itself was so tall and deep I couldn't really see how many bar staff were serving. A very drunk man put an arm around me, wished me a very merry Christmas, kissed me on the cheek and then whispered, 'I could give you a Christmas present you'll never forget.'

'And I could give you some crushed nuts,' I whispered back. Unfortunately my words didn't have a deterrent effect and he squeezed me even more tightly to him.

'Next, please,' said a voice. The queue had moved along and there was I sandwiched under a drunk's arm. I trod so hard on his right big toe that he yelped and let me go.

'Nigel Carter, I presume,' I said to the barman.

He stared at me in surprise. 'Do I know you?' he asked.

I shook my head. 'I've been looking for you.'

'I can't talk now,' he said, giving me a pleasant smile. 'I'll meet you when the bar closes about midnight.'

I had to be content with that, but I felt a crushing sense of anti-climax. I'd found the man whose disappearance had haunted me and led to an investigation punctuated by murder, and there he was, a barman, fit and well.

I ordered a white wine from him and sat down in a crowded corner of the room on the only empty chair. The drunk still watched me with a silly grin on his face. I think he was a man who liked to suffer.

My view of the bar was frequently occluded by various bodies who seemed to think I was with their group. When a young man asked me what I was drinking and I told him I was waiting for someone he said, 'Well, have a drink while you wait.' I tried to decline but he rushed off and some time later returned with a large cocktail that looked innocuous but definitely wasn't.

I did notice Nigel watching me occasionally with a puzzled expression, as though trying to work out who the hell I was and why the hell I was looking for him...

'Where do you work, then?' a voice asked me. It was the man with the cocktail, who now stood within a trouser width of my legs.

'I'm here on business.'

'What's your name?'

'Kate.'

'Mine's Carl.'

Carl moved forward slightly so that our knees touched. He was baby faced and all of twenty-one. By now I'd realized he'd had more than a cocktail too many and was gazing at me with that glazed lusty look some drunken men get just before they collapse.

'Excuse me, Carl,' I said as I stood up.

'You don't need excusing,' he said, breathing his alcoholic fumes at breast level. 'I like you just the way you are.'

I pushed past him quickly, through the jolly hordes, and made my way to the reception area and the front door. I stood for a while outside in the cold night air listening to the distant sound of the sea and wondering if Nigel would take my absence as an opportunity to run again.

I decided it was a chance I would take. I returned to my room, watched television and waited. Round about midnight car doors began to slam and goodbyes and Merry Christmases echoed loudly in the street outside.

The bar was almost empty and at first I couldn't see Nigel, but he must have been bending down behind the bar because he suddenly appeared. 'I won't keep you long. Would you like a drink while you're waiting?'

I shook my head. He was better looking than his photos, fair haired, a slight summer tan remaining and bright blue eyes. His mouth, though, was a little small for his face and his lips thin and tight.

I sat down and watched him clearing tables, washing glasses and generally tidying the bar. There was another barman but he was much shorter than Nigel and I'd really only seen a vague glimpse of him through the joyous throng.

'You go, Ed,' he said. 'This lady wants to speak to me.'

Short Ed smiled brightly at me and muttered to Nigel, 'Lucky ol' you.'

Once Ed had gone, Nigel drew up a chair beside me and said, 'You wanted to find me. You've found me. Now tell me the when, where, how and why.'

I introduced myself and told him that his aunt had employed me to find him.

'You've met my aunt?' he asked.

'I've only spoken to her on the phone.'

He shrugged. 'OK, so now you've found me you can tell her I'm well, can't you?'

'Yes, but she really wants to see you.'

'Does she indeed?'

'It has been difficult to find you, Nigel, and even if you're not very fond of your aunt you could at least pay her a visit before she dies.'

Nigel began to laugh then. I sat stony faced. After he'd finished laughing he said, 'You really don't know what you've done, do you?'

I was puzzled now. 'Well, I won't know, will I? Until you explain.'

'Have you any idea why I left Uplands Lodge?'

'Money troubles? Maybe you had a scam going which no one's discovered yet.'

'I had to leave.'

'Come on, Nigel,' I said in my best soothing voice, 'tell me why.'

Nigel sighed. 'I wasn't being a wimp. I'd put up with it for over a year. I just couldn't take it any more.'

'Take what?'

'The death threats.'

I sat back in my chair. 'Did you tell the police?'

'No.'

'Why not?'

'I don't think they take death threats very seriously.'

'They may have done. Especially after...'

'After what?'

Surely he knew Caroline was dead.

'Oh, you mean Caroline.' His voice held no trace of emotion.

'Yes.'

'I read it in the papers. I almost left here then but I thought I'd probably be found. And I've been proved right. How did you find me?'

'I wasn't told exactly, but the landlord of the Pig and Whistle gave me a clue.'

Nigel half smiled and shook his head in mock despair. 'For an intelligent man he's a stupid bastard.'

'Tell me about the death threats.'

He paused. 'They came by phone, by letter. Not very original or clever, but relentless. In fact they never varied. "You're a dead man." That's all they said, but I had the feeling I was being watched all the time. Stewart thought I was getting paranoid...'

'So Stewart knew about this all along?'

'He was sworn to secrecy. Yes, of course he knew. We

were partners, after all. I didn't read about Caroline's murder in the papers; Stewart rang me immediately and told me to go abroad.'

'You didn't think it would be sensible to help the police with their investigation?'

'And become prime suspect?'

'Why should you kill Caroline?'

'Why *not* me? That's the way the police would see it. She was killed on my property, we had once been lovers. And—' He broke off.

'And what?'

'Nothing.'

I stared at him. He looked away, uneasy. 'I'm pretty knackered now, Kate. I think we'll have to continue this conversation tomorrow.'

I sighed. 'OK. What time?'

'I'll meet you in here about nine thirty.'

'Fine. Could I just ask you one more question, Nigel?'

'Fire away.'

'About your aunt.'

'What about her?'

'Did she know about the death threats?'

He smiled. 'Unlikely that I'd tell her, Kate.'

'Why? Because of her age or her illness?'

'Neither, really. My aunt has been suffering from senile dementia for years. They call it Alzheimer's disease. She doesn't speak, she doesn't recognize me and she certainly couldn't use the phone. Whoever employed you was certainly not my aunt.'

I sat and stared at him. I was lost for words. Then it dawned on me.

'Oh my God, Nigel. I've found you for…'

'Yes, Kate. Whoever wants to murder me has been led here by you.'

SIXTEEN

THE NEXT DAY I waited in the bar, and waited and waited.
At ten thirty barman Ed turned up. 'Where's Nigel?' he
asked.

'I was hoping you could tell me.'

'I'll check in his room.'

Minutes later Ed came back looking worried. 'He's
gone. Everything's gone—clothes, shoes, books—the lot.'

I mumbled my thanks, went straight back to my room
and began to pack. I felt like crying. I'd failed, he'd been
there and I'd lost him. Why should he hang around?
Someone was after him, undoubtedly the same person
who killed Caroline, and I couldn't blame him for running. I just blamed myself. I should have insisted he in-
form the police. Too late, too bloody late, I told myself.

Even as I left the hotel I wasn't sure where I was going.
I was on the mainland, I told myself, and here I was going
to stay, but further inland—Longborough.

I WATCHED Hubert in the doorway of the Chapel of Rest.
He was arranging a posy of flowers in the hands of an
elderly lady's corpse and as I swung open the door and
said, 'Hi!' he jumped in surprise as though the corpse
itself had spoken.

'You shouldn't do that,' he said.

I waited for the welcome which didn't come, so I gave
my own. 'Well, hello, Kate, good to see you, I've really
missed you...'

'That's enough. You know I'm pleased to see you. You

just gave me a nasty shock. This dear lady was a clairvoyant. I thought she'd come back from the other side.'

I laughed. 'No, Hubert, I'm the one back from the other side—the other side of the Solent.'

'Found Nigel, then?'

I nodded.

'Well? Tell me the details.'

'Not here, Hubert. It's time for tea. Do you fancy a cream cake?'

'I think the bakery's gone bankrupt since you left.'

His face was so serious just for a second I believed him. 'What do you fancy, Hubert?'

He thought long and hard. 'A cream horn, and could you get Danielle a cream slice?'

I smiled between gritted teeth. 'Of course. I won't be long.'

When I returned Hubert and Danielle were sitting in the office and there were three mugs of steaming tea.

'Hello, Katie, love. You're looking well.' Her voice was as deep as a chief stoker and she looked as tartily feminine as always. I was convinced her description of me 'looking well' was another way of saying I'd put on weight, but I still ate my doughnut and enjoyed every mouthful.

'Don't keep us in suspense, Kate,' said Hubert. 'You found Nigel, so have you told his aunt yet?'

'It's not as simple as that.'

Hubert looked up at me with a pained expression. 'It never is with you. What happened?'

I paused as I brushed away the sugar from my lips. 'I found him working as a barman at the Metropole Hotel. I spoke to him after he finished his shift...'

'Yes,' said Hubert impatiently.

I sighed. Hubert knew me well enough to expect failure

and problems but Danielle didn't and I really didn't want to parade my dire performance in front of her.

'Come on, Kate. What have you done?'

'I haven't done anything,' I said irritably. 'Nigel arranged to meet me in the morning for another chat—but he didn't turn up. He's on the run again.'

'Who's he on the run from, dear?' asked Danielle as she arranged her legs and feet so that Hubert could see her thrilling insteps.

'I don't know. All I do know is he's definitely running and he's scared.'

'Is it money—that chap Renton?' asked Hubert.

'It's not money, Hubert. Someone wants him dead. It could be Renton or one of his hench men. But whoever it is has been sending death threats.'

They both fell silent and I sipped at my tea trying to work out my next move.

'What about the aunt?' asked Hubert.

I managed a wry smile. 'That's another complication. The person I spoke to on the phone was not his aunt. His aunt has Alzheimer's disease and isn't capable of speaking on the phone.'

There was a slight pause before Hubert said, 'So you were set up to find Nigel for whoever wants to kill him.'

'That was very well put, Hubert. I'm impressed.'

'I can be impressive when I try,' he said. Danielle looked as if she was about to agree, so I flashed her a glance which told her quite clearly 'I don't wish to know', and she stayed silent and thrust her head back in a way that could only be described as 'camp'.

'What's your next step?' asked Hubert.

'I was hoping you wouldn't ask,' I said. 'I'm not sure whether to go back to the Isle of Wight tomorrow or assume Nigel hasn't gone far away and keep searching for him.'

Danielle murmured, 'I should find his aunt if I were you, Katie. There might be a clue there.'

'I had thought of that,' I said sharply.

Hubert opened his desk drawer and produced a list of nursing homes. 'I pick up from most of these,' he informed me, 'but if it'll help I'll mark the ones that take Alzheimer patients.'

'Thanks, Hubert. You're a peach.'

Danielle nodded in agreement and once more I found myself resenting her. Hubert, I felt, was my exclusive friend and I knew that was being totally unreasonable but she/he seemed ever present and I was used to having Hubert all to myself. Well, I told myself firmly, you'll just have to get used to it.

I smiled sweetly at Danielle, and Hubert gave me a list of four that were known as homes for the elderly mentally infirm. There were two in Longborough and two in outlying villages.

My car wouldn't start. I swore at her and slapped the steering wheel a few times, but she still wouldn't start. 'You bitch,' I moaned. 'A few days I leave you and you get sulky.' I sat there turning the ignition again and again until I knew I'd flooded the engine and there was no option but to start walking.

Longborough was cold and breezy but not with the biting cold of so-called sea 'breezes', and the Christmas decorations didn't look quite so forlorn in the main street as they did beside the sea.

I had some idea of where Hazelwood Nursing Home was and I arrived at four thirty in the dark to face the gauntness of an Edwardian house with large bay windows, a general air of solid respectability and acute dullness. The door was opened by a resident, I presumed, with grey hair poking out from a navy blue fez-type cap, sharp grey eyes and a permanently smiling mouth.

'I'd like to see the owner if possible,' I said. 'I'm looking for a home for my grandmother.'

'Come on in,' she said, still smiling. 'I'm the owner, Avril Danes.'

She showed me through to her office. 'Do sit down. Would you like to tell me about your grandmother?'

I had just begun to formulate a nicely demented grandmother in my mind when Avril Danes said, 'Is there a house to sell?'

I nodded. 'Yes. She has a buyer.'

'That's good, that's very good,' said Avril Danes. 'Some people just have their savings and of course it doesn't take very long to use that up.'

'How much are the fees?'

Without blinking she answered, 'Three hundred and fifty pounds a week, plus you have to pay for hairdressing and chiropody and, of course, you have to supply all bath requisites such as soap and talcum powder. And we like them to have new underwear and at least one new nightie every six months.'

'So it's well over twenty thousand pounds a year.'

'I do like to get the financial position straight. Elderly people don't like to have to be told to go.'

'Does that happen?'

She stared at me. 'Oh yes. Some of my patients come in quite young, you know, and they live on and the money runs out. Social services haven't got the resources, so they send them somewhere cheaper.'

'How cheap is that?'

Avril continued to smile irritatingly. 'Cheapest is about

two hundred and fifty a week but some places are quite dreadful, you know.'

'Aren't homes inspected regularly?'

'Oh yes, once in a while, but nowadays it's only the paperwork that interests them.'

'You don't sound as if you approve.'

Avril lost her smile for a moment. 'I'm worn out, you know. I look as old as some of the residents. I *am* as old as some of the residents. I'd like to sell up and I've been trying for five years now. My husband left me; he couldn't take the strain. The staff don't stay. The relatives complain about everything.'

'Oh dear,' I murmured.

'I'm sorry, dear. I go on sometimes. I trained as a nurse before we all became pen pushers and had to write essays on client sexuality. Sexuality is the last of my poor residents' problems, since they don't on the whole know night from day or even how to feed themselves any more.'

I nodded sympathetically. 'Could I tell you about my gran?'

'Of course you can. Can she feed herself?'

'Yes, but she can only use a spoon.'

'Fine. Fine. Is she incontinent?'

'Sometimes.'

'Does she still recognize people?'

This is it, I thought, the crunch question. 'Well, she still talks about people,' I said. 'From way back. She did have a particular friend; she occasionally mentions her— Elizabeth Forrester.'

Avril looked blank for a moment, then she said, 'Oh, you mean Lizzie. We've always called her Lizzie. What a coincidence.'

'It's a small world, isn't it?' I said. 'Could I see her?'

'Of course, but she won't be able to communicate with you.'

'I'd still like to see her, and have a look round, of course.'

'Follow me, then,' said Avril. First home I walked into I'd found her. I was over the proverbial moon.

As she opened the office door a high-pitched wail began, followed by someone shouting, 'Mother, Mother.' A slightly stale but characteristic smell of urine and incontinence pads permeated the corridor, and together with the wailing and shouting even I felt uneasy.

'She's on the ground floor,' explained Avril. 'She still walks occasionally, so we have to be careful. Those that can't walk are nursed upstairs.'

As we walked along the corridor with its Indian restaurant red-flocked wallpaper I wondered why most nursing homes seemed so dimly lit and why so many of the staff looked like Sumo wrestlers. I knew nursing home work meant lots of physical work but the two members of staff who passed us were large with muscular arms and thin, grimly smiling lips. If I had a poorly gran I most certainly wouldn't let her live out her last few years in a place like this.

Mrs Elizabeth Forrester was slumped in an armchair that looked as old as her and sagged as much as she did. Her stark white hair straggled lifelessly beyond her chin and although she looked up as we entered the room there was no flicker of interest or animation in her vacant grey eyes.

'Hello, Lizzie,' said Avril. 'I'm showing this lady round.'

There was no response from Lizzie.

'It's a nice room, isn't it?' Avril continued with her sales pitch. 'A lovely view of the garden, and we have the en suite shower and toilet. Your grandmother could have the room next door.'

I stared out at the garden that Elizabeth Forrester could no longer appreciate, then turned to Avril Danes and said, 'Would you please leave me alone with Mrs Forrester for a few minutes?'

She looked a little surprised but nodded and said, 'I'll be in my office when you're ready.'

I sat down by Mrs Forrester and held her fragile white hands. 'I've seen Nigel. He's very well,' I said quietly but directly into her ear. 'Nigel. Your nephew.' There was no verbal response but she squeezed my hand. Her eyes showed no understanding, though, and I guessed her response was merely a reflex reaction.

Moments later she fell asleep, still holding my hand. Gently I slipped her fingers from mine and walked over to her bedside table to examine the few momentoes of a long life.

There was a wedding photograph of an unrecognizable Elizabeth with a balding groom, one of Nigel as a young boy and one more—this time a very elderly Elizabeth sitting in a garden with a young woman in nurse's uniform. The photo was small and blurred but the nurse interested me. She was buxom with red hair and a pretty face.

Back in Mrs Danes' office I waited for her to appear. When she did she seemed to have forgotten I was still around and looked slightly puzzled. 'I've been with Mrs Forrester,' I reminded her.

'Oh yes. Did she say anything?'

'No. Does she ever speak?'

'Not to me but to some of the nursing assistants she does. Just the odd word—father or mother—that sort of thing.'

'Who is the nurse in the photo?' I asked.

Again Avril looked puzzled; the strange hat combined with a very creased brow made her look decidedly odd. 'Let me think,' she said. 'Lizzie's been here about five years but she had private nurses before that. I think that one was her favourite.'

'Does her nephew Nigel visit her often?' I asked.

Avril gave a surprised look. 'I've never seen him. All I heard about him was there was no love lost between them. When Lizzie first came here she could speak; she was confused sometimes but she managed to make a will and she told me although Nigel was her only kin she wasn't going to leave him anything. "He's a waster," those were her exact words.'

'So who has she left her money to?'

'Charities, as far as I know. Why do you ask?'

I laughed. 'Just being nosy, I suppose.'

'What about your gran?' asked Avril.

I shrugged. 'It's difficult, I've got one or two other places to see before I make a decision. If Mrs Forrester had been able to converse then my gran would have felt less isolated, but I'm not sure.'

'I understand,' said Avril Danes. 'The trouble is with running a home like this, especially if an owner wants to sell, you do need full occupancy. It doesn't look good to have empty beds.'

'I'm sure it doesn't. I'll be in touch, Mrs Danes.'

I left Hazelwood with a sense of relief, glad I didn't have a gran to worry about but still very puzzled about Nigel. I realized my only hope in finding the nurse in the photograph was via Pauline Berkerly, my friend who ran the Berkerly nursing agency. She'd been in the area for some time and if she didn't know her personally there was no doubt she'd find out for me.

I rang her from my office at Humberstones.

'A plump redhead, at least ten years ago. You don't ask much do you, Kate?'

I murmured something about nursing her most difficult patient if she found out for me. Pauline laughed. 'I'll hold you to that. But you'll have to give me something to go on. Was this woman in the photo qualified?'

'She wore a blue uniform. I couldn't see any badges.'

'That doesn't mean anything. Trained nurses are always losing theirs. I'll see what I can do. I'll ring you.'

'Be an angel, Pauline, and make it quick. I've a client and I think his life might be in danger.'

'Is being a private investigator like the films, Kate?'

'You must be joking. This job has been one cockup after another. My suspects have alibis or no motive and it's like walking through treacle wearing shoes made of Velcro.'

Pauline laughed. 'I'll stick to my boring little number, then.'

It was ten p.m. when she rang back. 'Well, Kate,' she said. 'I've just got lucky. A home-help neighbour of mine who knows all the gossip from way back—and probably gossip that hasn't even started yet—remembers Mrs Forrester. In fact she used to clean for her until the ''nurse'' arrived. A redhead, plump and in her twenties. My neighbour was surplus to requirements then so she certainly hasn't forgotten.'

'Was Mrs Forrester OK mentally then?'

'That's just it, Kate. The Alzheimer's was just beginning and she was anxious and rather depressed and she grew very reliant on her nurse...'

'How long was she there?'

'Only about three months, but the gossip is—and it may

be just gossip—that Mrs Forrester kept cash under the mattress. A considerable amount.'

'Pauline, have you got a name for me?'

'Only a first name at the moment—Charlotte.'

SEVENTEEN

'CHARLOTTE.' I SAID the name over and over again as though somehow by doing that all would become clear. The mysterious Charlotte had once been Elizabeth Forrester's nurse and had been seeing Nigel. As there was no love lost between aunt and nephew the money for the hotel must have come from Charlotte. Had they made an arrangement that he'd pay the money back and then he'd reneged on the deal? And how was I going to find Charlotte with only her first name to go on and only a very sketchy description? I stared at the photo that I'd 'borrowed' from Mrs Forrester's bedside table. Charlotte's features were rather blurred but I could see they were neat. Hubert's footsteps outside my door caused me to pause and I waited for his knock.

He came in looking miserable. 'What's the matter?' I asked as I pulled up a chair for him.

He frowned. 'I've just had a row with Danielle.'

'That's not like you. What happened?'

'I asked her to live with me but she said it wouldn't work.'

Although I felt ashamed of myself my first reaction was 'Good!' but I managed to say, 'Why's that, Hubert?'

'She wants to be independent...' He paused. 'Do you know I think she's a...feminist.'

I tried not to smile. He made the word feminist sound like a cross between being a member of the Baader-Meinhof group and spy for the KGB.

'Give her time, Hubert. Working in an undertaker's and

living on the premises are two different things. And, let's face it, although your flat is very comfortable she'd always feel like a guest.'

'I didn't think of it like that,' he said thoughtfully. 'Perhaps if we bought a place together.'

That wasn't what I had in mind but I nodded and murmured something about the path of true love. He seemed to perk up at love's mention.

'What about you, Kate? How are you getting on?'

'I thought you'd never ask. I've been to see Elizabeth Forrester. She's not compos mentis. She disliked Nigel when she was well and she didn't leave him any money.'

'I don't like to say this, but this hasn't been one of your most successful ventures.'

'Thanks, Hubert, I needed that.'

My face must have registered either indignation or despair—even I wasn't sure what I felt at that moment—because Hubert suddenly felt inclined to stand up and put his arm around me. 'I'm worried about you, Kate, you look really knackered.'

I ignored that remark but thrust the photograph under his nose. 'That's Charlotte,' I said. 'Someone Nigel was supposed to see occasionally.'

He stared at the photo for a while. 'She's very pretty,' he said.

'Is she?' I looked again. Yes, I suppose she was.

'She could have changed,' said Hubert. 'How old is this?'

'Ten years, maybe a bit more.'

'I think some women improve with age,' said Hubert thoughtfully.

Suddenly I saw my rainbow. 'Hubert, you really are a genius,' I said, giving him a kiss on the cheek.

'I don't know what I've done to deserve that,' said Hubert with a mixture of embarrassment and pleasure.

We sat in silence for a while until Hubert decided we needed a nightcap and produced some malt whisky and American dry ginger. After a while he asked if I wanted to see his Christmas decorations so we decamped to his flat and sat by the light of a six-foot Christmas tree. He showed me his battery-operated Father Christmas that did a twirl while playing a medley of Yuletide tunes.

'It's a bit naff, isn't it?' I said.

'Not at all, Kate. I think it's quite tasteful. Danielle chose it.'

'She'll be here for Christmas, will she?'

'Of course. You'll be here too, I hope.'

'There's only a week to go, Hubert. I haven't bought a single present. I even forgot my mother this year.'

'You must get more organized, Kate.'

'Tell me about it,' I said sarcastically.

And he did!

I left early the next morning and Hubert insisted on driving me to the station. 'You should take your car,' he said.

'It's not worth the worry, and anyway that's purely academic because it's not starting and the Isle of Wight is so small that I can always hire one.'

'Just be careful, Kate. You don't seem to have any idea who killed Caroline, you've lost Nigel—'

'I did *not* lose Nigel,' I interrupted him. 'He lost me. And I will find out who killed Caroline...I just need a few more days.'

Hubert didn't look at all convinced. As I left he said, 'I'll be really disappointed if you don't make it back for Christmas. I regard you as family.'

I paused, feeling gratified and sad at the same time. 'That's the nicest thing you've ever said to me, Hubert.'

As I waved goodbye to him from the train I resolved that I'd be back for Christmas Day if I had to swim the Solent with one hand tied behind my back—and with my last-minute Christmas presents strapped to my back.

UPLANDS LODGE now sported fairy lights round the door frame and its hanging baskets and their brightness seemed a welcome contrast to the great bulging grey clouds and sleety rain. I was just taking off my jacket and scarf when Stewart appeared, flashing me a cheerful smile. 'Nice to see you back,' he said. 'Let me buy you a drink.' I reminded myself that he was a liar, although to be fair he had made a promise to Nigel, but that still shouldn't have caused him to lie so expertly.

The bar was only just beginning to gather in the pre-lunch drinkers but Stewart was quick to find a two-seater sofa in a corner, and while he ordered coffee I watched the guests, for the most part, struggling in.

'It could be depressing,' said Stewart, obviously guessing my reaction as he handed me my coffee. 'But our older guests are nearly always cheerful. More cheerful in fact than the younger ones who come in the summer.'

'I found Nigel,' I said abruptly.

'Oh.'

'You knew all along where he was, didn't you, Stewart?'

Stewart looked away, unwilling now to lie to my face. 'I wasn't sure, not a hundred per cent, but he swore me to secrecy. He was a frightened man; there was nothing I could say that would make him less frightened.'

'Was it just the death threats?'

'That was enough, I would have thought. They were regular.'

'What did he do with the written ones?'

'He tore them up straight away.'

'Were they sent from the island or the mainland?'

'From the mainland.'

'And who do you think they were from?'

Stewart shrugged. 'How the hell should I know?'

'Why didn't he go to the police, Stewart?'

'What would they have done? Nothing, because nothing happened.'

'Caroline was murdered.'

'Yes, but that was nothing to do with Nigel.'

'How do you know?'

'Well, I don't know, but why should it?'

'Why not? They had been lovers.'

This time Stewart really was surprised. 'I didn't know that. I always thought some woman had broken his heart at some point in his life. I know he only saw Charlotte occasionally and even then he didn't introduce us. Strange, I thought, but then some men prefer not to be committed.'

'Do you actually want Nigel to return or at least survive?' I asked him.

Stewart's eyebrows raised a fraction. 'What are you getting at?'

'Can't you see? Those death threats weren't idle threats, they were deadly serious. It was just a question of timing, Caroline came to the Isle of Wight and it was the right time for the murderer. Now that person must find Nigel.'

'Why?' asked Stewart pointedly.

'If I knew that, Stewart, I'd know who the murderer is. All I would say is that between them they caused someone a terrible need for revenge. Someone may have been har-bouring resentment for a very long time.'

We sat silently then, staring around us. I watched Nancy and Harold sitting near the bar drinking a pre-lunch sherry and holding hands and smiling at each other. Margaret was absent and I realized it was the first time I had seen the betrothed pair without her.

'Where's Margaret?' I asked.

'She's staying with a cousin over Christmas.'

'What about the wedding?'

'It's the day after tomorrow. I expect she'll turn up for that.'

I looked at my watch. It was nearly one o'clock. Time was running out for me. If I wanted to be back in Long-borough by Christmas Day I was going to need help or luck, preferably a bit of both. And, more to the point, I'd have to start missing a few meals.

'Stewart, I want you to be totally honest with me, especially if you want to save Nigel's life. Have you any idea where he may have gone?'

He shook his head. 'If I had any ideas I'd tell you. Perhaps he's with Charlotte, but I only know she doesn't live on the island. At a guess, though, I'd say she lived on the south coast because in the past he's been over on the ferry and back within a few hours.'

I stared at him for a few moments. He was telling the truth, I felt sure, so I smiled, shrugged inwardly at the loss of my lunch and hoped I could manage to fit dinner in.

ALEX FREEMAN was out when I called at the house but Tom and Adam were both in. It was Tom who opened the door to me and invited me in. Adam was sprawled between two chairs watching a horror video.

'What do you want?' he asked without taking his eyes from the screen. Tom now lay flat out on the sofa, also watching the screen.

'I want to ask you a few questions about your mother and Nigel Carter.'

Again he didn't move. 'Yeah. The police have already asked me. I said I didn't know anything.'

'Would you mind switching off the video, Adam?'

'I'm enjoying it.'

'I don't give a damn,' I said, striding over to the television and switching it off. They both sat up in surprise. 'Don't you care that your mother's been murdered?' I burst out. 'Don't you want the murderer brought to justice?'

He smirked in response and I had an overwhelming desire to smack his face very hard. 'I don't know why you're getting in a state,' he said. 'She was my mother; you didn't know her.'

'That's why I'm here. Someone she once knew, Nigel Carter, could be in danger.'

'So?'

'So, Adam, I'd like you to tell me a little more about your mother and Nigel.'

He stared at me for a moment with sullen resentment. 'She knew lots of men. Men and money, that's all she was interested in.'

'Could you explain that?'

'I'm not that clever.'

'Oh, I think you are.'

'Oh, for goodness' sake, Adam,' said Tom loudly. 'Why don't you tell her what she wants to know, then we can watch the end of the video.'

Adam struggled with the idea for a time then slowly, 'My mother wasn't a nice person. I quite liked her. She was good to me, really, but she did bring men along and...'

'And what?' I prompted.

'She wasn't very honest. She...I can't be bothered. You can have it. I haven't told the police I've got it but if it means I'll be left alone then I'll get it for you.'

I was mystified but he left the room and I waited. Tom switched the video back on and for a few minutes I watched zombies on the rampage until I could bear the suspense no longer. 'What *is* Adam doing?'

'He's getting stuff from the attic.'

Moments later I could hear something being dragged down the stairs. Adam appeared at the door carrying a large tin box. He held it out to me. 'It's quite heavy,' he said. It was. I almost staggered. 'This is the key,' he said, holding it in front of my face and then placing the key in my jacket pocket. I walked out carrying the tin box like a bow-legged chicken, with Adam walking in front of me to open doors.

At the front door I did manage to do a Columbo (ask a pertinent question on my exit). 'The night your mother was murdered, Adam, did you know she planned to break into Nigel's cabin?'

'She told me,' he said. 'She kept me informed.'

'I see,' I said. 'Did you tell the police that?'

'No, why should I?'

'Why not if you had nothing to hide?'

He stared at me nastily. 'If you had a mother like mine you wouldn't want people to know. She's dead now and I don't want anything more to do with her. That's why you've got the box. That's all that's left of her.'

'What exactly is in the box?'

He shrugged. 'I don't know and I don't care.'

'You haven't looked?' I was amazed.

He shrugged. 'No. I don't want to know. Anything to do with my mother is bad news.'

Somehow the box in my arms seemed to get heavier. 'I haven't got a car here, Adam, I forgot. Could you ring for a cab?'

'OK,' he said, his voice weighed with the sound of his perceived male superiority.

He walked back into the house and slammed the door. I placed the box on the ground and waited. It began to rain and after five minutes I felt very cold. I marked time on the spot, swung my arms and prayed that Adam actually had phoned for a cab.

Fifteen minutes later, when the rain had soaked me through, my hair hung in rats' tails and I was as cold as one of Hubert's corpses, the minicab appeared. As we drove away I saw Adam's face at the window. He was still smirking.

EIGHTEEN

I WAS AWARE OF some very strange looks from the guests as I staggered into Uplands Lodge. I was mortified to see Stewart, who seemed equally taken aback by the sight of me soaked to the skin and carrying a metal box.

'Here, let me take that,' he said. Strangely I felt reluctant to let go of my burden. 'Come on,' he urged. 'What on earth's in it?'

'I've no idea.'

He followed me up to my room. My shoes squelched as I walked and the rain dripped coldly from my head down my neck. He paused at the door and looked expectant as though waiting to be asked in. 'Thanks, Stewart, I'm going to have a really hot bath now.'

'What about the box?' he asked.

'Could you put it on the bed?' He placed it down carefully and even then stood expectantly. I smiled. 'Do you want to be there at the opening?'

'I must admit I'm interested. Whose is it?'

'Caroline's. The police don't know it exists. Her son kept quiet about it.'

'Intriguing,' he murmured as he brushed a wet strand of hair from my eyes. I wasn't sure if he meant me or the box, but I decided to ask him back anyway.

'I'll have the grand opening in an hour.'

'Have you had lunch?' he asked.

I shook my head.

'I'll bring up some sandwiches.'

I stared at the dull green metal box, placed the key

beside it and ran a hot bath. I lay in the bath, topping up the water occasionally, and thought about Caroline and Adam. Why had she said she was married to Lyle when in fact she'd only changed her name by deed poll? Why had she pretended she wanted to help me when in fact she merely wanted access to Nigel's cabin? Why pretend she didn't know Nigel at all? Another mystery, of course, concerned Adam. Whose son was he? And was he the mainspring of the mystery. More importantly would the box contain the answers?

Stewart appeared just within the hour carrying a tray of sandwiches and coffee.

'Do you want to do it now or shall we eat first?' he asked.

'Let's eat first,' I said. 'Why change the habits of a lifetime?'

We ate in silence for a while, then Stewart said quietly, 'Do you think Nigel could have had anything to do with Caroline's death?'

'What makes you say that?'

'Nigel disappears, which is a good enough way *not* to become a suspect and Caroline turns up dead in his cabin.'

'It's possible,' I agreed, 'but unless he came over from the mainland by submarine the chances are someone would have seen him, either on the ferry or simply skulking about.'

'Maybe someone did see him and hasn't come forward.'

I thought about that for a moment but no one in particular came to mind.

'Caroline gave the box to Adam a week before she died,' I said. 'So she must have genuinely thought her life was in danger.'

In unison we stared at the box. Its shiny gold-coloured

lock seemed to me like an all-seeing eye. We walked over to the bed and I picked up the key. 'At least it's not big enough for a whole body,' I said with a nervous laugh but thinking at the same time it *was* big enough for a severed head.

The lock, obviously an unwilling virgin, seemed to reject the key at first. I persevered, trying first one angle then another. Just as I thought I would need a hammer and chisel and was about to break out with a set of swearwords that would shock a brickie, the key turned.

I stared at the contents of the box with vague disappointment mixed with relief; there was nothing slightly messy such as severed body parts, no neatly stacked bundles of twenty-pound notes or interesting jewellery. There were simply mounds of paper, sheets of names and addresses, bank receipts, a passport, two building society books. I looked across at Stewart, who answered me with a wry smile.

'Needs a bit of sorting, doesn't it?' he said.

'I'll be up all night trying to organize this lot,' I murmured. 'My clerical skills are on a par with my detecting abilities.'

'Don't put yourself down,' said Stewart, giving my arm a reassuring pat. 'It doesn't look as if Caroline was that organized. She could have put them in appropriate bundles.'

'It looks like she did this in a rush,' I said, 'as if she had to leave somewhere in a hurry and she just threw the lot in.'

Stewart nodded. 'I'll come back later,' he said, 'and give you a hand. Just organize them into piles and we'll examine them properly in a systematic way.'

He left and I began sorting the loose papers into some kind of order. There were sheets and sheets of names and addresses from an organization called Finders in Birmingham. There was headed paper bearing the title Quick Finance, Prop. Caroline Uxton, 12 Menon Way, Southampton.

There was also a small number of leaflets entitled: 'WE CAN HELP. Underneath were the words:

CCJs no problem. Can't get a mortgage? No problem. Want to buy a business? A shop, hotel or nursing home but can't get the finance? No problem. WE CAN HELP.

During the last ten years WE CAN HELP has helped many, many people realize their dreams and released them from the frustration of 'black lists' and flat refusals.

WE CAN HELP will offer you sound advice and relieve you of the tedium and disappointment associated with trying to finance a new life when everyone you contact seems to turn you away. WE CAN HELP will not turn you away. Our name is our motto.

Underneath the blurb it said, 'Please contact Charlotte Uxton at WE CAN HELP, 4 Commercial Street, Bedford.

I stared at the name. Perhaps I should have realized that Caroline and Charlotte were the same person. What really struck me, though, was one word in the flyer—hotel.

I continued to sort through the rest of the papers and found a solicitor's letter relating to her change of name by deed poll—Caroline Charlotte Makepeace to Uxton. Also, Adam's birth certificate, a shortened version merely stating that he was born in Bedford on the fourth of January—Adam Makepeace.

I'd just started looking at bank statements when Stewart

came back. He stared at the assortment of paper on the bed. 'Pandora's box,' he said. 'Or is it a can of worms?'

'It depends,' I said cagily.

'What do you mean?' he asked.

'Tell me about buying this hotel.'

'Why? What's that got to do with Caroline?'

'I don't know yet, Stewart, but a good deal, I think. Did you in fact get a good deal?'

He frowned. 'Well, yes... We did buy this hotel at a bargain price. We were just lucky.'

'Luck may have had nothing to do with it. Was it a repossession?'

'Yes, but it was all legal. The previous owners went bankrupt. It seems they borrowed money for refurbishments and overstretched themselves.'

'Did you ever meet the owners?'

He shook his head. 'Nigel and I viewed the hotel empty. No guests, no owners, just an estate agent from Flowers and Tone.'

'And the mortgage?'

'From a small building society—South Downs. What are you trying to say, Kate?'

I shrugged. 'I'm not sure, but Caroline, also known as Charlotte, was a very shady lady.'

'You mean a crook.'

'I think she was a confidence trickster and a bit of a femme fatale. Only someone got their own back and I'm afraid Nigel is well in the running as a suspect.'

'Why?'

'I think she must have reneged on a deal and his disappearing was a chance to either plan her demise or establish a reasonable alibi. In fact it seems highly possible that he actually told her to go to the cabin. She made it seem a spur of the moment thing, but it may have been planned all along.'

'Who else could have known she planned to visit Nigel's cabin that night?'

I paused. 'She told Adam. She may even have told Alex.'

'So Alex could be in the running as a suspect.'

I nodded. 'Yes, but with reservations. The Isle of Wight police can't be that stupid that they would have overlooked him. His alibi must have been strong, or he had no motive, or…'

'Or what?'

'He's managed to commit the perfect murder.'

MY BEDTIME READING that night consisted of the names and addresses of hundreds of people. People in debt, desperate people like the Bottomleys. The tragedy for most of them was that their names would be removed from the blacklist but only temporarily. How the mortgage scam actually worked I didn't know, but I knew a man who did! How exactly I was going to get him to tell me was a different matter.

I rang his office in Cowes the next morning. Angel answered the phone sweetly, saying after a short pause, 'Mr Renton will be delighted to see you any time.'

I took the bus to Cowes and arrived at his office just before lunch. I was fully resolved to put on a tough act but when his large hand gripped mine and his burly frame towered above, I nearly changed my mind. 'I'd like to talk in private,' I said.

'Angel, go for your lunch now, dear.' Angel, wearing a red mohair jumper and short, tight black skirt, tottered out, smiling.

'Do sit down, Kate,' he said. 'Have you found anywhere you like?'

'Not exactly.'

He raised an eyebrow. I took a deep breath. 'I'm a private detective and I have in my possession incriminating evidence that I'm sure you wouldn't want me to make public.'

Only for a second did he seem surprised. 'Well, well, you had me fooled,' he said. He sat back in his black leather office chair and opened a drawer. After a few moments he produced a large Havana cigar and slowly peeled off the cellophane wrapper.

'So you're on the make, are you?' he said as he caressed the cigar slowly between his fingers.

'No. I simply want information in return for my silence.'

'What sort of information?'

I paused. What exactly *did* I want to know? 'Uplands Lodge Hotel—' I began, but he didn't give me a chance to continue.

'What about it?' he asked sharply.

'It was a repossession?'

'Yes, I believe it was.'

'Come off it, Mr Renton, I haven't got time to waste. I've got names and addresses, telephone numbers and if you're not worried on the business front I'm sure your wife would be interested in your more personal activities.'

For the first time I saw a genuine flicker of anxiety on his face, then he cut the end off his cigar with a pair of nail scissors, lit it, inhaled deeply and tried his best to look nonchalant.

'You're bluffing,' he said. 'I've got nothing to hide.'

'You've no worries, then, Mr Renton. I'll just let the *News of the World* have the story and they'll decide if it's newsworthy. I'm sure your wife will be most interested if they decide to print.'

He puffed on his cigar and I tried to guess his sexual secrets. It was then I noticed him glancing at a photo on his desk. Its back was towards me. 'Is that a photo of your wife?' I asked.

He nodded, looking quite miserable. 'I don't want her to find out. She'll leave me.'

'Your…secret…will be quite safe with me, Mr Renton. It's only your financial secrets I want to explore.'

He thought about that for a moment then said, 'OK. You've won. You want to know about Uplands Lodge…'

'And the scams in general.'

'Business acumen, I would call it,' he snapped as he stubbed out his cigar with as much ferocity as if he were grinding me into the ashtray.

'Looking after number one?'

'Yes. I don't believe in worrying about anyone else. Would they worry about me?'

I didn't answer that question. 'Tell me about Uplands Lodge,' I said.

'My memory could be a bit hazy. It was more than ten years ago.'

'I'm sure you remember how much profit you made to the last ten pence.'

He smirked. 'You're beginning to understand how, I think. Well done, love. I don't keep too much paperwork, it's not wise, but I do remember the main points. Uplands Lodge was called Fairview then. It was owned by a couple in their thirties called Cox—John and Denise. Someone in the family had put up the money and they did quite well for their first three years. Then Denise fell pregnant. She lost the baby and became depressed. The business went downhill. They came to me for help.'

He took another cigar from the drawer and laid it carefully in front of him on the desk. 'I suggested,' he continued, 'that to get extra funds they remortgaged.'

'So you arranged for a second mortgage.'

'I tried.'

'How hard?'

'That's the name of the game,' he said with a self-satisfied smirk.

'What do you mean?' I asked.

'I mean, Miss Private Dick, that I haven't made my pile of money running a charity. I run a finance company—the only people who come to me are already failures. No one else will even speak to them. I give them hope for a while.'

'Oh, how charitable!'

'The Coxes came to me. So for a thousand upfront I offer to spend my valuable time chasing their second mortgage. A few weeks later I say I haven't had much luck but I'm still trying and I ask for another thousand.'

'Then what?'

'They say they haven't got it so I suggest they borrow it from relatives. They do. Another five hundred, I say, we're nearly there. Then one day I ring them: would they come and see me? I explain I've had no luck and in all honesty their efforts should now be put into selling the hotel. I arrange for an estate agent to value the hotel, who only slightly undervalues it. They send in their surveyor who finds so many faults that they have to drop the asking price. Time passes, they have trouble paying their original business mortgage plus paying back relatives. I offer to loan them money, at a high interest rate, of course. They agree. Soon, of course, the bank is calling in their money—threats of repossession are made. A few months go by; they can see there is nothing to be gained by staying. They close up and go off into the wild blue yonder. The hotel goes up for auction at a knock-down price, previous interested persons are contacted and told that I can help them gain a loan at a reasonable interest rate. In this case there were three interested parties who all became clients of mine. Nigel Carter and Stewart Michaelson didn't need much of a loan and they were the lucky buyers. Everyone was happy, the estate agent and the surveyor got a pay-off, Nigel and Stewart got the hotel and I made a few pounds. It was a good deal.'

'Except for the Coxes.'

'They were losers. Life's like that. Some people win and some lose.'

'So what percentage of people who come to you for mortgages actually get one?'

He shrugged. 'About five per cent, I suppose. I have to be successful sometimes. People are so gullible, you know. I get them to tell me their outgoings and all their debts. I write them down on a sheet of paper with another sheet tucked underneath. So their last couple of debts are written on another sheet entirely. Then when they keep getting turned down I accuse them of not telling me of all their debts. They protest that they told me everything and I produce the sheet of paper minus the last couple of debts, which are on the other sheet. They are so stupid they apologize to me.'

I tried to keep my voice level. 'What about ordinary loans? How does that work?'

Renton shrugged and rolled his cigar on the desk backwards and forwards. 'Your ordinary Joes with their CCJs. They come in wanting one big lump sum to pay off their little debts. So I warn them that if they can't pay, their house is in danger, but being losers they take the risk. Most of them can't cope with the repayments and they lose their house anyway. Then, of course, there's a little extra for us all round.'

I watched his greedy face, his pudgy soft hands still rolling the cigar, the cellophane making a soft crinkly sound against his plush desk, and I wished him nothing less than plague and pestilence, financial disaster and full exposure in the *News of the World*. For someone like him, morals were for losers, losers were there to be fleeced for as much as possible and the broken lives and broken dreams of others were of as much importance as the pruning of a wayward tree.

'Why don't you light that cigar, Mr Renton?' I asked.

He shrugged and took my advice.

'What about Nigel and Caroline?'

'What about them?'

'Their death threats.'

He nearly choked on his cigar and I knew immediately he'd also been threatened.

'I'm surprised you dare have your phone number listed, Mr Renton. There must be more than one person wanting something nasty to happen to you.'

'You've outstayed your welcome,' he said. 'I've told you how my business works. If you don't approve, that's your problem. I shall deny this conversation, of course, and anyway nothing I do is illegal.'

'What about the backhanders?'

'Who's going to admit to that? Get real!'

'Among your dissatisfied customers have you any idea who might be sending you threats?'

He shook his head. 'I'm not that worried. Looney or loser, they'd be hard pressed to get past my dogs, my security system and my cameras.'

'Someone got to your *Havana Belle,* though, didn't they?'

Scowling, he puffed hard on his cigar, the cloud of smoke hitting me in the eyes.

'How did you find out about that?'

'Put two and two together, Mr Renton. I take it Caroline and Nigel were your protégés…'

'Un-bloody-official,' he snarled. 'She was the brains of that team. He didn't have her guts. I had to get rid of them both. They ripped me off, starting doing little private deals on the side. She was good, though.'

'Was she good in bed too?'

His mouth dropped slightly. 'How did you know?'

'Caroline liked to share and share alike.'

I was on a roll now and I didn't want to stop. I was loving every minute of his discomfiture. 'Did she tell you Adam was your son?'

His mouth dropped even more. 'He *is* my son—I've been maintaining that boy for years—' He broke off. 'Don't look at me like that. We had to keep it a secret— I was a married man. My wife can't have children—it would have broken her heart to find out I'd a child by another woman.'

'Mr Renton,' I said quietly, 'in the confidence trickster world I think Caroline surpassed you. At least three men think they are Adam's father. And I'm guessing now, but I think all three men have paid maintenance over the years.'

'You're lying. Adam is *my* son.'

'You're going to claim him now, are you?'

'No, but financially he'll be set up for life.'

I stared at him. 'Someone managed to kill Caroline. Nigel is still running and someone on this island is after you. I should always look over your shoulder, Mr Renton, because if there is any natural justice in the world you'll get yours.'

By now he was a tad puce in the face and on his feet. I'd rattled his cage and I was glad. 'Do mind that cigar,' I said as I left his office. 'Someone might just put it where it belongs.'

NINETEEN

I ARRIVED BACK at Uplands Lodge feeling jubilant that I was at last getting somewhere but that feeling was tinged with the depressing thought that society allowed people like Renton to carry on their very rough trade. Citizens were still going to prison for arrears of the now-defunct poll tax but loan sharks could legally wreck people's lives and escape any sort of retribution.

In my room I started writing a list. I wrote 'FIND NIGEL' at the top, as if by writing it down I'd as good as succeeded. Then under 'CAROLINE'S KILLER?' I jotted down my few suspects. I decided that I had to have two sections: Alibied and Non-Alibied. Alex was in the alibied section, along with Lyle Uxton. Renton fell between both camps. Nigel also had no alibi but he undoubtedly had a motive. My list was beginning to look messy so then I decided on a Venn diagram—A and NA. Lyle and Alex remained clearly in the A circle, Stewart and Nigel in the NA circle, Renton came in the cross-over of the circles, along with, and reluctantly, Adam. He was tall. He was strong enough and he certainly didn't seem grief stricken about his mother's death. But equally he didn't seem nervous or agitated as would be expected. The idea of a paid killer seemed a little off the mark in view of the use of the crowbar. Of course, my only experience of paid killers was either in films where they usually used guns, or from newspapers, where a considerable number of undercover police seemed regularly to pose as contract killers. That, of course, showed there was a market for hired killers and no doubt there were some who were cunning enough to make the murder seem both random and amateur.

I was on to my second Venn diagram and really thinking things through when someone knocked on the door. I guessed it was Stewart so I called out, 'Come in.' I guessed wrong. At first I didn't recognize him; he wore a cream Aran sweater, tweed jacket and brown cords. He looked no more handsome but he did seem fairly relaxed. I wasn't, I was on edge. 'What on earth are you doing here?' I asked Lyle Uxton.

'I'm sorry to barge in. There was no one in reception so I came on up.'

'Why are you here?'

'May I sit down?'

I nodded. He wasn't a tall man but I felt more comfortable once he'd sat down.

Seeing his face in repose, its roundness gave him a slightly younger look than I remembered from our brief encounter, and together with his minimal hair and rimless glasses he gave me the impression of an ageing baby.

'I know where Nigel is,' he said quietly.

'You do?'

He nodded. 'He's staying with me. He turned up at my home...my ex-home. My wife told him where I was living.'

'What did he want?'

Lyle Uxton smiled, which made him look cherubic. 'I think he wanted sanctuary. He's scared, he's convinced someone is after him.'

'I'm sure they are,' I said.

His glasses slipped slightly down his small nose and he stared at me with a worried expression. 'Do you really think so?'

'Could you persuade him to come back? After all, he

could have information that would help catch Caroline's killer.' There was a long pause in which he seemed to be deep in thought. 'Do you want to tell me about your relationship with Caroline?'

'I've told the police. I may as well tell you.'

'You start,' I said. 'I'll make us some coffee.'

I sacrificed my last two sachets of coffee and was just pouring boiling water into the mugs when he said, 'I met her on the ferry going over to the mainland. She was having some sort of panic attack...'

I nearly scalded myself, but he didn't notice.

'I know now that she feigned those attacks whenever she travelled. That way she always met someone who was a "soft touch". Anyway, she met me, she had a face like an angel and she told me that she was escaping from an abusive relationship and that she had nowhere to live. I was married but I knew of a flat she could rent and I suggested she took it. That's how it all began.'

'Did you divorce your wife?' I asked.

He shook his head. 'Caroline didn't want me to. She said she didn't want to be known as a home wrecker.'

'Have you got children?'

'Only Adam. Caroline became pregnant almost immediately. I was delighted but she only allowed me to visit once or twice a week. I gave her money, of course...but I soon realized I wasn't the only man in her life.'

'What about your wife?'

'I told her about Caroline. For years she put up with me and the situation. There was, of course, a lot of bitterness and resentment. I lived for the time Caroline consented to see me. I suffered agonies of jealousy when I thought she was seeing other men.' He sighed loudly. 'Most of the time I was miserable and unhappy. Stupidly I thought, given time and the fact that Adam was my child, she would settle down as she grew older, and we would be together. But she didn't change. Caroline was fond of me but she didn't love me. I don't think she loved anyone. She loved money most.'

'I've seen her building society accounts,' I said. 'Very impressive. How did she make that sort of money?'

Lyle's bottom lip trembled. 'She wasn't too greedy at first. I knew she was running a small business but I didn't take that much interest.'

He paused and I could see his eyes had begun to water and he stared straight ahead as if lost in his own world of betrayal and misplaced love. To bring him back to the present I asked, 'Did she want more money from you?'

He didn't move for a moment, then he shook his head slowly. 'I was assistant manager at a small bank. I'd been in the area some time. She started asking me to introduce her to estate agents and surveyors and builders. We entertained, she spent her money. Then she started wanting information on client accounts, names and addresses, that sort of thing...'

'Those in the red?'

'How did you know?'

'I know. Just keep on talking, Lyle, get it off your chest.'

He smiled wanly. 'Yes. I loved her, you see. I thought if I did this for her she might...well, love me back. I know that sounds pathetic and perhaps I am. But I went along with her plans because I couldn't live without her. I tried to reason with her but she pointed out I wasn't stealing clients' money, that what she was doing was perfectly legal, so I was weak and I carried on doing just what she wanted.'

'Did you get found out?'

'No. Six months ago my wife left me for another man.

I didn't love her but she was honest and good and worth ten of that evil bitch Caroline.'

'Why did Caroline come to the Isle of Wight this time?'

'I think she was just customer hunting. Strange about her…activities. With her it was the thrill of the chase. She made money but she hadn't got expensive tastes. She still lived in her flat in Southampton. In my calmer moments I used to think she was doing it all for Adam but in bad times when I could have strangled her I thought she did it all for herself. She was promiscuous, selfish, amoral and I still loved her, so what does that make me? A pathetic…stupid…moron.'

I wanted to offer him a comforting platitude but I knew it wouldn't help. Instead I said, 'Did you want her dead?'

He sighed. 'Sometimes. Mostly I just wished I'd never met her. She'd wrecked my marriage, I've resigned from my job and worse than that I have no claims on Adam. He has no regard for me, considers me more like an uncle or a family friend. He's so like her, he absorbed all her attitudes, only connects with people who can be useful.'

'Did Caroline make a will?'

'Yes, about two years ago—everything goes to Adam.'

'Did she tell you about the death threats?' I asked, guessing that she'd received plenty.

Lyle rested his head in his hands. 'Yes, I knew about them.'

'What did you think?'

'I didn't think anything. I sent them.'

'*You* sent them?' I asked in amazement. 'Why?'

He looked me straight in the eye. 'Why? Because I wanted her weak and vulnerable. I wanted to demoralize her, make her lean on me, cause her to give up her activities.'

'But it didn't work like that.'

He smiled. 'She was a tough nut. She told me to pull myself together. She also said more than one person wanted to kill her.'

'It may have been bravado.'

He shrugged. 'I really don't think she was scared. She had no sense of guilt and no fear of death.'

'I wonder, then, why she gave Adam a box of papers containing her passport, bank books and business papers? It was as if she knew someone was about to kill her.'

'Maybe she had a premonition. She believed in all that spiritual stuff.'

'Did you know about her previous relationship with Nigel?' I asked.

He nodded. 'Oh yes, I knew. I sent him death threats too.'

'Have you admitted that to him?'

'No. Do you think I should?'

'Yes. He might come back here if he didn't think he was being pursued by a homicidal maniac.'

'I've got to know him in the past few days. He'd fallen under her spell years ago but he hasn't said much about recent years. It's as if he's ashamed of loving her too.'

'Or perhaps he's done something of which he's ashamed. They did work together for a while.'

'She wanted everyone in her power, you know,' murmured Lyle thoughtfully. 'She was strong and we were weak.'

'Or too nice or too trusting or just too loving.'

He shook his head miserably. 'I don't know anything anymore. My life's in ruins. No job, my wife's gone, my house is up for sale. My son doesn't want anything to do with me. Once he even said to me he didn't think I was his father. That was very hurtful. The day he was born was the happiest day of my life.'

I sighed, wondering if Nigel, Alex and James Renton had all heard the news of his birth with jubilation. Had they all offered her maintenance or had she demanded it? Surely James Renton and Lyle couldn't have seen any genetic likeness in the gangly boy, or was their pride in fatherhood as blind as their feeling for Caroline?

Lyle suddenly looked tired. 'I'd better go now. The police need to see me one more time.'

'Before you go, Lyle, will you answer me one more question about Caroline?'

He nodded.

'Her looks. Has she changed much over the years?'

He smiled. 'Oh yes. When I first met her she was plump as a little cherub, then she got very slim about a year after Adam was born. She often changed the colour of her hair, sometimes red, blonde or brunette. Sometimes she changed the style of her clothes—ethnic, power dressing, smart casual—she was a different person to different people.'

'Did she ever do any other sort of work—non office work?'

'No.'

'Did she ever go away?'

'After Adam was born she nursed her elderly aunt for a while. She was more of a companion, really. Somewhere in the Midlands, I think. The aunt died, she came over here, but as I said, her previous relationship was violent and she decided to settle in Southampton.'

'Was *your* relationship violent?'

'I slapped her a couple of times but I'm not really a violent type. She could bring out the worst in me.'

'You're sure it was only a slap?'

'Yes,' he said firmly. 'And I was very ashamed of myself.'

'So you don't think Caroline had ever been frightened of you?'

He stared at me and then smiled. 'Caroline wasn't frightened of anyone. She was tough. The sad thing is, I still love her. I know she was selfish, perhaps even evil, but I'll never stop missing her.'

'Why did you follow her to the Isle of Wight, Lyle?'

He shrugged. 'I suspected she was seeing someone. I watched her leaving the bungalow, followed her to the hotel and assumed she was meeting a man. I'd been drinking, I was at the end of my tether. That's why I got violent. I would never have harmed her.'

'Someone else was also at the end of their tether, Lyle. I just wish I knew who.'

TWENTY

AFTER LYLE'S VISIT I sank into the private investigator's doldrums or the 'What the hell do I do now?' syndrome. I tried ringing Hubert, only to be told by Danielle that the cold room was 'chocca' because influenza was rife in a local nursing home and he was fully booked with funerals until the day before Christmas Eve.

The weather had taken a turn for the utterly dire with gale force winds and rain that didn't seem to fall—it was thrown! Who did I see next, anyway? As far as I could guess, only Adam remained without an alibi and of course young Tom. Boys of their age did occasionally commit murder but surely not matricide? As far as motive was concerned, all the usual ones might count—jealousy, money...even love.

I went down to breakfast, chose a full fried one and didn't feel a whit of guilt. After all, it was raining hard and today I decided was a day for reflection and a full stomach. The dining room was noisy and busy, but I managed to bag the only two-seater table in a corner and for a while sat in splendid isolation. Until, that is, Stewart came over to join me just as my vast breakfast arrived. He smiled at my bacon, egg, sausage, tomatoes, mushrooms and—oh, most heinous item of all—fried bread and said, 'I like a woman with a hearty appetite. Do you mind if I join you?'

'Not at all, as long as you too have the full breakfast.'

'I'm man enough for it,' he said, somewhat suggestively.

Trying to concentrate on my food I merely smiled, although I've always suspected as far as suggestive smiles go, on men they look like a leer and on women they look simpery, so I hoped my smile was simply a reflection of food enjoyment.

After a while the silence between us made our chinking knives and forks, swallowing and then crunching on the fried bread seem exaggerated, so I said, 'Lyle Uxton came to my room yesterday.'

Stewart swallowed hard. 'What the hell for?'

'To tell me Nigel was staying with him.'

'Why on earth should he go there?'

'Why not? They had Caroline in common.'

'How is he?'

'Fine. Lyle says he'll try to persuade him to come back.'

Stewart pushed his plate away, his breakfast only half eaten.

'You do want him to come back?'

'Of course I do.'

I knew he was lying, but why? 'You don't look pleased,' I said.

He shrugged. 'I suppose I've got used to being in sole charge. The power must have gone to my head.' He was trying to be light hearted but not succeeding.

'Stewart,' I said quietly. 'Don't you think it's time you were honest with me?'

He glared in response. 'I don't know what you're talking about. I've got to go now, Kate. I'll see you later.' With that he left as quickly as if pursued by a charging rhino.

I continued eating my toast and told myself firmly that of course being a private investigator wasn't easy, why should anyone want to give me information, I was lucky to have got this far... I was well into my own little pep talk when I gazed up from my toast to see DCI Form-bridge standing in front of me.

'All right if I join you?' he asked. A smile from Form-bridge would have been asking too much, but he did man-age to incline his head.

'They'll give you breakfast if you want,' I said.

He looked undecided. 'Was the full breakfast good?'

'Delicious.'

'Hmm. I should be watching my cholesterol.'

'I'll watch it for you,' I said. He didn't appreciate my little joke. I thought breakfast might cheer him up, so I said, 'It's just the once, Chief Inspector, and anyway you won't need lunch, so that's a saving.'

'That's true,' he said as he signalled to a waitress.

While he waited for breakfast he stared round the guests, then unexpectedly said, 'Nigel Carter rang this morning. He's coming back.'

I didn't say anything.

'You'd already found him, hadn't you?' He was obvi-ously disgruntled.

I nodded. 'Have *you* made any progress?' I asked.

'Of course we have. But we've found quite a number of people were less than distressed by Caroline's death so it's made the investigation a bit slower. We're getting there, we persevere and I do have a strong suspect.'

'Why are you here today?' I asked.

'Just taking a look round,' he said cagily.

'So you think someone staying in the hotel murdered Caroline?'

'Oh yes,' he said. 'Don't you?'

'Well, I did think that at one time but anyone fairly agile could have got into the garden without having to go via the hotel. The wall's high but not that high.'

'Our scene of crime boys didn't find anything to indicate that anyone came over the wall.'

'What did they find?'

At that moment the waitress arrived with his breakfast and as he began to eat hungrily I realized he wasn't going to answer that question. After a few mouthfuls he said thoughtfully, 'Caroline Uxton had a colourful life—a poverty-stricken childhood, an alcoholic single mother who bought booze before food. They lived like gypsies, moving from one place to another, but each place got worse, more run-down, more problems. She left home at sixteen, worked as a chambermaid for a while, then later for James Renton, who runs a so-called finance company.'

'How did you find all this out?' I asked.

'Diaries we found at her flat in Southampton.'

'So you know the men she was involved with?'

'We certainly do.'

I waited for him to expand on the male front but he didn't, he carried on eating. After a while he said, 'We do know who benefits from her death…'

'Adam?' I queried.

He shrugged. 'In time.'

He sipped his tea, helped himself to some of my cold toast and flashed me a rather sickly smile as if saying, 'We know something you don't know.'

'Are you going to tell me, Chief Inspector?'

'Why not? She left all her money, a considerable amount…to Lyle Uxton. We've just told him, it was a do-it-yourself will but it's been verified as perfectly legal so he's come out of it quite well.'

'What about Adam?'

'His school fees are to be taken care of by Lyle and he'll have some money when he's twenty-one. It was her wish that Adam kept in close contact with Lyle as, in her words, "Lyle has always been a good father to Adam."'

'Does Adam know about this?'

'He will do today. That's where I'm going from here.'

'It may not come as a surprise.'

'That's true.'

'Could he have killed his mother?'

'Of course he could.'

'Have you questioned him?'

Formbridge's lips set once more into their near-normal angry position. 'This force may not be the Met but we do maintain our standards. Yes, he has been questioned very carefully and sympathetically.'

'Not by you, then,' I said, just as a joke but he glared in response.

'I'll be talking to him today,' he said coldly.

He left then, merely nodding at me again and I felt slightly peeved because if there was anyone I'd brave the wind and the rain for it would have been Adam.

'Hello, Kate,' said a voice at my side. 'You look as if you've lost a shilling and found a tanner.' He was wearing one of those zipped-up cardigan-type jumpers, olive green with brown suede panels at the front, and cream trousers. He certainly looked sprightly enough at that moment for the rigours of his forthcoming wedding day.

'Hello, Harold. I don't remember shillings but I know what you mean.'

'I hope you'll be coming to the wedding. We're not sending official invitations to those at the hotel. Everyone's welcome. Nancy is getting really excited. Mind you, she hasn't even found a frock to wear yet.'

'When exactly is it?'

'The twenty-second. It's at three p.m. at the Baptist Church, then back here for tea and a dance.'

'I'm looking forward to it,' I said, making a quick mental note not to forget to buy them a wedding present. 'Is it just as exciting the second time around?' I asked.

Harold looked at me thoughtfully. 'It's different,' he said. 'Just different.'

'Why don't you sit down, Harold?' I suggested.

Resting his walking stick against the chair, he sat down heavily and, after a short pause, said, 'I've just been out for a walk. I go for the paper every morning, rain or shine.'

'Why don't you have them delivered to your room?'

He smiled. 'It gives me a reason to go for a walk. I used to have a dog called Jasper, just an old mongrel but I walked him every morning and twice in the evening, so even when I do go for a walk it's not the same. I like to have a reason to walk and buying a paper is as good a reason as any.'

'What happened to Jasper?' I asked.

Harold looked at me then, so sadly that I wished I hadn't asked. 'When I lost the business,' he said slowly, 'and had to move, I couldn't keep him, so...he was old and arthritic and I had him put down.'

'I'm sorry,' I murmured.

Harold shrugged. 'It's a pity people can't be put down as easily as dogs. There's no suffering. He didn't even blink when the needle went in. He just kept looking at me—I didn't know he was gone.'

I was struggling to find something appropriate and comforting to say when I saw Nancy approaching slowly. When she finally reached our table, she said, 'There you are, Harold. I've been looking everywhere for you. You're always disappearing.'

He smiled. 'Never mind, love, I'll soon have the ball and chain on.'

'That's not a nice way of putting it, is it?' she said. 'Come on, love, we've got things to discuss.'

Harold gazed heavenwards. 'Women and weddings,' he said as though talking directly to God. 'They make such a palaver.'

'And men,' said Nancy, 'do nothing but moan about the cost.' She smiled at me, they smiled at each other and then Nancy helped Harold to his feet and they walked off arm in arm.

I wondered as I watched their retreating backs if I'd have to wait till I was in my seventies to meet the man of my dreams. And would I think him worth the wait?

A short time later, with my door sightly ajar as I dithered about going out in the still-torrential rain, I heard the chambermaids chatting. I'd only seen them fleetingly before and in no way could they be 'maids'. One was well into her sixties with slightly bowed legs and the other was fortyish with varicose veins and her bleached hair was only memorable because of its black roots.

I stood with my ear to the door hoping they wouldn't notice it was slightly open and listened.

'Untidy!' said one. 'Number eleven. You're lucky you're not doing my floor this week, Jean. Number eleven, they're old enough to know better.'

Jean laughed. 'Will they win this week, do you think?'

'They won last week. I think I'll bet on that couple in six.'

'He looks a bit past it, Mary. My old man looks as if he's got more life in him than that fella in six.'

'Looks can be deceiving, you know, Jean. What about Harold and Nancy. They won the WFL three weeks in a row.'

'I know. I mean, they can hardly walk, let alone... Maybe getting married will cure 'em.'

They both laughed and I heard the sounds of packets being removed from their trolley and then doors opening and closing. I picked up my coat and umbrella and crept out of my room as if I'd just eavesdropped on a royal tryst.

TWENTY-ONE

I PAUSED AT the entrance to the hotel and decided I needed to hire a car. I could hardly practise surveillance in a downpour standing under a brolly for hours at a time. I assumed that Formbridge, if he had visited Adam, wouldn't have spent long with the surly youth, so my timing might just be well judged.

An hour later, having used some more of my camera money, I sat, slightly steaming, in a warm new car sucking Polos, listening to the radio and waiting for Adam to leave the Freeman house. Of course there was a chance he wouldn't go anywhere at all but being an optimist I convinced myself was all part of the job. I sucked enough Polos to rot gold fillings and though I occasionally gave the windscreen wipers a quick swish I could quite easily have been sitting in a car wash for the amount of the outside world I could see.

Two hours later the rain eased off somewhat and I was relieved to see I hadn't wasted my time. Adam and Tom were on the move by minicab. I'd always wanted to say, 'Follow that car.' It didn't have quite the same cachet when spoken aloud to myself but it galvanized me into action and I drove behind the cab at a safe distance, keeping virtuously to the speed limit.

I soon became aware they were going towards Ryde. Perhaps they were simply going Christmas shopping or to the Arcade to play the fruit machines. Once in Ryde I realized they were not on a fun trip because the minicab stopped at the boatyard and the two boys took shelter under the stone-built gents' lavatory.

From my car, between soft rivulets of rain running down my windscreen, I could see them waiting. Was the gents' loo significant? I wondered. After about five minutes they grew fidgety and were obviously cold, because they wore only sweaters and jeans. Adam, in particular, began pacing along the edge of the small building. There was no one to be seen and even Robbo's office looked deserted. The boats bobbed up and down noisily, a few seagulls wheeled overhead and we all continued to wait. Once or twice the boys glanced over to my hire car but luckily they couldn't see me because of the rain on the windscreen.

It was then he appeared. I'd looked down for a moment to switch on the radio and when I glanced up a figure with his back towards me was talking to the boys. He carried a large black umbrella, but I knew from his width who it was—James Renton. They talked for a few moments, then I saw Adam stuff something into the pocket of his jeans. Renton turned and walked away and the boys, seeming more jaunty now, walked in the opposite direction towards the town. They'd obviously booked the minicab for the journey home, because the same car turned up at the entrance to the boatyard.

I assumed they would be going home, so I followed behind and once I was sure that they were at least going in the right direction I allowed myself to lose sight of the car without worrying.

Outside the house there was no sign of the minicab or the boys and I cursed myself for losing sight of them. I ate my last Polo and was about to drive away when one of the downstairs lights came on.

I knocked several times before I heard answering footsteps. It was Tom who opened the door. He stared at me questioningly for a few moments, then shouted, 'Adam, it's that woman asking questions again.'

'The name's Kate.'

'Kate!' he yelled.

'I'm coming. Just hang on a minute.'

'You'd better come in,' said Tom.

As I walked into the hall Adam came slowly down the stairs.

'Why are you hassling me?' he asked. 'I gave you that box so that you'd leave me alone. Do you want me to tell the police you've got it?' His smile seemed tight and nasty.

'Are you trying to blackmail me, Adam?'

He shook his head. 'I don't suppose you've got any money.'

'So if I had you would consider blackmail?'

He shrugged. 'Why not? Dickheads deserve all they get.'

'Like Renton?'

He couldn't hide his surprise. 'You followed us?'

I nodded. 'Yes. I saw what went on. I take it with your penchant for blackmail he was giving you a payoff.'

Anger flashed in Adam's eyes and Tom moved to stand beside his friend. Suddenly they both looked threatening. Even more so as they moved closer so my heel touched the wall and I began to feel a sense of claustrophobia at their sheer physical nearness. They were invading my space and I would have sworn on oath that both boys were exuding dangerous amounts of testosterone.

'I think you two should stand back,' I said firmly. 'I would hate to have to assault your manhood with a Japanese twist. Quite incapacitating, I can assure you. You'd have to crawl away.'

My threats seemed to have the desired effect. Tom's right hand moved swiftly to protect his manhood and Adam suffered a brief cringe before moving back and pulling Tom with him.

'What's a Japanese twist?' asked Adam.

'Similar to a Chinese burn but agonizing. Do you want me to demonstrate?'

'No thanks. Just ask your questions and then go.'

'That's not very polite, Adam,' I said, emboldened by my success. 'You could invite me in properly and I'd love a cup of coffee.'

'All right, then,' he answered reluctantly. 'Come into the kitchen. We have got other things to do, you know.'

The kitchen sink and drainer were cluttered with take-away food containers and I counted at least six glasses and four unwashed mugs.

'Your father isn't here, then Tom?'' I said.

'He's gone away for a few days on business.'

'And the cleaning lady?'

'Her husband's ill. She hasn't been in for several days.'

'When will your father be back?'

He shrugged. 'Don't know. He said he'd be a few days looking at property on the mainland.'

The coffee, when I was eventually presented with it, was vile, but I thanked them anyway, sipped it slowly and stared at them between sips. I was deliberately trying to make them uneasy, and it worked.

'What's your game?' asked Adam.

'I'm not playing games, Adam. I'd like to find out who killed your mother, because although I was hired to find Nigel Carter I subsequently found out about the connection between him and your mother...and I'm a person who needs to know.'

'She's dead. Nothing's going to bring her back.'

Just for an instant I thought I saw genuine sorrow in Adam's eyes, then, just as swiftly, his usual surly expression returned.

'Whoever killed your mother may kill again,' I said. '*You* could be a target.'

He grinned. 'What have I done?'

'You tell me, Adam. Today you met with James Renton and it seemed to me he was giving you money. What was he buying?'

'He just wants to help,' said Adam. 'He knew my mother.'

'I know he did. Come on, Adam, be realistic. Renton could be the man who killed your mother, perhaps not personally but he could have hired someone to do it.'

'He wouldn't do that.'

'Why not?'

'Because he thinks he's my dad and he knows if I found out he'd killed my mum I'd kill him.'

'Do you think you could kill someone?'

Adam smiled lazily. 'Yeah. I'd shoot them. But I'd have to have a really good reason.'

'I'm glad to hear it. In your opinion, then, killing isn't wrong.'

'I didn't say that,' said Adam indignantly. 'Of course it's wrong, but you have to look after yourself, don't you? You think I don't care about my mother being killed, but I do. I'm looking for him too and when I find him—he's dead!'

'What did Renton pay you for, Adam?'

Adam's mouth tensed into a sulky line. 'I'm not saying anything. He didn't give me any money and I don't know why you think he did.'

'I saw him.'

'You couldn't have.'

'I saw,' I repeated.

Simply by the expression in his cold bright eyes I knew Adam wasn't going to give in. Crossing his arms he said, 'Prove it. Go on, prove it.'

I was well aware I had lost my way with him on this point. Of course I couldn't prove it, but equally I didn't want a fourteen-year-old to have the last word. 'Think about it, Adam. Very carefully. If you have information that could trap the killer, and he knows, you could be next.'

'I'll be ready,' he said.

'Your mother probably thought that—until the first blow.' He winced. 'Leave me alone. Just leave me alone.' His voice sounded higher, slightly scared.

'Remember, Adam, if you want to talk I'm at Uplands Lodge Hotel.'

I left then but one thought did strike me. I was fairly sure Adam wasn't trying to protect Renton, but what about Alex? Of course Alex did have his alibi but what if *he* had paid someone to do the terrible deed. Or maybe his alibi wasn't as cast iron as the police assumed.

BACK IN MY hotel room I was debating the pros and cons of chasing up alibi witnesses when there was a knock on the door. It was Nancy. 'I've got it!' she said excitedly. I was about to say 'Got what?' when I saw the large shiny plastic bag. 'Your outfit?'

She nodded. 'Will you come down to my room, Kate, and tell me what you think? You're young and I'm sure you'll know if it's suitable.'

'Yes, of course. Where's Harold?'

'He's gone off to the hire shop for his suit. So we'll be all on our own.'

Although the room was large and the furnishings standard hotel issue, Nancy had made it home with many little extras, fresh flowers and potted plants, two matching footstools and various knick-knacks from across the years. She seemed to guess my thoughts. 'It's home to us now, dear. Strange to live in one room but we're ever so happy. Harold goes out quite a bit. He enjoys a walk even in winter.'

It was while Nancy changed into her wedding outfit in the bathroom that I moved to the window and gazed out. Behind the trees I could see the cabin and by craning my neck I could also see a man's back. He straightened up, turned round and began walking back towards the hotel.

It was Nigel.

'Well, what do you think, Kate?'

Nancy stood before me in a pale blue two-piece suit, the jacket slightly fitted and showing at the neck a white silk mandarin collar. Her cheeks were pink, her hair a shimmering silver, her eyes bright with excitement.

'You look lovely,' I said. 'Harold's a very lucky man.'

Having seen the outfit now, and having seen Nigel, I must have moved towards the door without realizing it.

'Don't go yet,' said Nancy. 'You haven't seen the hat. I've got two to choose from. Are you sure this outfit looks all right? It's such a worry. I do so want everything to be perfect on the day.'

'You'll look perfect,' I said as I resigned myself to catching up with Nigel later.

Nancy was putting on a matching blue pill-box hat with half-veil and a confection of tiny flowers when she said, 'I'm surprised you've never married, Kate.'

'I haven't given up. After all, you're getting married for the second time.'

'True,' she said. 'My first husband was a good worker

but he gambled. We got into money difficulties. He wouldn't retire. Work and worry killed him in the end.'

'What about Harold's first marriage?'

Nancy stared at herself in the mirror. 'Harold says all that is in the past. I don't know the full story, but losing his plumbing business was a real blow. He worked long past retirement age, you know. Then his business went bust... He doesn't talk much about that time in his life but sometimes I catch him with a funny look in his eye as if he's remembering...' She paused, adjusted the veil, smoothed down her skirt and said softly, 'At our age all those old memories seem so fresh as if everything happened just the other day.'

Two cups of tea and two custard creams later I left Nancy and began the search once more for Nigel.

There was no sign of him in reception or the bar and I was just about to go down to the kitchen when Stewart appeared.

'If you're looking for Nigel,' he said, 'he's gone.'

'I seek him here, I seek him there...' I began.

'I'll tell you what he came for,' said Stewart, 'if you promise to have lunch with me.'

I smiled. 'Done!'

Stewart suggested we ate lunch via room service in his room. As we waited he said, 'I'll put you out of your misery. Nigel's gone to see the police.'

'To confess?'

Stewart smiled. 'No, not to confess. To tell the police that a key he had hidden outside the cabin has gone missing. He'd forgotten about it. Last year he'd mislaid his keys and as he'd only got one to the cabin he had two cut. For some reason he decided to place one under a stone outside the cabin. He did tell me once he left his keys in the Pig and Whistle.'

I couldn't quite fathom the significance and must have looked blank, for Stewart seemed to know I needed an explanation.

'Someone had access to his cabin even before he left. Nigel said he sometimes had the feeling that someone had touched papers on his desk, but he thought that was just his increasing paranoia. He's only just remembered about the key, and the morning Caroline was killed the murderer could have used the door and even been in the cabin for some time before Caroline was killed. She would have heard someone scrabbling through the hole you two forced.'

'Which is why she didn't put up much of a fight,' I murmured. 'Perhaps they talked first; maybe it developed into a row.'

'We'll probably never know, Kate.'

I shook my head. 'I'm sure the police have a good idea who did it. Maybe they can't prove it yet but I want to be at least equal with them.'

Stewart gave me a slightly patronizing smile, so I said in retaliation, 'Stewart, do you remember a short time back we were talking about Caroline and I called her Charlotte—you didn't bat the proverbial eyelid.'

'I knew she was Caroline Charlotte so I didn't comment.'

'I see. I also find it really strange Nigel didn't give you a spare key to keep in the hotel? Are you sure he wasn't frightened of *you?*'

Stewart stared back at me so coldly I shivered. 'Are you frightened of me?' he asked.

Suddenly I wasn't sure.

'Are you?' he repeated.

'Of course not,' I said sharply, but I was lying.

TWENTY-TWO

ALEX FREEMAN phoned me later that evening. 'I'm sorry I missed you, Kate,' he said, as if I'd made a social call. 'The boys told me you came round. If there's anything I can help you with I'll be in all evening.'

I paused before I answered. I felt suspicious, as though he wanted to check me out, find out what Adam had told me.

'Fine—about nine?'

'Come earlier, Kate, I'll do a stir-fry. Say, eight?'

'I'll be there.'

I arrived at the house at five to eight, waiting as long as I dared without knocking, and thought as I stood there that time-keeping is really a psychological trial. Arrive early and you can look too keen, too eager; arrive late, you feel inefficient and lazy. Being punctual to the minute indicates a certain rigidity of personality and an attention to detail you might not be able to keep up. All in all I guessed that I admired the unpunctual person most, who turns up cheery and unconcerned. Lateness to me meant embarrassment, whereas to some of my past friends being late was one way of showing they were unconventional, free spirited and couldn't give a damn what anyone thought about them.

When I did knock on the door it was opened so promptly by Alex that I suspected I'd been watched—merely waiting for time to pass.

'Kate, I'm so glad you could come,' he said with a very welcoming smile.

'Why's that?' I asked.

He smiled again. 'I don't often get a chance to share my brilliant chicken stir-fry with an attractive woman.'

'I'm sure that's not true,' I said, feeling at that moment quite unable to make flirtatious smalltalk.

'Come on through to the kitchen. You don't mind eating in the kitchen, do you?'

'I prefer it.'

The kitchen had resumed its usual pristine condition and Alex poured me a glass of wine, assuming I'd drink it.

'I'm driving Alex. I've hired a car. Could I have a soft drink?'

He shrugged. 'I could phone for a minicab, then you could keep me company.

I shook my head. 'I'd love some orange juice.'

I watched him as he reluctantly poured me out some orange juice. He was tall, he was attractive, supposedly he cooked a good stir-fry, but he was just too sure of himself, too convinced of his own desirability.

'The boys are out,' he said as he handed me a tall glass of juice. 'It'll give us a chance to talk.'

'What in particular do you want to talk about, Alex?'

He smiled easily. 'This and that—but it can wait till after we've eaten.'

Within minutes Alex and his wok enjoined in a routine of smoking oil, fiercely frying chicken and bean shoots, which he shook and tossed as if his life depended on it. *Or* he was merely showing off. A short time later, with a huge bowl in front of me, I tasted his oriental delights. I had to admit, although it didn't taste like a Longborough Chinese takeaway, it was pretty good.

'This is wonderful food,' I said, looking him straight in

the eye, 'but I didn't come for the food. I came for information.'

'What do you want to know?'

'I want to know more about Caroline.'

'Why?'

'Why?' I repeated. 'Because she was murdered.'

Alex put his hand out and touched mine. 'Have you found anyone who's sorry she's dead?'

'Well no, but...'

'You're going to keep pecking away, aren't you, Kate?' he said gently as he stared at me with those Paul Newman blue eyes.

'I suppose I am, although I do want to be home by Christmas, which leaves me only three days.'

We finished the meal in a rather strained silence.

As Alex stacked the dishwasher, he said without turning towards me, 'Perhaps it's time I told you the truth.'

He finished stacking, poured himself a whisky and sat down again at the kitchen table. 'I've spoken to Nigel and we both agree that we have to tell the police what really happened. Not because we're overly concerned about Caroline's death, but to ease our consciences and prevent anyone else dying.'

'So you think this person could strike again?'

He nodded. 'The police seems to think so. You see, Nigel has been in contact with them, they now know that some incriminating papers were removed from the cabin, presumably at the time Caroline was murdered. The murderer knows our names and addresses.'

'What do you mean, ''our''?'

He sighed. 'In those days we worked together—Renton, Nigel and me and, of course, Caroline. Mortgage rackets, mostly. That's how I acquired so much property.'

'And now you feel ashamed of yourself?'

He smiled wryly. 'Partly, perhaps, but I'm totally legitimate now, except...'

'Except what?'

'Caroline couldn't leave me alone. She'd ring me wanting false references—that sort of thing—and she wouldn't take no for an answer.'

'Why not? Surely you could have told her you didn't want to be involved any more.'

He shifted uneasily in his chair and finished his whisky in one gulp. 'It wasn't that easy. You remember I told you I slept with Caroline. I was married at the time, which was bad enough, but Caroline also found out I was bisexual.'

'I see,' I murmured.

'Do you? I don't think you do. Gay awareness is gaining ground but bisexuality is still a bit of a mystery and I do have a penchant for young men. I've always been terrified that if it became public I might lose Tom. I've always helped maintain Adam and kept in touch with him and I know he wants to stay with me rather than Lyle, whom he seems to despise.'

I nodded. 'What did she have on the others?'

Alex had stood up and was refilling his glass. 'Are you sure you won't have one?'

I shook my head. 'I think you're trying to change the subject, Alex. I did ask if you knew what she had on the others.'

Alex stared for a moment into his whisky and I thought he was going to ignore my question entirely. 'I'm not sure, but I wouldn't tell you even if I were. Their private lives were and are no concern of mine. Anyway, I'm glad the bitch is dead.' He took another mouthful of whisky. 'She had no conscience, no morals. Her only motivation was power and accumulating money. She manipulated us like puppets.'

'And you let her.'

He shrugged. 'Yes, we did. Perhaps we were weak but we had so much to lose.'

'Is your alibi kosher?' I asked quietly.

He smiled. 'Oh yes. The tenant in question is very law abiding and the police are perfectly satisfied I was where I said I was at the time of Caroline's death.'

'And the boys? Are you sure they didn't leave the house?'

'What's that supposed to mean?'

'They could have killed Caroline, or at least Adam could...'

'Nonsense! Don't be so bloody ridiculous.'

'It does happen, Alex.'

He stared at me, his eyes losing their blue friendliness and taking on more the colour of a turbulent sea. 'I think you'd better leave now. Neither Tom nor Adam has violent natures. They are perfectly normal teenage boys, selfish but not, I repeat *not*, killers.'

'Did you know Adam is capable of blackmail?' I asked, but I didn't really expect an answer. He continued to stare at me with a mixture of anger and bewilderment as if he couldn't quite believe I could dare say such a thing. I felt I still had a point to make and I was going to make it. 'Adam has been taught by an expert. From all I've learned about Caroline she could probably have made a criminal of Mother Teresa.'

'You're talking nonsense, woman. I don't have to listen to any more of this.'

I shrugged. 'I'm going now, Alex, and I'm sorry if I've upset you, but it is possible that Adam's desire to be with you and Tom may have been motive enough to kill his mother. Murder has been committed for less.'

His answering glance seemed to confirm that murder could be motivated by merely casting aspersions, so I made a hasty exit, but I knew as I left that he was uneasy and would remain so until he could talk to both the boys. Even so, I wasn't convinced that Alex would shop either of them. *If* they were killers, they could quite unconsciously have committed the perfect murder.

WHEN I GOT BACK to the hotel I bumped into Harold and Nancy as they were returning to their room. Nancy's face looked a little pinched and her eyes were slightly red.

'You don't look well, Nancy,' I said.

She forced a wry smile. 'I'll have to put on a brave face for tomorrow,' she said. 'I can't let Harold down.'

Harold squeezed her hand in response and she smiled up at him.

'Has something happened?' I asked.

Nancy nodded. 'It's Margaret. She's phoned to say she's not well enough to come tomorrow.'

'Is it serious?'

She shook her head. 'I don't think so, but she was…well…strange. As if she didn't want to come.'

'I'm sure she does,' I said.

'Maybe,' said Nancy, sounding unconvinced.

'Come along, dear,' said Harold. 'We've got a lot to do.'

As I watched them walk slowly away I felt a little puzzled. Was Margaret jealous of Nancy's happiness? I was just thinking I'd probably never know the answer when Amanda appeared.

'Hello, Kate. Have you seen Stewart?'

I shook my head.

'He's never around when I want him,' she said, frowning.

'Problems?'

She smiled and shook her head. 'Not really. It's just a catering problem.'

'The wedding?'

She nodded.

'I've just seen Nancy,' I said. 'It seems Margaret isn't well enough to attend the wedding.'

Amanda gave me a quizzical look. 'I don't know if I should be telling you this, but a friend of mine works in a guest house called the Rosedale, just outside Ryde, and Margaret's staying there.'

'How strange,' I murmured.

'You won't tell Nancy, will you? She's under the impression Margaret is staying with relatives.'

'No, of course I won't.'

Once in my room I stared out of the window for some time. I decided I had two options. The first was that having found Nigel for an albeit bogus aunt my mission was accomplished and I could go home. The second was that I had a duty to find out who murdered Caroline. I had a feeling that going back to Longborough would win over the high moral ground, but first I would visit Margaret. I was curious about her sudden defection, and even if I left the Isle of Wight immediately after the wedding would I enjoy Christmas...wondering?

TWENTY-THREE

ON THE WAY TO Margaret's new abode I bought a bottle of sherry from the off-licence. It seemed faintly unethical to encourage her to drink but at her age and in her frail physical condition it was, I thought, a justifiable indulgence.

The Rosedale Guest House was a large Edwardian house just outside the centre of Ryde. The front door had a brass knocker and stained glass of rather gaudy red roses. It was opened by a tall, middle-aged woman with ultra-black hair cut short in a spiky fringe. She carried a cloth in her hand and wore a plastic rose-covered apron.

'I've come to see Miss Margaret...' I announced. She dabbed at the woodwork on the door before answering me.

'She's in her room,' she said, polishing some imaginary speck on what to my eyes seemed absolutely pristine paintwork. 'Along the corridor first room on the right.'

The hall carpet obviously reflected the rose theme and the pictures on the walls didn't deviate but depicted every rose from dog rose to full blown. Outside Margaret's room were several small framed collages made of rose petals and I had a strong impression of rose-smelling polish until I realized my eyes had deceived my nose and it was really lavender.

'Come in,' Margaret called at the sound of my knock. When I entered the room, she lifted her head slightly to see her visitor and I knew by her anxious expression I wasn't welcome.

'Nancy doesn't know you're here, does she?' she said sharply.

'No, Margaret, she doesn't. I came to see what was wrong.'

'I'm a bit tired, that's all. There's nothing wrong with me.'

'May I sit down?'

She nodded.

'It's a lovely room,' I said as I sat next to her on a high-backed grey chair with rose-embroidered chair antimacassar.

'I like it,' she said and she moved her head slightly to look round.

The carpet was a plain rose pink, the lampshades a darker pink with tassels; even the cornices of the high ceilings were rose shaped. In the bay window on a drop-leafed table stood a vase of red roses. 'It's much bigger than your room at Uplands,' I said. 'More like a bedsitter.'

'I'm quite happy here,' she said, the emphasis on the 'quite'.

'Did you move because it's cheaper?'

'I did not,' she said indignantly. 'I heard it was a nice clean place and the food was good, so I moved. I wasn't happy at that hotel.'

'I'm surprised at that, Margaret. I thought you, Harold and Nancy made a great team.'

She paused. 'Things change.'

'What things?'

'Kate, I don't want to be rude, but I don't want to talk about Harold and Nancy.'

Simply to change the subject I said, 'What about Christmas? Will you stay here for Christmas?'

'Of course. Mrs Munro, the landlady, will be here and

there are four other permanent guests. I'm looking forward to it.'

'I'll be leaving after the wedding, probably. Nigel's appeared and I'm sure the police are making headway with Caroline's murder, so there's no reason for me to stay.'

'No,' she murmured. 'None at all, I suppose.'

Margaret's head hung painfully low and for a moment I thought she'd fallen asleep. I was getting nowhere fast, but I was determined not to leave until I found out about the rift, because it seemed so sad that three people who were such good friends should be estranged.

Suddenly Margaret lifted her head slightly. 'Would you like a cup of tea?'

It was then I remembered the sherry, so I produced it with a flourish from my shoulder bag.

'Even better,' she said as she smiled for the first time since I'd entered the room.

'I've got some gin to go with it,' she said as she stood up slowly and walked over to her bedside cabinet.

'Gin with sherry?' I queried. A mixture like that seemed more like slow suicide than mere indulgence.

'You've never tried it?' she said.

'It sounds lethal.'

She gave a dry laugh. 'Oh, it is, dear, but it's delicious.'

Producing two large schooner glasses, she'd poured the gin in before I could tell her I didn't want it.

We sipped slowly on our drinks and I had to admit this was one way to drink gin, the pleasure being you couldn't actually taste the stuff.

'Nancy's found a lovely outfit to wear for her wedding,' I said.

'Blue?'

I nodded.

'Blue's always been her colour.'

'I think Harold's wearing dark grey.'

'Nancy's too good for him,' said Margaret and I noticed she'd very nearly finished her glass.

'What makes you say that?'

'Intuition,' muttered Margaret.

I knew then that Harold was the problem and not Nancy, and a few reasons sprang to mind. Perhaps Margaret had found out he was a bit of a womanizer or maybe even a gold digger. Perhaps Nancy's finances were in better shape than Harold's, but even so the difference wasn't likely to be that great. Finishing my gin and sherry in a final gulp, my mind quickly toyed with ideas of Harold as a flasher, a peeping tom and a paedophile. But I firmly rejected them all.

'Time for another,' said Margaret, holding out her glass to me.

In her glass I added a generous measure of gin; in mine I was a little more parsimonious, because I'd realized that Margaret could drink me under the proverbial table.

'I never married,' she said as I handed her the glass.

I smiled. 'Are you glad or sorry?'

Raising her head so that she could look directly into my eyes she said, 'Very glad I didn't marry, but I would have loved children. I was born in the wrong era. As a school teacher now I could perhaps have been a single parent.'

'It would have been hard.'

She nodded. 'I suppose it wouldn't have been fair on the child either.' She smiled briefly. 'Men do have their uses, I suppose.'

There was a pause then. I desperately wanted to get back to the Harold and Nancy question but I wanted to be tactful so I said eventually, 'I've been to quite a few weddings, but I can never imagine myself being married.'

'Why's that, dear?'

I shrugged. 'My relationships just seem to go wrong. Or maybe I don't have very good taste in men. The steady reliable types frighten me. I imagine the life. He comes in at just after six each night, jaded and tired and expecting a meal even if you've just got home yourself. Then he switches on the TV and after a little moan about work and colleagues he falls asleep. Once a week together you do a supermarket shop and perhaps on a Sunday, in the early days, he takes you out for a pub lunch but after a while he says, "Your cooking is so much better, darling, let's stay in." So you stay in. If you want to go out with a girlfriend he doesn't exactly object but goes all quiet and sullen so after a while you stop bothering.'

'What's the alternative, though, Kate? Hours and hours spent alone. No one really caring if you live or die. It can be very hard living alone. I talk to myself quite a bit. Once I did have some single friends but they are gradually dying off.'

'Hey, come on, Margaret, we must have drunk too much—we're getting maudlin.'

'On the contrary, my dear, we haven't had enough. Drink up and I'll pour us another. If you want the bathroom it's just next door.' Was she psychic? I wondered.

By the time I came back into her room the third drink awaited me. I wouldn't be driving my hire car back to the hotel tonight. I was drinking on an empty stomach; it was five p.m., the wedding was tomorrow and as yet I hadn't bought a present for the happy couple.

'Have you bought Nancy a wedding present?' I asked.

Keeping her head down she said quietly, 'I didn't have the heart.'

'Why not?' I asked. 'Harold hasn't got a terminal illness, has he?' This seemed to me the most logical explanation.

'Not of the sort you mean.'

'I only know one sort. Why don't you tell me about it?'

'I couldn't do that, Kate. I have to keep my secret.'

'But surely if it's something that will affect Nancy, don't you have a duty to...at least warn her?'

'She'll find out in time.'

'But in the meantime this dark secret could spoil their marriage. Perhaps it would be better in the open.'

'I think not,' said Margaret firmly. 'Some things are better off not being exposed and anyway I could be wrong.'

'She's your friend,' I said. 'If you were marrying Harold wouldn't you want to know and would it make a difference? I mean, would you still marry him?'

Margaret seemed to think about that for some time, staring at her hands and rubbing them nervously together. 'I probably would still marry him,' she said. 'And live in hope.'

I sighed. 'Margaret, think about it. If it was you, would you rather be forewarned, at least?'

'I suppose it wouldn't come as such a shock,' she said. 'But who wants bad news on their wedding day?'

'Come on, Margaret, what bad news? Other than him having a dire condition I can't see what else could be so bad.'

'You're not drinking, Kate. Drink up.'

I stared at her glass, which was empty. I couldn't let the side down. I finished my drink in one.

'That's better,' she said. 'You won't be anxious soon.'

'I'm not anxious, I'm just puzzled.'

'You'll stay for supper, won't you?' she said. It wasn't

really a question and at the moment I felt hardly able to stand, but I was sure I could eat.

'If it's no bother,' I said.

'It's no bother to me. I'll just tell Mrs Munro you'll be eating tonight. She'll bring it along to us.' She stood up then and staggered a little. 'I'll need my trusty frame,' she said. 'Here in my room I try to do without, but for the corridor I need help.' From a huge walk-in cupboard she lifted out her Zimmer frame, patted it fondly and began walking slowly to the door. 'I won't be long. I keep it hidden away so it doesn't remind me I'm disabled.'

'Shall I pull the curtains?' I asked.

'Good idea,' she said, twisting her neck to speak to me. 'It's always best to cast out the night.'

Once she'd left the room I stood up, then sat down again quickly. My head was spinning and all blood flow seemed to have stopped in my legs. I felt my top lip; it was numb. This is a sure sign, I told myself. You're drunk! I tried to stand up again by using my hands to lever myself from the chair, but I couldn't move. I sagged back down into the chair and held my head. I felt ill, really ill. The room started to go round and round, the black sky outside was moving too, dots of light shimmered before my eyes, my stomach knotted and unknotted, but worse than that was that I couldn't seem to think properly. Thoughts drifted in and out of my brain like goldfish in a fancy tank—I had seaweed floating in my brain—in and out and round and round. I knew I was drifting but I couldn't hold on to my thoughts.

I had nightmares in my horrible drifting, nauseous world. Mrs Munro was doing things to me. Undressing me. Moving my chair around the room. Doing things to my arms and legs. The word dying flitted into my head. That must be it. I was dying. Dying, I thought. Now my past life would flash before me—but then there was nothing.

Nothing until a face appeared. Black, black hair, spiky fringe like tiny daggers. Pale face close to mine. From some distance I heard my name being called. It was then I became aware of the pain in my head, an iron band. I tried to open my eyes. When I finally succeeded, a bright light seemed to scorch them and I closed them quickly. 'Meningitis,' I croaked. 'I'm dying.'

TWENTY-FOUR

'HERE, DRINK THIS,' said a voice I recognized as Margaret's.

'What is it?' I managed to croak.

'It's just warm milk, it'll do you good.'

'I don't like milk,' I managed to say. 'I'm feeling a bit better.'

'Drink it,' said Margaret firmly. I drank it. It tasted foul but I was thirsty. 'I'll help you to the bathroom,' she said as she held my hand to sit me upright.

'I'm in your bed,' I murmured in puzzlement as I gazed at her floral duvet cover. 'I thought I was in hospital.'

Once I was on my feet I managed to get to the bathroom without help. I splashed my face with cold water and noticed my wrist watch had been removed.

Margaret was waiting for me by the bed. 'You can't go yet; you're not quite well enough,' she said. 'Rest in bed for a bit longer.'

'I'm just a bit groggy,' I said. 'I'll be fine in a few minutes.'

'Get back into bed, dear,' she said, holding the corner of the duvet up. I struggled back into bed and minutes later, when I felt the strange and awful tiredness creep over me...I knew.

'You've poisoned me!' I burst out as I struggled to sit up.

Margaret pushed my shoulders back down on to the bed.

'Not poisoned, dear. That's a bit dramatic. I've drugged

you. Just some more of my Ativan tablets crushed up in the milk.'

'Why?' I asked, but my voice didn't seem very loud, so I asked again, trying to make my voice louder. 'Why?'

'I'll tell you when you wake up, dear. You have a lovely sleep.'

'Sleep!' I thought. 'Sleep! I could be dying,' but the effects of the drug soon meant I didn't really care. Sleep was fast engulfing me and I felt no anxiety.

WHEN I DID wake up Margaret sat by my bedside more like a worried gran than a treacherous poisoner. 'You've woken up at last,' she said, as if I were being lazy and having a lie-in. 'I'll make some tea.'

'No thanks,' I said quickly.

Margaret laughed. 'It's all right, Kate. Just plain tea this time. You can go as soon as you feel better.'

Emboldened by the fact that I was still vaguely alive, I said, 'I'm not leaving here until you explain why you've done this to me.'

'All in good time. All in good time. Would you like something to eat? Mrs Munro will cook you anything you fancy.' Pride wouldn't allow me to say yes to food, so I shook my head.

'I'll go and tell her you're feeling better and you can get dressed.'

Once she'd left the room on her Zimmer frame I raised myself from the bed feeling, I'm sure, less well than Lazarus, and dressed myself as quickly as I could. I found my watch on the table in front of the window and stared at the time—six p.m. I pulled back the curtains—it was dark. What day was it? Saturday—the day of the wedding. I'd missed it. Margaret had wanted me to miss it. Why?

Why the hell should she have wanted to keep me here so that I couldn't attend the wedding?

When Margaret came back she seemed genuinely pleased. 'You do look better,' she said.

'I'm so glad,' I said sarcastically. She didn't seem to notice my sarcasm; in fact she seemed almost excited by her deed. 'Mrs Munro is bringing you a tray of tea and toast. She was worried about you last night. I told her about the gin and sherry but not the Ativan.'

'Of course not.'

Margaret walked slowly toward me without her Zimmer frame and rested her hand on mine. 'I'd rather you didn't tell Mrs Munro that I...spiked...is that the word? your drinks. I think she'd understand, but on the other hand she might think it was a bit dramatic.'

'Dramatic,' I echoed. 'I think that's an understatement.'

'I did it for the best.'

'Whose best?'

'Nancy's, of course.'

At that moment there was a knock at the door, which I jumped up to answer. Mrs Munro, carrying a tray of tea and toast, stood there. 'Well, I am relieved to see you up and about. I was really worried. I thought you were ill, but Margaret told me you hadn't got much of a capacity for drink so it was to be expected.'

I wanted to give her a sharp retort but merely said, 'I'm sorry I was so much bother.'

'No bother at all, dear. I should stay off the alcohol, if I were you. Some people it just doesn't agree with.'

'I'll remember that in future.'

When she'd gone I turned to Margaret. 'Are you going to tell me why you wanted me to miss the wedding?'

Margaret gave me a sly glance. 'I thought you had put two and two together and that was the reason you had come to see me. Nancy and Harold are the two most precious people in my life. I couldn't let you go, just in case you guessed and Nancy's wedding day would have been spoilt.'

I poured out tea for both of us and began eating the hot buttered toast. 'For some reason, Margaret, you practically told me anyway.'

Margaret nodded slowly and thoughtfully. 'I'd had a lot to drink. It made me loose-tongued.' She paused. 'I've always had a problem with alcohol. It was those two who saved me...' Her eyes filled with tears, then she added miserably, 'They are only...suspicions.'

'Mine too now,' I said, but as I thought of Harold, all neatly pressed and happy, I found it very hard to believe.

'What makes you think Harold is a murderer?' I asked.

'I didn't say that,' she said. 'I just have my...doubts.'

'You realize I shall have to find out more, don't you?'

'Of course,' said Margaret. 'At least Nancy is married now. It's just so much more respectable. I never did approve of them sharing that room. To me they were living in sin.'

'Margaret, are you going to tell me the basis of your suspicions?'

'No,' she said firmly. 'I'm not. I've decided that I'm going to develop a really bad memory. When the police do come, and they will after you've spoken to them, I'm going to act dotty. Without my evidence they won't have a case.'

'Is Nancy so special to you?' I asked.

Margaret smiled. 'They both are. I told you before, they saved my life. I feel I have an obligation to them.'

I finished my tea and toast in silence. As I left, Margaret said, 'I do hope you'll come to see me again.'

Outside, the shock of the cold fresh air made me shiver,

my head felt more muzzy and I prayed I'd be able to drive. Once in the car I kept the engine running for a while until the heater came on, then opened the window slightly and drove back to Uplands Lodge very slowly and very carefully.

In reception I could hear the wedding celebrations still going on. Even the Christmas tree had a smattering of confetti. I was creeping towards the lift when Stewart appeared.

'Kate, where've you been? I was just about to call the police. I've been really worried.'

'I'm OK Stewart, I was delayed.'

He frowned. 'You look awful. In fact you look ill.'

'I'm not too chipper,' I said, and I had to admit I felt worse now than I had earlier on.

Stewart put an arm around me. 'You could do with a drink,' he said.

I couldn't even force a smile. The idea of alcohol nauseated me. 'That's the last thing I need. I'm just going to my room to lie down for a while.'

'I'll take you.'

'There's no need. I'll be fine.'

'I'll take you,' he repeated, and I didn't feel up to arguing, so I let him take me by the arm and to my room. 'Lie down on the bed and I'll make you a cup of tea.'

I watched him making tea and he watched me drinking it, but at least he let me finish it before he started asking questions. 'Now then,' he said as I swallowed the last drop. 'What happened?'

'I was slipped a Mickey Finn.'

Stewart's expression moved from disbelief to concern. 'Who the hell by?'

'I'd rather not say at the moment,' I murmured.

There was a long pause, in which Stewart looked

peeved, but eventually he said, 'OK…I'll ask you again later. But I would like to know why this person didn't want you to attend the wedding.'

I paused now, debating with myself. Could I trust him? There was no suggestion he'd had dealings with Caroline, and yet…

'Come on, Kate,' he said irritably. 'Out with it. This sounds serious.'

'I was drugged by someone who suspects Harold killed Caroline.'

Stewart immediately began to laugh. 'Come off it. Does Harold really strike you as a man capable of murder?'

'He was in the army.'

'Probably the catering corps.'

'Just because he's old, Stewart, doesn't mean he wasn't capable of wielding a crowbar.'

'I'm not saying he's not physically capable, but in God's name—why?'

'That's something I've yet to find out. And I've got twenty-four hours to do it in.'

'Why such a short time?'

'I want to be home by Christmas.'

'You could have Christmas here.'

I smiled. 'It's not the same as being at home. Hubert wants me there.'

'Is he on his own, then?'

'No, he does have a girlfriend.'

Stewart shrugged. 'So you'd be playing gooseberry?'

'Well… Yes, I suppose so.'

He smiled and patted my hand. 'If you can't make it home I promise you'll have a good time here. But in the meantime I think you ought to tell me who has these suspicions about Harold.'

'Let me rest for a couple of hours, Stewart, then I'll

come down to the bar about nine and drink orange juice with you.'

'It's a date,' said Stewart. 'If you don't appear I shall come looking.'

I felt relieved when he'd gone. I wanted to lie on my bed and think. What exactly did I know about Harold? He'd been in the army, he'd run a plumbing business, he was a widower, he'd had some financial trouble, he gambled on the horses, he enjoyed walking, he loved Nancy and he liked a drink. He liked to drink in the bar! And that's where he was the night Caroline died.

I closed my eyes and tried to remember the scene that night. Harold, Nancy and Margaret had sat on the three-seater sofa, Caroline and I were at a corner table. They had waved to us and Harold had fiddled with his glasses—gold-rimmed. Had he worn them before? I couldn't remember. Was he fiddling with them because they were new? I'd remembered his blue eyes being bloodshot and he hadn't worn glasses then. So were they new that day? If he was wearing them at night in the bar they weren't reading glasses. In that case they were distance glasses, which meant he could see more clearly. And what did he see more clearly? Caroline. He'd recognized her at that moment. After the visit by Lyle, perhaps he guessed she would stay in the hotel. Did he see us go to the cabin?

I fell asleep fully dressed and when I woke my head was aching, but I did feel more alert. It was nearly nine. As I ran a bath I debated the pros and cons of telling the police of my suspicions, but what did they amount to. Harold once wore gold-rimmed specs and liked an early-morning walk. Really I had no more than that to go on.

I'd just got out of the bath when I heard knocking at my door. I threw on my bathrobe feeling irritated that Stewart should dare to come and rout me out for being a

mere twenty minutes late. I opened the door with a flourish and there stood Harold and Nancy, both pink faced
and a little bleary eyed but still smiling.

'We're so sorry you were too poorly to come to the
wedding,' said Nancy. 'We've saved you some wedding
cake, though.' She handed me the cake wrapped in silver
foil. 'There's still food left downstairs if you fancy it.'

'Thank you. Aren't you going to dance the evening
away?'

Harold leaned on his stick. 'To be honest,' he said,
'we're really tired. We've had a smashing day, but it's
been a long one.'

'It wouldn't have been so long, Harold, if you hadn't
got up at the crack of dawn as usual.'

Harold didn't answer. He wasn't wearing glasses either.

'You're not wearing your glasses, Harold,' I said, trying
to sound casual. 'Don't you usually wear them?'

Harold opened his mouth to reply but Nancy answered
for him.

'He should wear them, Kate. He can walk past people
without recognizing them. He's walked past me before
now. He's vain, he says a stick is bad enough but, as I
told him, he is over seventy so what can he expect?'

Harold managed a smile. 'I'm going to bed. I know
you want to stay and chat for a while. Don't be long.'

Nancy watched him walk away and I saw a flicker of
anxiety cross her face. 'Have you got time for a little chat,
Kate?' she asked.

'Of course, come on in.'

Nancy refused tea and once she'd sat down she began
playing with the cuffs of her sleeves.

'You seem troubled,' I said.

She gazed at me for a moment with bright but anxious
eyes. 'I'm worried about Harold.'

'His health?'

'Yes…his mental health. He's got something on his mind. I thought it was the wedding. He stares out of our window for hours at a time. I think the murder upset him. He watches the cabin. And he walks all the time. He says he's keeping fit but I think it's a waste of shoe leather. His shoes don't last five minutes—' She broke off, as if remembering something. 'He's upset about Margaret too. Once he got quite angry, saying he didn't believe she was ill and she was a nosy, interfering busybody. That upset me for days too, but there it is—friends come and friends go. And of course it was a little sad for him today—his son not being there.'

'Does his son live abroad?'

Nancy shook her head. 'No, dear, he's dead. He committed suicide in the eighties. In the car. The worse part, though, was that he didn't die alone. The family went. His wife and teenage son too. Harold doesn't talk about it much, he keeps it all bottled up inside him.'

'Was there a suicide note?' I asked.

'I don't think so, but I do know that when interest rates went up and the housing market collapsed it affected the plumbing business very badly. Harold tried to help out his son but Andrew had already got involved with a loan shark and it was too late—he was bankrupt and Harold had to sell up at a great loss.'

'Poor Harold,' I murmured.

Nancy gave me a sad little smile. 'I'd better go. Harold will be waiting for me. After all, it is my wedding night.'

TWENTY-FIVE

I MET STEWART in the bar just after ten. It was crowded and most people seemed to be drinking heavily. The Christmas tree glittered in all its artificial glory and barman Frankie sported a sprig of holly behind one ear. Stewart, I thought, seemed a little subdued.

'You're very quiet,' I said.

'All this will wreck Christmas for the guests,' he said. 'Some of them may even decide to leave.'

'So you're worried about profits?'

'I didn't say that, but police still swarming everywhere and asking more questions won't exactly create an atmosphere of good will to all men.'

We both drank orange juice and although we sat alone at a corner table lit by a red candle I felt there was a coolness between us that I couldn't quite explain. Eventually I said, 'Is there something else wrong, Stewart?'

He stared at me for a moment. 'I'm sorry I seem a bit distracted, Kate. I've just spoken to Nigel. I think he's suffering a crisis of conscience. He wants us to sell up and...'

'Give back the money he stole from his aunt?'

'You knew about that, then?' he asked in surprise.

'I knew Caroline posed as a nursing assistant and stole the money his aunt hoarded.'

He nodded. 'It seems she called herself Charlotte and because the old girl was already confused she stayed just long enough to clear out the several thousand pounds she'd hidden in the house.'

'You won't give up the hotel without a fight, will you?'
I asked.

Stewart managed a smile. 'If we can sort out the Harold
situation with as little fuss as possible, then maybe I can
persuade Nigel to stay, if not I shall have to find a new
partner.'

'I wonder if the police are on to Harold.'

Stewart shrugged. 'I think they'll get round to him
eventually, but if he had an alibi for the time in question—'

'Nancy!' I exclaimed.

'What's that supposed to mean?'

'She must have said he was with her at the time, and
who would disbelieve a sweet-faced elderly woman?'

'He could get away with it. It might be better if he did,'
muttered Stewart.

'I know Caroline wasn't in the running for a Nobel
Peace Prize, but she didn't deserve to die like that.'

'That's a matter of opinion,' said Stewart.

'I thought you didn't know her.'

'I've heard a few things since she died. None of them
good.'

'So people who aren't whiter than white should just be
bumped off.'

'That's an over-reaction.'

'Is it? Quite a few men were happy enough to sleep
with her. I'm surprised you didn't.'

'Calm down, Kate. I wouldn't tell you if I *had* slept
with her, but then I think she was quite resistible. I'm not
keen on thrusting, ambitious types.' He smiled at me as
if suggesting I was the opposite of thrusting and ambitious—which was, I suppose, laid back and lazy. Suddenly I felt I had to show Stewart I really couldn't care

what he thought. Abruptly, I announced, 'I'm going now, Stewart. I'm still a bit hung over from last night.'

'Was it something I said?' he asked with the faintest of smiles.

'No, of course not. I just want to make an early start in the morning. Maybe even before the chambermaids arrive. What time do they start?'

Stewart looked puzzled. 'Six thirty. They help out in the kitchen first.'

'Thanks. I'll see you tomorrow.'

I felt guilty as I walked away and I was aware of his eyes following me, but I couldn't let him influence me. I was determined to find a little more evidence, because after all there was only circumstantial evidence at the moment; then I would contact the police. After that, I'd hopefully make a quick exit back to Longborough. The last ferry I knew was on Christmas Eve. And I wanted to be on it.

MY ALARM TRILLED at six a.m. and in a half-awake state I was washed and dressed by six fifteen. I deliberately left my door open, sat on the bed and waited for the trolley to trundle along the corridor. It was just after seven when I heard sounds of activity outside. I looked along the corridor to see Mary, who was the older of the two, going into a bathroom carrying a plastic box of cleaning materials.

'Do you want to use the bathroom, dear?' she asked when I approached.

I shook my head. 'I just wanted to ask you a couple of questions—I'm a private detective.'

'That's nice, dear, but I'll have to keep working as we talk. We're a cleaner short so we have to do the bathrooms pretty sharp in the mornings. Not many need to use the bathrooms, mind; most of the rooms have baths or showers, but there's always one who wants to use it when it's not convenient.'

'I wanted to ask you about Harold James; he's on the floor below. The man who got married yesterday.'

She grinned and began spraying the bath with a foam spray. She cleaned and talked at the same time. 'Not my floor, but he's more spritely than he looks.'

'In what way?'

From her bending position she twisted her head and winked at me. 'You know what I mean.'

'Have you noticed that he goes out early every morning?'

Mary paused at the tap end of the bath. 'Jean has. She talks to Nancy quite a bit. Nancy sleeps like a log in the mornings. He's up with the larks.'

'Do you remember the morning the body was found in the cabin?'

'Course I do, love. What a day. I didn't see anything, though. I was on this floor that day. We swap floors sometimes.'

'What about Jean?'

'She was a bit late that morning. She didn't notice anything.'

I waited until Mary had finished polishing the taps and was about to ask her another question when Jean walked in. 'I've run out of bloody teabags again,' then, seeing me, she said, 'Sorry, didn't see you there.'

'I've been asking Mary a few questions. I wondered if you'd mind answering a few.'

'What about?' she said suspiciously.

'Harold James.'

'Why him?'

I shrugged. 'Just something I need to clear up.'

A reluctant expression crossed her face. 'Look, tell you what, I'll do a deal with you. I'm dying for a fag and we're not supposed to smoke, so I'll stand here and have one and answer your questions as long as you don't grass on me.'

I smiled. 'Done!'

Taking a packet of cigarettes from the pocket of her blue overall she lit one, inhaled deeply and said, 'Righto.'

'I must get on,' said Mary, gathering up her cleaning materials and bustling away.

'Did you notice anything strange about Harold James the morning the body of Caroline Uxton was found?' I asked Jean as she took another puff of her cigarette and blew the smoke just past my face.

'No, I don't think so.'

'Did you see him that morning?'

'I saw him and Nancy come out of their room.'

'He didn't seem unusual in any way?'

She shook her head. 'Well, only one thing, I suppose. Well, two things. I didn't tell the police because you get a bit confused, don't you? And you don't want to look stupid. It's nothing really, just that... He'd had a shower and he made a right mess—water everywhere. Not like him at all. I think Nancy had got up in a bit of a hurry and I don't think she noticed. Ever so neat and tidy, they are.'

'You said two things, Jean.'

'Oh, yeah. The paper. He buys the *Sun* and I like the *Sun*. But as soon as he's read it he bins it 'cos they have the *Radio Times* so he doesn't need it for the telly. Sometimes he cuts out the racing page but that doesn't interest me. So every morning when I do his bin I take out the *Sun* and read it during my tea break.'

'Yes...'

'Well, that morning it wasn't in the bin. I just wondered why he hadn't got his paper.'

'What time does he usually go out for it?'

'It varies. I've seen him going out as I come in at half past six, but Nancy says he'll sometimes be out as early as five thirty, just as the shop takes delivery of the papers.'

'Thanks, Jean, you've been a great help.'

'Have I? That's good. I've helped two people today, then. Funnily enough, I saw Harold about half an hour ago as I came along the corridor. He was off to get the paper but we stopped for a little chat and I told him I knew where Margaret was staying. She's at Rosedale; my friend Di works there as a cleaner. Anyway, he was really pleased, said he'd take her a piece of wedding cake.'

'Oh, my God...'

I rushed straight to Harold's room. Nancy opened the door; she wore a pink dressing gown, her hair had not yet been combed and her eyes were puffy and dull looking, as though she'd had a sleepless night.

'Is Harold here?' I asked.

'He's gone for a walk, dear. Why?'

'I just wanted to ask him something,' I mumbled.

'There's nothing wrong, is there?' she asked anxiously. Even as she asked I guessed by the expression on her face that she knew. And I knew there was nothing I could say at this moment.

'No, Nancy, nothing's wrong. Don't worry. I'll see you later.'

I left the hotel immediately and began driving. As I drove through the narrow, empty streets I realized Harold might just as easily have gone for his newspaper, but Nancy didn't say that, did she? She said he'd gone for a walk. I glanced at my watch; it was still only seven thirty. I was sure I'd be there in time.

There was very little traffic but the clouds were grey and low, I needed my side lights and I knew I was driving too fast. Once I clipped a kerb, risked a red light and narrowly missed a man on a zebra crossing and although I slowed down a little I was still over the speed limit. My car screamed to a halt outside Rosedale and I ran out of the car leaving the keys in the ignition and the door wide open.

My demented knocking brought Mrs Munro, one sleeve in, one sleeve out of her dressing gown, black hair in clumps on her head. 'What's the matter? What's happened?'

'Margaret!' I yelled as I rushed to her room. I burst into the room.

Margaret lay on the bed wearing a high-necked nightie and a dressing gown. One fur-lined slipper had fallen off. I couldn't bear the thought of her lying there with only one slipper on and I bent down to pick up the stray slipper and stood there holding it and staring at her pale face. Her false teeth had dropped slightly, the room smelt of... alcohol! I stared at her chest and saw the slight rise and fall. She wasn't dead! She was dead drunk.

I rubbed her hands and patted her face. 'Margaret. Wake up! Has Harold been here?'

'Harold,' she slurred eventually. 'He came to the window. He didn't come in. I opened the window and spoke to him—' She broke off.

'Margaret, stay awake! What did he say?'

There was a long pause. 'Say... He didn't say much. He said... I should look after Nancy and he was going for a swim.'

'Oh, my God...'

From behind me I sensed Mrs Munro shuddering. 'Call the police, Mrs Munro.'

She looked about to faint, so I said firmly and slowly, 'Leave the room, Mrs Munro, and call the police.'

She began to tremble but she started to move and murmured, 'Yes, yes the police.'

I DROVE straight to the beach, all the time looking for Harold. I heard the police sirens long before I saw them. The sea itself was black and choppy and as I ran on to the beach I desperately scanned the horizon. Although I stared and stared I could see nothing but the black sinister waves. Until, that is, someone shouted, 'There he is!' I followed the pointing finger of a constable and saw one black-sleeved arm, far out, just a flash and then it was gone. For a moment we all stood motionless, then two constables started stripping off their clothes. Suddenly Formbridge's voice rang out. 'Get your kit back on. It's too bloody late. He's a dead man. The current out there is lethal, he's dead from the cold anyway.' His men hesitated and then began dressing. Formbridge turned to me and said almost apologetically, 'I can't risk my men's lives for a corpse. The divers are on their way. Believe me, he's a goner.'

We all stood watching for some moments the vast, black, treacherous sea that was now Harold's grave and I thought of newly wed Nancy who so soon had become a widow and felt tears welling in my eyes.

As I walked back to my car Formbridge said, 'We were on to him. We just didn't have any evidence. I think his coming to Uplands Lodge was all part of his plan to wreak revenge on those he held responsible. Undoubtedly he planned to kill Nigel but Nigel did a runner and then Caroline appeared, he recognized her and bingo!'

'Did Nancy give him an alibi?'

'She said he didn't budge from her side until seven a.m.

Strangely enough, Margaret alibied him as well. They never lock their door and she expected Harold to be up and she said she looked in on him wanting an aspirin and he was fast asleep in bed. No one believed it, but she wouldn't change her story.'

'He could have done the deed and then gone back to bed.'

'He could indeed, but proving it was another matter. We'd found out about his son's connection with Caroline Uxton and Renton. Harold wrecked his own business trying to save his son's. They both went under in the end.'

'Why didn't he go for Renton? And who fired Renton's boat?'

Formbridge shrugged. 'I think Harold, probably. He was building up to murder. It was a sort of warning.'

Back at the hotel I stayed with Formbridge while he broke the news to Nancy. She was dressed now in a navy roll-neck jumper and skirt. A stray tear escaped down her cheek but that was all. She remained remarkably self composed.

'I knew he'd kill himself if he was found out,' she said.

'So you knew he'd killed Caroline Uxton?'

For a moment she gazed at Formbridge as if pitying *him*. 'Of course I knew. He thought he had a chance of getting away with it. She made it easy for him coming to the hotel that night and being in Nigel's cabin.'

'How did he get into the cabin?'

Nancy smiled wanly. 'Silly Nigel hid a key outside the cabin. Harold had been in the cobblers collecting some shoes he'd had repaired and he saw Nigel getting a key cut. It was a special offer—two for the price of one. So Nigel got two keys cut. Harold started to go to the cabin occasionally, just looking for evidence against Nigel, I suppose. After Nigel disappeared he used to go there more often—' She broke off. 'Harold wasn't a violent man. He tried the legal way, consulted solicitors, even barristers, but in law it seems crooks can cheat, lie and ruin lives and there is nothing anyone can do.'

'Did he plan to kill Renton too?'

Nancy shrugged. 'Harold was always neat and methodical. And that's all I'm going to say at the moment.'

'Could I ask you a question, Nancy?' I said.

She looked at me steadily for a moment. 'I know what you're going to ask. You're going to ask who telephoned you and paid you to come here. Harold organized that. He wanted Nigel found. His sister made those calls. She'd heard there was a private investigator in the area and Harold thought you might be capable enough to find a missing person.'

'I see,' I murmured. Not meeting a prospective client was one mistake I wouldn't make again.

Formbridge moved forward then and touched Nancy on the arm. 'You'll have to come to the station, Mrs James, to make a formal statement.'

'I'll just get my coat,' she said calmly.

As she fastened her buttons and picked up her handbag she turned to me. 'I think, Kate, for the funeral I'll wear my wedding outfit. Blue is my colour. Harold liked me in blue.'

I nodded and smiled. There was nothing I could say.

A WPC waiting outside led Nancy away. Formbridge gave a sort of satisfied grunt, then smiled. 'Remember this, Miss Kinsella, and you can quote me at any time. "Behind any man's decision is a woman's permission."'

'Will she be charged with being an accessory to murder?'

He frowned. 'I'm not sure. In view of her age I don't think she'll get a custodial sentence.'

There were so many questions I wanted to ask Nancy and Formbridge but I knew I'd have to wait. The Chief Inspector was obviously in a hurry to close his investigation. He shook my hand and I was instantly grateful he wasn't Sicilian or Italian because then he might have kissed me.

'Merry Christmas,' he said, with resignation.

TWENTY-SIX

IN A SLIGHTLY DAZED state I walked to the shops. Other shoppers had that frantic Christmas-shopping-at-the-last-minute look. Some seemed totally desperate. The loose ends of my investigation seemed to me to be as numerous as dandruff, and combined with worrying about presents, buying the camera, checking the times of the ferry the next day, taking back the hire car, no amount of Salvation Army carol singing could make me feel less agitated.

I bought Hubert's present first. I knew exactly what to buy him. Danielle was a bit more difficult. In the end I decided on a complete hand-care kit—nail varnish, false nails, nourishing cream, emery boards—the works. With male hands to care for, I reasoned, she needed as much help as she could get.

The camera shop fazed me and I would have needed a salesperson with time to spare. The salesman on duty looked more demented than the queue of shoppers. I moved on to a supermarket where I felt more at home and I started buying the sort of treats you buy only at Christmas: sugared almonds, turkish delight, chocolate-covered nuts, expensive tins of biscuits.

Back at the hotel the atmosphere seemed subdued. Even the bar was empty, almost, it seemed to me, as a mark of respect.

A few of the guests gathered in corners and stared at me as I came in laden with Christmas shopping.

As I collected my key Amanda said with a worried smile, 'Stewart's been looking for you.'

I nodded. 'I'm going up to my room. I'll be leaving in the morning.'

'That's a pity,' she said. 'I think he was hoping you'd stay.'

I was still wrapping presents when Stewart came to my room.

'You're really going, then,' he said.

I smiled. 'This was not one of my most successful investigations, Stewart. I just want to put it all behind me.'

'Don't be so hard on yourself. Caroline was a fraudster on a grand scale and fraud cases take years to clear up.'

'What about you?' I asked. 'Is Nigel still wanting out?'

'I think I can persuade him to stay. I just wish I could do the same with you.'

I shrugged, half wishing that I could stay. After all, Stewart was attractive and he'd not been swayed by Caroline. 'I'm a loner, Stewart. I can't help it. My experience of sharing my life with someone wasn't that joyful.'

'We could take it slowly. Learn to trust each other.'

I shook my head sadly and then stretched up to kiss him. His lips were cool and soft and for a few seconds I wavered. I *could* stay here for Christmas.

'Just stay on for a few more days,' he murmured in my ear. 'You'd enjoy it.'

I wavered for several more seconds, then gently I pushed him away. 'Hubert needs me,' I said.

'What for?'

'Just to be there.'

Stewart realized then that he wasn't going to change my mind. He kissed my hand. 'Come back in the summer, Kate. And write to me.'

'I'll do that.'

'Goodbye, then.'

Once he'd gone I started to snuffle.

In the morning I rang Hubert to let him know I was on my way home but disappointingly only the answerphone spoke to me.

The rattling sound of the chambermaid's trolley reminded me about Jean and Mary. Jean was having a surreptitious smoke in the bathroom and Mary was acting as look-out.

'Hello, dear. We heard about what happened yesterday. Terrible—really terrible. I'd never have thought it of Harold. I mean, he didn't seem like a murderer, did he?'

'No, he didn't,' I said.

As I handed them each an envelope with money in it I had to ask the question even if they did think I was stupid. 'Mary, I overheard you talking about the WFL,' I said. 'It's been puzzling me.'

She laughed and Jean emerged from the bathroom laughing too.

'I'm surprised you didn't guess, dear,' said Jean. 'You being a private detective. We had a little bet each week. Harold won a few times.'

They laughed again. 'It's the Well Fucked Look.'

'I thought it was that,' I lied.

The crossing was cold, choppy and packed with last-minute Christmas returners. A middle-aged woman weighed down with plastic bags full of presents fell just outside the ladies. She'd fallen on her wrist and seemed in some pain. This time I hesitated. 'Does anyone know first aid?' I asked in a loud voice.

'I'm a doctor,' answered a female voice as she waded in through the concerned onlookers. I slipped away unnoticed and congratulated myself on being so sensible.

Once we'd docked and left the boat I stood and searched the faces of waiting friends and relatives for Hubert. He wasn't there and I experienced one of those moments in life when you feel totally alone and abandoned.

Then suddenly I heard a voice calling 'Kate!' and there he was. Looking sombre and tired, his face seeming paler than ever.

'I've driven like the clappers, Kate. I rang you last night but you must have been out.'

'I went to bed early. I put the phone on mute.'

'I spoke to the owner. He told me you were leaving early in the morning. Come on, let's get to the car. I'm perished.'

The 'car' was a hearse. 'Why do you do this to me, Hubert?'

'Danielle wanted to use my car,' said Húbert. 'This was all there was. Just be grateful for a lift.'

On the way back to Longborough I was grateful for the smoothness of the ride and for the blanket Hubert provided.

'So, what happened?' asked Hubert.

'I can't say it ended in a blood bath, Hubert, but…someone died.'

'Not Nigel?'

'No. Nigel's fine.'

'Well then, Kate. Mission accomplished.'

I tried not to laugh. 'Oh, Hubert,' I said. 'You make things seem so simple.'

On the journey I told him in great detail about Caroline and her scams, how lives had been ruined. I even told him about the Bottomleys.

'Only one thing to do about that sort of fraud,' said Hubert. 'Get the media involved. Ring the tabloids, TV, radio stations. That sort of publicity will ruin their little racket.'

'You're right,' I said. 'But then you usually are.' He smiled, highly gratified.

OBVIOUSLY UNDER Danielle's influence Hubert had decorated his flat in very dubious taste. There seemed as many baubles and as much glitter as in the whole of Ryde itself. The enormous Christmas tree stood in the corner of the lounge with flashing lights, shiny balls and glittering silver strands.

The three of us ate a huge cooked breakfast washed down with Buck's Fizz and then we exchanged presents.

As Hubert opened the box and saw his gift his eyes lit up as bright as the lights on the tree.

'I suppose it's a joint present, really,' I said, smiling at Danielle. 'I bought the largest size—an eight. Will they fit?'

'I'll make them fit, darlin',' said Danielle.

Holding the black strappy creation with stilt-like heels, Hubert gazed at them for several reverential seconds as though they were icons. Then he passed them solemnly to Danielle, who forced her at least size nine feet into them. She tottered around the room. Hubert watched her and smiled happily. He was in his own personal heaven.

I smiled through a haze of Buck's Fizz and Christmas bonhomie, aware that I could get maudlin and sentimental. But I didn't care. I was home, it felt like home and I was amongst friends.

Take 3 books and a surprise gift FREE

SPECIAL LIMITED-TIME OFFER

Mail to: **The Mystery Library™**
3010 Walden Ave.
P.O. Box 1867
Buffalo, N.Y. 14240-1867

YES! Please send me 3 free books from the Mystery Library™ and my free surprise gift. Then send me 3 mystery books, first time in paperback, every month. Bill me only $4.19 per book plus 25¢ delivery and applicable sales tax, if any*. There is no minimum number of books I must purchase. I can always return a shipment at your expense and cancel my subscription. Even if I never buy another book from the Mystery Library™, the 3 free books and surprise gift are mine to keep forever.

415 BPY A3US

Name	(PLEASE PRINT)	
Address		Apt. No.
City	State	Zip

* Terms and prices subject to change without notice. N.Y. residents add
  applicable sales tax. This offer is limited to one order per household and not
  valid to present subscribers.

© 1990 Worldwide Library.

MYS-796

FOWL PLAY

A MOLLY WEST MYSTERY

Birds of a Feather

After fifteen years in rural Ohio, Chicago native Molly West is still considered an outsider, but as director of the local meals-on-wheels program, she's becoming more at home. The murder of a local woman and the abduction of a prize rooster are on everybody's minds.

Intrigued, Molly starts digging into the mystery. The trail leads to illegal doings and into the sport of cockfighting. However, the fowl deeds of the ring are minor compared to the blood sport of murder....

Patricia Tichenor Westfall

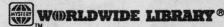
WORLDWIDE LIBRARY ®

WPTW273

UNTIL IT HURTS
AN IKE AND ABBY MYSTERY

WHO'S GOT THE SHOOTER?

When a shotgun blast drops basketball superstar the Big Chill at Madison Square Garden, it's another murder for Ike and Abby, co-workers at TV's "Morning Watch." As the bickering exspouses dive into the world of New York's biggest hoop gods and into their strange rivalries on and off the court, a trigger-happy killer nearly cancels Ike and Abby permanently.

One thing is for certain: the divorced duo must keep moving because this killer is playing a game of sudden death.

Polly Whitney

WORLDWIDE LIBRARY ®

WPW272